AN A

An Amish Surprise

Shelley Shepard Gray

THORNDIKE PRESS
A part of Gale, a Cengage Company

GALE
A Cengage Company

Thorndike Press® Large Print Romance.
The text of this Large Print edition is unabridged.
Other aspects of the book may vary from the original edition.
Set in 16 pt. Plantin.

LIBRARY OF CONGRESS CIP DATA ON FILE.
CATALOGUING IN PUBLICATION FOR THIS BOOK
IS AVAILABLE FROM THE LIBRARY OF CONGRESS.

ISBN-13: 978-1-4328-8959-3 (hardcover alk. paper)

Published in 2021 by arrangement with Gallery Books, a division of Simon & Schuster, Inc.

Printed in Mexico
Print Number: 01   Print Year: 2021

*For the many librarians I've
gotten to know over the years.
Thank you for touching so many
lives in so many ways.*

Dear Reader,

Do you like surprises? The older I get, the more I seem to like them! By nature I'm a fairly steady person. I usually follow rules, I like to know what to expect, and I basically do the same things every day — write books and walk dogs. But every once in a while, something surprising happens that shakes things up and gets me out of my rut. Sometimes it's news from my agent or fun family news — or even an unexpected snowstorm in September.

Just yesterday I received one of the most special "surprises" ever. Just an hour after I'd finished writing *A Christmas Courtship* and sent it to my editor, Sara, my husband, Tom, came up to my office and said he needed to show me something. I honestly thought a group of deer were back in our front yard! Rather reluctantly, I got up and followed him down to admire the deer, but then Tom turned me toward the dining room instead of the front door. I was completely confused — until I saw what had just arrived.

There, in the center of our dining room table, was the biggest bouquet of roses I'd ever seen in my life. My agent had sent me one hundred roses to celebrate the upcoming publication of my one hundredth book. I was so shocked, I burst into tears. Tom grinned and handed me a bunch of tissues. Of course, the rest of yesterday was spent admiring those roses and not doing too much else!

I hope you enjoy *An Amish Surprise* and the many unexpected surprises the characters experience in the novel. Some were wonderful, some almost heartbreaking, but all of them serve to remind the characters to keep their eyes and hearts open to the Lord's many blessings.

Happy reading, and here's wishing you have a wonderful surprise or two during this coming year.

Blessings,
Shelley Shepard Gray

Open my eyes to see the wonderful truths in your instructions.

— Psalm 119:18

One of the most complicated tasks modern man faces is trying to figure out how to lead a simple life.

— Amish proverb

ONE

SARAH ANNE MILLER'S GUIDE TO DATING AFTER AGE SIXTY

(I compiled these tips from both my experience and advice from friends.)

· **TIP #1** ·
If all else fails, remember this:
It's never too late to fall in love again.

Sarah Anne Miller often wished she had two more hands and another set of eyes. Well, that wasn't exactly the truth. She only wished she had such things when Ruth Schmidt led her brood into the bookmobile.

Yes, whenever the Amish woman arrived with her six *kinner,* Sarah Anne wished she had those extra hands, more eyes, an unlimited supply of earplugs, and extensive experience in crowd control. Maybe even a degree in psychology as well. Honestly, anything would be more helpful than her twenty-eight years at Pricewaterhouse-Coopers followed by a two-year online course in library sciences.

One needed a great many tools in order to survive the Schmidt triplets and whatever assorted children dear Ruth happened to be fostering at the time.

But since wishes and dreams were for other people, at least in this case, Sarah Anne was on her own.

Summoning her best kindergarten-teacher voice, she clapped her hands. "Children, please. Do gather around me. And speak one at a time."

Three out of six complied. A ten-year-old boy, a sweet little boy around seven, and a rather shy eight-year-old girl sat down immediately in front of Sarah Anne, their legs crossed like pretzels and their hands in their laps. "Ah, look at you three. Would you like to hear a story?"

The oldest boy nodded before gazing warily over his shoulder at the three remaining children. The five-year-olds didn't seem to understand the concept of following directions. Mary, Jonas, and Ian, also known as the triplet terrors, were currently gallivanting around like they didn't have a care in the world.

Sarah Anne didn't even attempt to hold back a sigh.

"No worries, Sarah Anne!" Ruth called out merrily. "You go right ahead. I'll tend to these wild *kinner.*"

Just then a triplet — Jonas, perhaps? — held up a picture book. It had a badly ripped cover page. "Lookit!" he yelled.

"Ah. Yes. I see that." Sarah Anne smiled weakly before turning back to the three who were sitting down. Each was still patiently waiting for a story.

What to do? What to do? The children needed their story, but that book needed to be saved before Jonas began his next round of destruction.

When the door opened again, Sarah Anne felt like screaming . . . until she realized who had arrived. It was Calvin Gingerich.

Calvin, the twenty-something-year-old Amish farmer who was so solemn, so kind, and so quiet. Who loved books and small children. Who visited every week to pick out a history book or a biography during his lunch break.

She knew he loved his few moments in the peaceful bookmobile. Probably looked forward to the time to do nothing but peruse her new titles. Unfortunately for him, this wasn't one of those days. He was

13

simply going to have to step in and help.

"Calvin, you are an answer to my prayers! Come here," she commanded, just as Miles, the oldest child in the group, sighed.

After giving the seated children a wary smile, he faced her. "*Jah,* Sarah Anne?"

Sarah Anne handed him *Mr. Brown's Barnyard Friends,* her go-to book in times of trouble. "Calvin, do me a favor and read to these children for a few minutes, would you, please?"

He took the book — not that she'd given him much choice — with obvious reluctance. "Well, now . . . Sarah Anne, I don't have much time. Fact is —"

She interrupted. "It's a short story. It won't take you long. *Please,* Calvin?"

Whether it was the plaintive tone in her voice, the faces of the sweet children who were still sitting and waiting, or the way Jonas was grabbing at another poor, unsuspecting book, Calvin sat down on the floor with the three little ones. "Hiya," he said. "I'm Calvin. What are your names?"

"I'm Miles. This here is Ethan and Minnie."

"Nice to meet ya. Are you ready to hear about some farm animals?" After the three all nodded, Calvin opened the book and began to read.

And then, praise the Lord, a miracle happened.

His deep voice resonated around the room, presenting a calming influence like a big dose of lavender aromatherapy. By the time he got to page four, even the Schmidt triplets were sitting down and listening to him.

Calmed by his words, Sarah Anne quietly picked up Jonas's injured book, taped the ripped page, and leaned against one of the bookshelves.

Even Ruth stopped inspecting cookbooks and listened.

The wonderful sense of peace lasted almost six more minutes. Six blessed, wonderful minutes. Until Calvin closed the book. "Well, now. That was a *gut buch*. Ain't so?"

"*Jah,*" Miles said, smiling for the first time since he'd arrived. "It was a real good book."

Sarah Anne was so pleased about that, she felt like her heart was about to burst.

Then chaos erupted yet again. In a flash, Mary shoved Ian, he pushed her back, and then, with a shrill squeal, she scrambled to her feet and ran to her mother.

When Jonas grabbed two more books off the shelf, Sarah Anne knew she couldn't take another second. "Mrs. Schmidt, I'm sorry, but you all are going to need to check out your books and be on your way. I'll need to be getting to my next stop soon."

Ruth blinked. "Oh! Oh, *jah.* Of course." Taking hold of one of her children's hands, she smiled at them all. "I think it's time we moved on, *kinner.* Everyone, take the *buch* you chose to Miss Sarah Anne and then come to the door."

Wonder of wonders, the children began to do just that.

After glancing at Calvin and mouthing "Thank you," Sarah Anne was busy again. But not too busy to notice that Miles seemed very taken with Calvin. He was gazing up at him with wide eyes.

Calvin bent down to speak with Miles, then walked him over to a section of chapter books and pulled out *Charlotte's Web.* From the way Calvin was smiling at the boy, it seemed like the admiration was mutual.

Ten minutes later, Ruth guided all six of the children out the door. "See you next week, Sarah Anne!" she called out. "Goodbye!"

"Goodbye," Sarah Anne replied with a half-hearted smile.

The door slammed.

And then, amongst the displaced books, a wad of discarded tissue, and what looked to

16

be the remains of two pretzels, gratifying silence returned.

Calvin looked shell-shocked. "Is it like that every time Ruth Schmidt visits?"

"Oh, yes." Looking through the window to where Ruth was still attempting to organize the six children and double that number of books, Sarah Anne chuckled. "Sometimes, things are even worse."

He gaped. "How can that be?"

"Every once in a while, some of the children she's fostering are as unruly as her own. It can be headache-inducing."

"Wait. Those aren't all hers?"

"Oh, no. Only the three youngest. Those are her triplets."

"One would think three would be enough."

Sarah Anne smiled. "I've never been blessed with children, so I can't say for sure, but I would have thought that, too." Realizing she wasn't sounding very kind at all, she added, "As unruly as the children are, I know the foster kids are in good hands. Ruth and her husband have been foster parents for years. Do you not know Ruth and James Schmidt? I thought you would, since they're Amish as well."

"I know who they are, but we're in different church districts."

"Ah. Well, it may not seem the case, but Ruth has a knack for fostering. She's a very caring woman . . . with a high tolerance for noise."

Calvin folded his arms over his chest. "Sarah Anne, what will happen to the foster kids after they leave the Schmidts? Will they get adopted?"

"If I'm not mistaken, I believe each case is different. Some of the boys and girls will go back to their parents. Others will go to another foster home. And, God willing, hopefully some of the children will get adopted. I, for one, would love to hear that each goes to a place where they feel wanted and loved."

" 'Wanted and loved,' " he murmured.

"Calvin, thank you again for helping me today. If not for you . . . Well, I don't even want to think what could have happened!"

"You caught me off guard, I tell you that. But I liked reading the book. I enjoy *kinner.*"

A shadow appeared in his eyes. Sarah Anne wondered what made him so sad but didn't dare pry. She'd already intruded upon him enough. "Do you need any help finding books?"

"*Nee.* I came in for a couple history books I've been thinking about. I'll go see if any

18

are available."

She pointed to the computer station. "You can always order books, and I'll bring them next time. That way you won't have to read to children. You'll be on your way."

"I know it might be quicker, but I didn't mind reading to them. It was kind of fun." Obviously still thinking about the foster children, he turned to face her again. "Sarah Anne, about how long does Ruth keep each foster child?"

"How long? Oh, I don't know. Usually a couple of months. Sometimes longer. Why?"

"No reason."

He smiled in a distracted way before walking to the small nonfiction section.

She watched him, wondering what was on his mind. Anxious to not be caught staring, Sarah Anne sprayed some hand sanitizer on her hands — really, those kids were a messy lot — then busied herself by putting the picture books back to rights.

She was going to need to get on her way in thirty minutes' time.

Glancing at Calvin again, she slowed her pace. She might be a little late departing after all. Calvin seemed to really *need* this visit today. Since her goal was to serve her patrons and their needs, Sarah Anne was happy to give Calvin as much time as he wanted. After all, he'd just saved her day.

TWO

· **TIP #2** ·
Your smile is your best feature. Don't
forget to use it. No one wants to date a
grumpy senior suitor.

Two Weeks Later

Calvin was late for lunch. Again. Standing
at the kitchen window, Miriam searched the
garden and adjoining fields for him. When
Calvin had first started designing their
house, he'd asked her where she wanted the
kitchen window. She'd known the exact
spot. It looked out at the front of their
thirty-acre farm. From that spot, she could
see her flower garden, currently abloom
with daffodils, irises, and a profusion of
petunias and marigolds she'd just planted
last weekend.

Also in view was the gravel path to the
barn, the paved road leading to the state
highway heading to the center of Berlin, and

the small pond where box turtles liked to sunbathe in August.

She'd loved this window to the world. From this one spot, she could do dishes and watch the world go by. Four years ago, when Calvin, his father, and his uncle had built their three-bedroom home, Miriam had been sure she'd soon be standing at the sink and watching her family. She'd imagined lifting the pane to call for their children to come inside for supper. Or watching them play a game of tag in the field.

Or sitting at the kitchen table, feeding a baby while the day's first rays of sunlight streamed through sparkling windows.

But, of course, none of that had happened.

They hadn't been blessed with any children. Despite four very long and difficult years of trying, an ectopic pregnancy, and two miscarriages. Miriam wasn't sure why the Lord had been so cruel. When they'd been courting, she and Calvin had often talked about their love of children and big families. Calvin, especially, had been excited to be a father. Each time she'd shared that she was pregnant, he'd been over the moon. Each time she'd lost a babe, his pain had been so acute, it had been hard for her watch, even though her disappointment had been just as strong. She'd begun to feel like a failure.

Now they had essentially given up. The fancy *Englischer* doctor specialist in Columbus that Calvin had taken her to had said that while there was a slim chance she could conceive again, the chances were even slimmer for her to carry a baby to term. The news had been so dire, neither she nor her husband had even wanted to think about going to other doctors for second opinions or trying any of the scary procedures that held only the smallest rays of hope. Especially when the price tag for that one visit had been hundreds of dollars.

Instead, with heavy hearts, she and Calvin had decided to leave their chances up to the Lord and tried to put their dreams of parenthood out of their minds. Or at least they pretended to do that.

So far, Miriam wasn't doing very well. She'd attempted to take up quilting, but she found it boring. Making jams and preserves and canning quarts of applesauce and tomatoes only served to remind her that she was just filling a pantry for two people.

Calvin had tried to move on by throwing himself into work: laboring out in the fields until it was near dark or helping out some of their friends and family with their machinery. But that meant he was gone a lot. And as the months passed, it was becoming harder and harder to believe that Calvin wasn't disappointed in her . . . and that maybe, one day, he'd fall out of love with her, too.

So now the only time she spent at that kitchen window was when she was waiting for her husband to come home.

Unfortunately, even that undertaking was beginning to feel futile. Calvin now seemed to arrive later and later for their noonday meal.

Especially on Thursdays.

Tired of looking for him, Miriam turned away. Paddy, their black and brown spaniel, lifted her head and gazed up at her with big brown eyes. Kneeling down to pet her, Miriam felt her heart melt. Three years ago, when she'd been in a particularly blue mood after far too many women at church had asked her about her childless state, Calvin had driven her in the buggy to a nearby farm.

He'd joked and teased when she'd tried to guess where they were going, reminded her over and over again that patience was a virtue. Just when she was threatening to not make his favorite banana pudding for dessert, he'd pulled into the Barretts' yard and helped her down.

"Come on," he'd said with a big smile.

She'd held his hand as they'd walked into the barn and then gasped when Jack Barrett stood up and motioned them over to a nearby pen. Inside that pen were six eight-week-old springer spaniel pups, each one cuter than the next. They'd frolicked and yipped and greeted her with the kind of exuberance only puppies seemed to be able to have. Not caring one whit about the dirty straw, she'd knelt down in the middle of their pen and played with them all.

She'd cooed and mooned over them and then had gotten tears in her eyes when Calvin told her to pick one out. Thinking that the little pup who'd been sitting in a corner by herself needed her as much as she'd needed it, Miriam had cradled her in her arms. When they'd gotten home, she'd promptly named her Paddy in honor of her favorite childhood toy bear.

Ever since, Paddy had helped her through any number of blue days and melancholy moments. But for once, even the dog's devotion wasn't going to help her overcome her newest set of worries — a husband who didn't seem all that eager to come home.

"Miriam, where are ya?"

Startled, she jumped to her feet to find

Calvin peeking into the kitchen from the laundry room right by the back door. "I'm here. I didn't hear you come in."

"No worries," he said as he turned on the faucet and washed his hands. "I'm running a little late anyway."

He was twenty-five minutes late. Struggling to keep silent about that, Miriam attempted to adopt a nonchalant demeanor. "Where did you go this morning?"

"Hmm?"

When he turned off the faucet, picked up one of her dish towels, and rubbed it against his face, she was once again struck by how very handsome her husband was. Even in early May, his face and arms had begun to bronze, and his usually dark blond hair was beginning to lighten. His beard, like his arms and chest muscles, was filling out, too. Yes, at twenty-eight years of age, her Calvin was a mighty fine-looking man. Everyone had noticed and taken to teasing her about having such a handsome husband.

Maybe too many people had noticed.

She leaned against the doorway and tried to sound only slightly curious. "Where were you? Did you go to the Olsons' to help with their generator?"

He tossed down the towel. "At the Olsons'? Oh, no. Sarah Anne and her bookmobile were down the road. I went to get a book."

"I wish I would've known you were going. I would've gone with you."

"Sorry. I guess I should've told you." He straightened. "Is lunch ready?"

She remained where she was, essentially blocking his way. "Where is it?"

"Where is what?"

"The book you got. Where is it?"

Calvin looked around, as if he was hoping a book was going to magically appear. "Um, I didn't find anything I liked."

"You spent your morning at the bookmobile but didn't find a thing?" She knew her voice was brittle, but she couldn't seem to help herself. "I find that hard to believe."

Calvin's usual easygoing demeanor tightened. "Miriam, what is the point of this? You're acting like I've done something wrong."

"I'm not acting like that at all." Which, of course, was a fib.

"Nee?" His brown eyes darkened as he folded his arms over his chest. "If you have something to say, you should just tell me. I have no time for games, you know."

His comment stung, though she wasn't exactly sure why. "Since you don't have much time to spare, we should go eat.

Lunch has been ready for some time, and it's getting cold."

"Of course." He strode to their table, pulled out a chair with enough force that two of the legs scraped the floor, and sat.

Miriam took the chair across from him, pushing out of her mind memories of sitting to his left so she could be closer to him. That was back when he'd come home ten minutes early because he couldn't wait another minute for a kiss.

And sometimes just one kiss wouldn't be enough. Remembering those days, those marvelous, middle-of-the-day stolen moments, she felt her cheeks heat.

"Miriam?"

"Hmm?" She turned to him.

Everything in his expression signaled his impatience. "Are you ready to bow your head in prayer?"

"Oh. *Jah.* Yes, of course." She bent her head and gave thanks for their blessings before adding another prayer, asking for patience and strength.

By the time she raised her head, Calvin was already eating.

She'd made roast beef sandwiches on toast with gravy and potato salad. It was a hearty meal, a good meal for Calvin, who farmed all day and usually ate breakfast

28

before the sun rose.

She'd taken special care to put spicy mustard and a good amount of crunchy celery in the salad. Since it was already half gone, she assumed he was enjoying it very much.

As the silence wore on, she cleared her throat. "So, how was Sarah Anne?"

"Who?"

"Sarah Anne," she repeated, this time with a bit of a bite in her tone. "How was she today?"

"Ah, fine, I think."

He thought? "Did she ever get the lift on the side of the bookmobile repaired for the wheelchair customers? Last time I saw her, she was complaining about how much the company was charging to even take a look at it. Is it working again?"

"I couldn't say. I didn't ask her about the lift." He shoveled another bite into his mouth.

"You know, that does remind me. I didn't know she was going to be near us today. How did you know?"

"I didn't. I just happened to see her when —" He stopped, obviously caught in his lie.

"When . . . ?" Miriam raised her eyebrows, impatiently waiting for him to explain himself.

But all he did was set down his napkin. "I've gotta go check on the corn."

"Already?" He hadn't even been at the table for fifteen minutes. His sandwich was only half gone, too.

"The corn is what keeps us fed, Miriam. You know that." He didn't wait for a reply before he walked out the back door.

Remaining frozen where she was, Miriam stared at his empty chair. Calvin had been anxious to leave, and she knew in her heart that it wasn't because he wanted to spend more time among the cornstalks. No, he hadn't wanted to talk to her.

He hadn't wanted to be with her.

Tears filled her eyes as she forced herself to acknowledge something else as well — her husband had absolutely not been at the bookmobile. If he had, he would've shared news about Sarah Anne. He would have known about the lift because he was interested in things like that. And, at the very least, he would have picked up two or three books because he was like a child in a candy store whenever he was inside that bookmobile.

Calvin had been someplace else, someplace he hadn't wanted her to know about.

Maybe it was time she stopped pretending and admitted that her worst fear could very well be happening. Her husband could have his sights on another woman. And who could blame him? There were likely lots of women who could give him what he wanted so desperately. A family. A son of his own.

All she could give Calvin was her love.

31

THREE

· **TIP #3** ·

Look for that someone special wherever
you happen to be — even at the library.

Calvin didn't know how much longer he
was going to be able to continue visiting
Sarah Anne's bookmobile on the sly. Lying
to Miriam was not only a sin, but it also
made him feel nauseous. For a moment, he
had feared he was going to lose his lunch
right there at the table. Something needed
to be done.

What was sad was that if he'd just gone
ahead and told Miriam the truth, she
would've likely responded better. At the
very least, she wouldn't have looked as
disappointed in him as she had fifteen
minutes ago. Miriam was smart, and she
had an innate sense about things. She knew
he had avoided her questions.

Yes, Miriam absolutely knew he was being

sneaky, and he could tell she wasn't pleased about that in the slightest.

Which made two of them.

Carrying the large, sturdy canvas bag across his shoulders, like always, he walked down the rows of corn and inspected each stalk like a proud parent. They were coming along nicely — almost knee high, as they should be. When he found a stray weed or an ear that needed pruning, he tossed it in his sack. Just the way his father had taught him years ago.

However, unlike in years past, the success of his corn crop brought him no feeling of satisfaction. All it brought was a nagging feeling from the Lord that he was still not doing His will. Which was, of course, figuring out what he was going to do about Miles.

Unable to stop thinking about the boy, Calvin had been going out to the bookmobile a lot. No doubt too often. Today, after waiting around for almost an hour, he'd spied Miles tagging along listlessly behind five other *kinner.* He'd looked so completely alone that Calvin hadn't even bothered hiding his dismay. Sarah Anne had noticed, and that's when she'd whispered that Miles had been in the foster system for several years already and that she'd noticed he usually kept a bit apart from the other kids in the Schmidts' care.

She'd also mentioned that Miles had already been in a number of foster homes. And, because of his age, his chances of being adopted were becoming less and less promising as each year went by.

The boy sure looked defeated. Why, he looked as somber and wary as an old mare. Calvin couldn't even begin to compare the boy's demeanor with his own self at age ten. He'd been happy, curious, and even a bit full of himself — all because he'd grown up secure. Miles's situation had clutched his heart and held on tight.

Today, the boy had grinned when he'd spotted Calvin. And, after getting a nod from Ruth, he'd walked right over to him.

"Hiya," Calvin had said.

The boy's smile had been so good to see, Calvin had felt like the ten-year-old had just given him a hug. But, knowing how skittish Miles could be, he'd tried to temper his reaction. "How are you today?"

He'd shrugged. *"Gut."*

Calvin told him about how hard he'd been working in the field, while Miles relayed how he'd been glad that last weekend's storm had cooled things off. In the grand scheme of things, none of it really mattered.

But to Calvin it did. Honestly, every word the boy spoke meant the world to him.

Later, while Sarah Anne was reading a story to the *kinner,* Ruth had walked to Calvin's side.

"I noticed that you and Miles are getting along real well," she murmured.

"We are. He's a nice child." Worried that Ruth might be wondering why he'd been giving Miles so much attention, Calvin added, "I hope you don't mind me speaking to him."

"Not at all." After peeking at the children, she said, "You're making a difference in the boy's life, Calvin. Today, Miles actually seemed happy to go on our long walk to the bookmobile. I know it's because of you."

"Well, now . . . I don't know about that."

"*Nee,* it's true. Miles likes you a lot. He talks about you often."

Not sure where the conversation was going, Calvin cleared his throat. "Ruth, I hope you don't mind. I don't mean him no harm."

Her expression softened. "Calvin, James and me have been fostering children for years and years. We like giving children a solid home when they are in need. And, if I've learned anything, it's that there's never too much love or attention. If you like

35

spending time with him, I hope you will."
She paused. "Why, you could even stop by
our house to see Miles from time to time."

"That's allowed?"

"*Jah*. It is." With a smile, she added, "It
might be easier on you, as well. I mean, then
you won't be having to stand around the
bookmobile wondering if we're going to
show up."

He smiled back. "Sarah Anne probably
doesn't know what to do with me."

Ruth looked like she was ready to say
something more, but she seemed to change
her mind. "Ah. I think I better go save Sarah
Anne before she kicks us out, *jah*?" she
joked as she walked back to the squirming
group of kids.

Now, remembering her offer to come by
their house to visit Miles, Calvin couldn't
stop thinking about it.

And, what would happen if Miriam discovered what he was actually thinking.

They would argue something awful, no
doubt. After all, they'd discussed their childless state many, many times. Each discussion had been full of hurt and tears, especially of late, ever since her last miscarriage
and the fancy *Englisch* doctor's warnings
that she would likely never be able to carry
a child to full term — if she happened to

conceive in the first place.

Calvin had never felt so forlorn. He wanted to help his wife, wanted to encourage her, but there didn't seem to be anything he could say that would make a difference. It was his fault, no doubt. He'd been so overwhelmed by their losses; he'd sometimes forget to hide his feelings around Miriam. His disappointment would make her feel worse — sometimes even guilty. He knew she was harboring a lot of guilty feelings, no matter how many times he'd told her he didn't blame her one bit.

And sometimes, when Calvin couldn't sleep in the middle of the night, he would find himself admitting that he would probably feel the same way if the shoe was on the other foot.

Which was why he'd recently been bringing up the idea of adoption again.

Unfortunately, his wife did not want to adopt a babe. They'd had this discussion many, many times before. Miriam still held out hope that they'd have a child of their own — one who was really theirs, a little boy or girl who looked like them — and she had made it clear that if they started thinking about adoption, she'd be giving up that dream.

Calvin hadn't exactly agreed, but he had

also begun to learn that it was different for women. After all, they had sole responsibility for the babe during pregnancy. One could only assume that holding another woman's child would never feel the same.

But he was starting to wonder if the child they adopted needed to be a baby who was theirs from birth.

After all, the Lord had put Miles in Calvin's world for a reason. Maybe it was so Calvin and Miriam could learn that all children were precious and that children could come into their life through many paths.

Unfortunately, Calvin had no idea how to share that thought with Miriam. He had no idea how to even begin.

FOUR

· **TIP #4** ·
One could meet a nice man in an
exercise class, at the grocery store, or
even out walking in a park.
I've had the best luck at the library,
however.

They'd eaten a silent breakfast. Calvin had
kept sneaking looks at her, obviously trying
to figure out what he could say to make
things better.

She, on the other hand, had been trying
not to throw up.

The moment he went to the barn, Miriam
had run upstairs and deposited her whole
breakfast into the toilet. Barely in time.

Then, just because it was starting to look
like that kind of day, she'd burst into tears.

An hour later, she was sitting in their
bedroom, staring at the unmade bed and
attempting to focus on the source of her

weepiness instead of how much she would rather be sleeping. Which was, of course, yet another source of confusion. She didn't laze about. She never had. Even as a child, she'd refused to take naps.

So why was it sounding like the best idea in the world?

But perhaps a nap — her mother's favorite remedy for a blue mood — wasn't such a silly idea, after all. Back in those difficult years before she'd become a teenager, Miriam had had a terrible time with her best girlfriends. Some had already been looking forward to graduating eighth grade, flirting with boys and practically planning their weddings in hushed, giddy tones on their way to and from school. And some had wanted to stay firmly entrenched in childhood, by their mothers' sides. Miriam's problem had been that she'd floated somewhere in between. Anxious not to lose a friend, she had tried to fit in with everyone. But that plan had backfired all too quickly. For a time, she'd lost both sets of friends. That loss — and her confusion about who she should be — had propelled her into a depression. She'd cried, felt lethargic, and took as many naps as she could.

Was that what was happening now?

Was everything so bad with her marriage

that she had returned to coping the way she had at twelve? The very idea that she was regressing like that scared her half to death.

Determined to get some help, she decided to walk to her parents' house. It was an easy walk down a windy road, but because it was a far more difficult, uphill journey on the way back, she often asked Calvin to take her in the buggy. But the weather was nice, and maybe some exercise would help lift her spirits.

As she expected, the walk was relaxing. Though it had been a blustery, cold, wet April, May had brought many changes. Today was a perfect spring day. It was sunny and warm enough to go without a sweater, though she would need one soon enough. A lingering chill still permeated the winds, so when the sun went down it would grow cold once again.

As she approached the rambling white house she grew up in, Miriam was surprised to see that her sister, Lavinia, was there instead of her brother, Eli. Eli, his wife, Bethy, and their two children lived in the *dawdi haus*. But Lavinia lived in Sugarcreek, about thirty minutes in a car and far longer than that by buggy. She wasn't a frequent visitor.

Lavinia and their mother were sitting on

the front porch, snapping peas into a large metal bowl. Both paused as she came into view.

"Hi, Mimi!" Lavinia called out, using her family's pet name for her. "What brings you over here?"

No way did she want to tell her perfect sister about her marriage worries. "No reason. I'm uh, going to be canning tomorrow and the next day, so I thought it would be good to take a walk today."

Her mother's eyes narrowed, but she merely stood up. "It's a good day for me, then. I've got both of my daughters here at the same time."

"Would you like some help with the peas?"

"*Nee.* We've almost got it done."

Looking around, Miriam realized it was quiet. "Where are Bethy and the twins?" she asked. "And where's your John, Lavinia?"

Lavinia smiled. "He's with my neighbor Audrey for a few hours."

John was only ten months old. "Why?"

"She asked if she could watch him for a bit. Hers are in school now, you know." Her smile grew. "Besides, I've been so tired, I was happy for a break."

She was tired, too? Maybe something was going around. "Why do you think you're so tired? Could you be catching a cold or something?" And yes, she probably sounded too hopeful about that.

"Only a nine-month cold." She took a deep breath and blurted, "I'm pregnant again!"

"Oh!" Miriam's topsy-turvy mood plummeted again. "That's . . . that's wonderful. I mean, congratulations." She hurried over and gave Lavinia a hug.

"*Danke.*" Lavinia's voice rose, as it always did when she was very happy. "Roland and I could hardly believe that we conceived again so fast. We'd rather hoped to wait a bit longer, but it seems the Lord has His own plan."

"Yes, it would seem so." Miriam tried to sound pleased, but it was hard . . . especially since all she could seem to do was wonder why the Lord wasn't blessing her and Calvin the same way.

She was faithful, she really was. But sometimes, she worried that her faith was wavering. Why, nowadays, she wanted to yell her frustrations every time someone told her their good fortune was the Lord's will. How come He seemed to only want her to suffer and wait for a baby? Did He really not want her and Calvin to be happy?

Or, did He believe they shouldn't have

43

good things happen to them? Had they done something awful she wasn't aware of?

Her mother held out a hand. "Miriam, come help me with the kettle. I have some peppermint tea I've been saving for a special occasion. You may help me prepare it."

"*Jah,* Mamm."

She followed her mother inside, taking note that everything looked exactly as it did when she was little. The dark green sofa and matching chairs were in the same spots they'd been in for the last twenty years. So was the hard, uncomfortable wooden rocker. Her mother's quilting frame was set up in front of the living room windows, just like always.

Nothing seemed to change here at all.

There was comfort in that, she supposed. But sometimes she did wonder if her mother ever had a notion to shake things up a bit.

Miriam rinsed out the kettle in the sink and filled it with cold water, then lit the gas burner on the stove. She noticed her mother wasn't getting out cookies, cups, or tea bags. "Mamm, what else do you need for tea?"

"Only a moment."

Her insides tensed. "Why?"

Pressing a warm hand on her daughter's arm, Mamm spoke again, each word soft and carefully measured. "I have to admit

44

that I brought you inside to make sure you weren't too upset about your sister's news. Sometimes Lavinia can be rather obtuse."

No way did she want to start crying again. "I'm not sure I know what you mean," she said.

"Of course you do, dear," Mamm said softly. "There's no shame in being happy for your sister but sad for yourself. The Lord doesn't ask us to only think of others, you know. I feel He would understand if you sometimes focus only on yourself." She patted Miriam's arm again. "Your time will come. One day."

Yes. One day. It was obvious that coming over had been a very bad idea. Now she was feeling even more depressed — and dreading the long, uphill walk back to her own house. "Where's Daed?"

"Daed? Oh, he is in town with your *bruder.* Why?"

"No reason."

"Let's sit inside. Go get your sister, and we'll catch up."

"Okay." She walked out to the porch and tried to keep a smile on her face. "Lavinia, Mamm said to come on in."

"Oh, of course." Looking down at the big metal bowl, she added, "Carry that inside, won't you, Mimi? Roland doesn't like me

45

carrying anything too heavy in my condition."

She was gone before Miriam could reply, but maybe that was a good thing, since right at that moment, all she wanted to do was tell her sister exactly how inconsiderate she was being. Couldn't Lavinia see how much she was struggling?

Though, of course, this depression she was feeling wasn't going to magically evaporate. If the Lord determined that she would never have a child, Miriam knew she was going to have to accept that.

But it was going to be so hard.

She already felt like she was letting Calvin down and had become a source of pity for her parents and her siblings. Almost as bad was the realization that she was going to have to suffer in silence. People would think she was being selfish if she wasn't happy for their large families.

Feeling a burst of nausea hit her again, she pushed it away. She picked up the bowl of peas. She would go sit with her mother and sister and pretend to be happy. Again.

However, Miriam was starting to wonder if she was ever going to truly feel happy. At the moment, she just wasn't sure.

FIVE

· **TIP #5** ·

Nowadays, it doesn't matter who makes
the first move. Yes, I realize that can
be confusing.

"Miles, you've barely touched your dessert.
Do you not care for strawberries and ice
cream?" Mrs. Schmidt asked from the other
side of the picnic table.

"I like it fine. Sorry."

The other kids looked at him and snick-
ered but didn't say anything. They wouldn't
because Mr. and Mrs. Schmidt were in
hearing distance. But Miles knew that the
moment they were out of earshot, one
would ask why he was so quiet all the time
or why he couldn't even eat dessert without
someone having to make a fuss over him.

He supposed he couldn't blame them,
though.

He spooned another big bite into his

47

mouth and quickly swallowed.

He didn't exactly love strawberries, but the fruit didn't have anything to do with his lack of appetite. The truth was that he kept thinking about the bookmobile and Calvin Gingerich. The man was really nice and always went out of his way to talk to him. And, when they talked, Calvin listened, like Miles had something interesting to say, like what he thought mattered. Hardly anyone did that anymore.

Not that they ever did, he reminded himself.

Hating that he had started thinking about his real parents, Miles scooped up the last of the ice cream and stuffed it into his mouth. At least he'd done that much.

"Everyone, time to rinse your dishes," Mr. Schmidt said.

Dutifully, Miles got in line behind Minnie, Ethan, and the triplets and waited his turn. Mary looked back at him and smiled.

He smiled back.

Mary, Ian, and Jonas weren't mean; they were just spoiled and had a lot of energy. And the trio seemed to love to egg one another on. Miles reckoned he would do the same thing if he had close siblings, too.

At first, their loudness had caught him off guard, but soon he had realized they were just like puppies. The three five-year-olds were sometimes a mess and didn't always mind their parents, but they were basically harmless.

In any case, he'd rather be around them than in his previous foster home. At the Hershbergers', he'd been one of three foster kids. Sam and Aaron had been at the home longer. They were sullen and kept to themselves, rarely speaking out loud. Instead, they'd conversed through long, secret glances. He'd never felt comfortable around them.

So, it really was fine at the Schmidts' house. It wasn't their fault he was once again the odd one out. He'd always been that way.

"Miles, would you mind helping me with these dishes for a moment?" Mrs. Schmidt asked.

"Nee."

Mr. Schmidt took the others upstairs. It was now shower time. One by one they'd all have to stand in line, waiting their turn while Mr. Schmidt timed them with an egg timer. They were on a rotation, so Miles knew he was going to be second to last tonight. All things considered, he'd much rather wash dishes than stand in the hall while holding the towel Mrs. Schmidt had given him for the week.

"Do you want me to wash or dry?" he asked.

"How about you dry?" After he picked up the dish towel, Mrs. Schmidt added, "There's actually another reason I asked you to stay behind and help me, Miles. I wanted to talk to you about something."

"What?" Boy, he hoped it wasn't about leaving their house already. He'd only been there three months.

"It has to do with Calvin Gingerich. Does that name ring a bell, by chance? He is the man we sometimes see at the bookmobile."

"I remember him."

She smiled as she sprayed water on a bowl before passing it to him. "He's nice, isn't he?"

Miles dried the bowl, then set it on the counter. "*Jah.* He reads *gut,* too."

"You know, I thought the same thing. He has a deep, calm voice. Everyone seems to like that very much." She handed him a coffee cup.

He carefully set it down on a dishcloth while he finished drying the second bowl. "What about Calvin? I mean, Mr. Gingerich?"

"Well, it seems that he's taken a shine to you."

50

"What does that mean?"

She handed him four newly scrubbed teaspoons. "It means that he asked me and James if he could spend more time with you."

"Why would he want to do that?" He immediately wished he hadn't just sounded so hopeful.

For the first time since he'd met her, Ruth got tears in her eyes. "Miles, I'm sorry. I'm sure you're thinking the same thing I was, that he would like to adopt you. But I don't think that's the case. I think . . . well, I think he's hoping for the two of you to perhaps become friends."

Calvin wanted them to be friends? But why?

"What do you think?" he finally asked Ruth.

She shrugged as she walked to the corner of the kitchen and folded her arms across her chest. "I've been thinking a lot about this, and I'm of the mind that it might be a good thing for you both. Calvin strikes me as a rather quiet sort. And Sarah Anne has told me he and his wife, Miriam, are mighty nice people. That said, Calvin is a farmer, and Miriam spends a lot of time on the farm, too. I think they might be lonely people."

51

They sounded kind of like him. "Hey, Ruth? How can someone be lonely if they're not all alone?"

"You'd be surprised how easy that is," Ruth said. "People can be unhappy, or in a rut, or well, I don't know. I just know that it is possible."

Of course, Miles knew that it was very possible to feel alone in the midst of others. He'd pretty much felt like that his whole life — he just hadn't believed others could feel that way, too.

Ruth picked up another bowl. "Anyway, I'm not saying you act like you're lonely, but I have noticed you aren't quite so, um . . ."

"Loud?"

She laughed. "*Jah.* 'Loud' is a good way of putting it indeed. Right. So, because you aren't as loud as the other *kinner,* I thought you might appreciate a break from time to time. Calvin mentioned that maybe you two could go fishing. Do you like to fish?"

"I don't know. I've never gone fishing."

Ruth grinned like he'd just said the smartest thing in the world. "Well, there you go, then. You could go fishing with Calvin. But maybe first he can come over and tend to the goats with ya."

"I hope he likes goats." There were a lot

of them, and most were bossy, too.

She laughed. "Come now. Our goats are a far bit quieter than the six of you."

"That is true."

"So, why don't you think about it tonight and let me know how you feel about this tomorrow?" Ruth placed a hand on his arm. "If you'd rather not spend time with Calvin, I won't be upset, and I'm sure Calvin will understand, too."

Miles couldn't remember the last time he had a choice in anything. Even his own father — no, he wasn't going to think about him now.

"*Jah,*" he said at last. "I'll tell you tomorrow."

"Very well." She patted him on the shoulder. "Now, you'd best go grab your towel and get in line."

He smiled at her before walking down the hall. Then he realized that he was also smiling for another reason. He now had something to look forward to. He already knew what he was going to say. He should have told Ruth right then and there.

But there was something special about having a secret, and there was really something nice about getting to make a choice for himself. So, he would keep it in his head and think about fishing some more.

After all, chances were pretty good that Calvin might have already changed his mind.

People did that all the time.

SIX

Save yourself the headache and inform
your family that you are dating again. I
promise, you don't want them to
be surprised.

Miriam was all teary-eyed, and Calvin had
no idea how to help her. But even though
everything he did seemed to upset her, he
knew he had to try. She was his *frau,* and
he loved her.

"Miriam, want to take a walk around the
pond?"

She looked at him blankly. "Why?"

Sometimes, the way she questioned even
his most innocuous offers felt so cruel. "It's
a pretty evening, and we used to enjoy it.
Remember?"

"*Jah.* I remember."

Since she didn't seem to be any more
motivated, Calvin took a different tack. "We

55

could count bunnies. I'm sure they're out and about right now."

Her eyes widened. "Do you think so?"

"Oh, *jah.*" He held out a hand. "Come now. Let's see if we can spy twelve of them."

"You won't shoot any, will you?"

He laughed. "I would never encourage my *frau* to watch me kill her favorite rodent."

As he'd hoped, she retorted, "Calvin, rabbits aren't rodents. They're adorable and so sweet."

But she did take his hand and allowed him to lead her down the drive toward the small pond. Just to egg her on, he teased, "Those sweet bunnies also feast on your strawberries."

"Only some." But her lips quirked up.

"When they're not sampling strawberries, they're chomping on your tulips."

"The deer do, too."

"I *canna* argue with that, can I?" Pretending to be mighty put-upon, he shook his head. "*Jah,* we are surely surrounded by gutsy interlopers." When she giggled, he squeezed her hand lightly and kept his pace slow. It was a lovely May evening. Sunny and gorgeous and still not too warm. For once, there was hardly a cloud in the sky. Its bright blue had faded to a steel color, and it was so clear Calvin felt as if he could see for miles.

It was perfect.

"Oh! Calvin. There are two!" She pointed to a pair of rather young-looking rabbits, happily nibbling grass in a shady spot.

"There's another one." He pointed in the other direction to a much bigger hare who looked to be contentedly sleeping.

"That makes three!"

Oh, but it was good to see her smile again. It had been far too long since he'd seen her look so carefree. "Now, if all rabbits were like that one, snoozing in an empty field, I'd have no problem with them. But most are brazen, Miriam."

" 'Brazen'? Hardly that."

"It's true. Why, the other day, I just about had to pick one up in order to get it out of my lettuce patch. And when he ran off, he still had a lettuce leaf trailing out of his mouth." That wasn't a lie, either. Miriam's sweet bunnies would try to rule the world if they were bigger. He was sure of it.

She giggled. "Oh, stop exaggerating."

"I swear it, they are eating all our lettuce."

"They're hungry."

He frowned, as if he really cared all that much about lettuce. "As am I."

"They're God's creatures, Calvin. Plus, I love them."

He knew she did. That was one of the things he'd always loved about her. Miriam had a beautiful, oh so kind heart. Back when they were newlyweds, he'd had to be so very careful to guard it. If he ever complained about the laundry or his supper, she would cry, and then he would feel terrible.

Remembering those days, and those first few months in their home, he pointed to a little box turtle lying on the bank of the pond. "Do you remember when we first got married and we had all those turtles on the driveway?"

"Oh, my stars. I do. My, but they seemed to multiply every day. What made you think of them?"

"I don't know. It's a good memory, I guess." A mighty good one. For some reason, that year the turtles had enjoyed an exceptionally good mating period and they'd all decided to sun on the driveway and the usually quiet road right outside their farm every afternoon. He'd ignored them — until a car drove over one and Miriam had cried.

After that, he'd joined her on a nightly walk, picking up turtles from the middle of the drive and depositing them in the grass.

"I guess all these bunnies made me think

of your turtle rescuing mission."

"We were saving one turtle at a time," she said. "You didn't want to see them harmed, either."

"That's true. I did not." He'd always thought the tiny creatures had needed a helping hand, given their slow feet. That said, he was fairly sure he wouldn't have been quite as vigilant if not for Miriam. Looking at her fondly, he added, "You got to be mighty skilled at it."

"The first time I picked one up, and that little turtle's head popped out, I squealed."

"I remember. It was loud enough to be heard for miles."

"Then I got brave." Her pretty features filled with pride, nearly taking his breath away.

"I started thinking that those turtles took you for granted. They'd venture out to lay in the sun, knowing that you'd give them a ride to safety," he teased as they made their way around the pond. Oh, the time they'd had! Every night, they'd practically march up and down the driveway, combing the pavement for turtles. He'd often wondered what he would have done if she hadn't been there. Would he have ignored them all? Maybe only picked up one or two? He didn't like to think that he might have done only that.

She laughed. "I haven't thought about those days in years. Those turtles did indeed have me working for them. On some days, I threatened to make turtle soup!"

"I've never seen them since. Not to that extent, at least. I wonder why?"

"I don't know. Maybe they didn't want to press their luck. Or perhaps they decided it was less work to simply lie on the old tree limbs around the pond."

Looking to where she pointed, Calvin spied three turtles lined up next to each other, their little heads, tails, and limbs practically splayed out, as if they were intent on getting a suntan.

"I daresay you're right. Four!" he called out, pointing to another rabbit.

"Five, six!" she said, pointing in the other direction.

And so it continued. Walking, looking for animals, talking about things that had happened so very long ago but felt just a week or two in the past. "I'm glad we came out on this walk, Miriam. I needed it."

"I guess I needed it, too." She stretched her arms out to her sides. "I feel more relaxed than I have in days."

"Miriam, I wasn't going to mention anything, but you've seemed upset with me lately. What have I done?"

Everything in her body language changed. She pulled her hand from his and stepped a little farther away. "Do we have to talk about this? Now?"

He felt like a heel. Here, they had been having such a good time and his wife had just told him how glad she was that they were spending such an enjoyable time together.

But he couldn't ignore the facts. Some things could be covered up, but they were always there. "*Jah*. I don't want you mad at me."

She folded her arms over her chest. "I'm scared, to be honest. It might be like letting one of those awful jack-in-the-box clowns out of its cage."

"Hopefully it won't be anything as scary as that. But even if it is, I'm willing to risk it." He meant that, too. He loved Miriam. He didn't want to continue to walk on eggshells around her.

"Fine. Calvin, I think your eye has strayed."

Of all the things he thought she was going to say, that was the very last. He was shocked. "Miriam . . . are you saying . . . do you really think . . ." He caught his breath and tried again. "Miriam, do you think I'm cheating on you?"

"Don't act so shocked." Her voice was bitter. "All the signs are there."

What signs?

"Miriam, just so you know . . . I'm not *acting* shocked. I *am* shocked. What have I been doing that is making you think I would do something so wrong?"

"You've been coming home late for supper. And I know you've been covering up something." Her voice hardened. "I know you, Calvin. I know what you're like — you can't lie worth beans. Your right eye twitches, and you look sick to your stomach. So, don't even try to deny it. I *know* you're up to something."

He'd been a fool to think she wouldn't notice even the smallest change in his routine. He noticed everything about her. Hadn't their conversation about bunnies and turtles proved that?

"All right. I have been doing something that I wasn't comfortable telling you about. But it has nothing to do with another woman."

She turned to him. "Stop stalling. What is it?"

Miriam's face looked pale, and hurt shone in her eyes. He had to just tell her. "One day when I was at the bookmobile, I met

Miles. He's a ten-year-old foster child living at the Schmidts' *haus.*"

"What . . . what does a little boy have to do with anything?"

Everything.

He weighed his words carefully. It felt like this moment was not just important to him and Miriam, but to that child, too. "He needs a friend. So, I've been trying to see him when Ruth Schmidt takes her brood to the bookmobile."

"That's what you've been doing? You've been spending time with a little boy?"

He nodded. "He's a sweet child, Miriam. And even surrounded by all those other children, he still seems so very alone. There's something about him that's special to me." He paused, then blurted, "So much so, I decided to do something else."

While she stared at him, her eyes still filled with confusion, he felt his stomach knot, hoping that what he was about to say wasn't the worst idea in the world.

Seven

For a first date, meet in a public place.
Not everyone acts the same out of
the spotlight.

Miriam's head was spinning. She'd been so sure that her husband had been sneaking around on her. And she'd been right — Calvin had. But, of course, it wasn't what she'd thought. Never could she have imagined that he'd been going to so much trouble to spend time with a child.

Though she was puzzled and more than a little dismayed by the fact that he hadn't trusted her enough to talk about it, she knew she had to tread lightly. She was afraid if she didn't convey the right tone, Calvin might be reluctant to share everything he was thinking.

"Calvin, what have you decided to do?" she asked slowly.

He studied her for a few seconds before replying. "I asked Ruth if I can spend more time with him," he replied at last. "I thought maybe I could visit his house, go for walks, maybe help him with a project." He shrugged. "I really have no idea. But it would be just the two of us."

Just the two of them. Though she knew her husband well enough to know he would never intentionally make her feel bad, she was still hurt. "I see."

"Plus, Miles seems to feel the same way about me, which Ruth says is rare for him. I feel like the Lord has opened up my heart to this boy. I don't want to ignore His will."

"Ah."

"Miriam, what are you thinking? And please be honest. I need to know."

The desperation in his voice was what caught her. This boy, *this boy she'd never known about,* mattered to him. She wanted to say the right words, yet everything inside her was a jumbled mess.

On the one hand, Calvin was doing the exact thing that had made her fall in love with him. He was reaching out to someone in need and giving his heart without reservations. It was lovely.

But he'd also been keeping it a secret from her, and he would have continued to do it if she hadn't said anything.

Weighing her words, she said, "I am feeling confused. Why didn't you tell me about this child two weeks ago?"

"I know how you feel about adoption. And though I'm not trying to adopt Miles right now, I was afraid you'd tell me you didn't want me to spend time with him. He and I have developed a bond, a good one. I *canna* betray that."

His explanation actually hurt her heart. It was true, she hadn't ever felt called to adopt. Though she'd known Calvin didn't feel the same way, she'd never imagined that he would be contemplating adoption again without speaking to her about it. "I'm not so unfeeling that I would hurt you or a child on purpose."

"I know."

It didn't sound that way. It seemed like he'd found another flaw in her. "Do you, though? Calvin, I'm not trying to be difficult or mean, but here you've just gone and told me that you've been developing a relationship with a small boy on the sly — all because you didn't think I wouldn't support it. I feel like I've failed you somehow."

No, it felt like she'd disappointed him yet again.

How could Calvin be so fond of her saving tiny turtles but think she'd turn her back on a little boy who was so obviously alone in the world? Surely he realized that just because she'd yearned to give him his own child, it didn't mean she didn't care for other children. After four years of marriage, had he really thought she was that type of person?

"Miriam, you haven't failed me." He sighed. "To be honest, I don't know why I didn't tell you. I've meant to talk to you about Miles and Ruth and reading stories at the bookmobile, but every time I started to bring up the subject, it didn't seem to be the right time."

"Ah." Of course she wanted to rail at him, to remind her husband that she was always happy to speak about any subject. Goodness, sometimes she felt like she had to badger conversation out of him at their midday meal or during the one or two hours they sat together in the fading light before bedtime. But then she recalled the many days she'd been too depressed to do much at all. She'd been feeling like such a failure, because she hadn't become pregnant, that she'd sunken into herself.

Now they could either turn this into another squabble or she could take advantage of the situation and change things.

There was only one choice. She loved Calvin. There was no doubt in her heart about that.

"Tell me about him now, then. I mean, tell me about Miles." She smiled encouragingly. She wanted to know everything about the little boy who had stolen her husband's heart.

Calvin brightened right up. "Oh, Miriam. He's such a fine boy. But he's in the midst of all those Schmidt *kinner.*"

The name rang a bell, and she slowly put two and two together. "Wait, the Schmidts have the triplets, *jah*?" More than one person referred to those triplets with a shudder. She was one of them, too. The children seemed to have no manners or boundaries. They were a troop of banshees, without a doubt.

"That's the family, for sure. The Schmidts have a set of triplets and now three foster *kinner* as well."

She raised her brows. "That's a lot of children. It must be a *verra* full *haus.*"

Calvin nodded. "A busy one, too, since they are all under the age of eleven."

Just imagining all the noise made her want to cover her ears. "I don't know how Ruth Schmidt does it."

"She's a kind woman, but it's my opinion

68

those tiny triplets run roughshod over her. Sarah Anne practically winces whenever they arrive at her bookmobile."

"Poor Sarah Anne." Lavinia was in the same church district as the Schmidts, and her sister had once declared that the triplets could create a path of destruction in mere minutes, like a cyclone, but louder. "How did you and Miles strike up a friendship in the middle of all that chaos?"

"Well, it was the strangest thing. I just happened to walk into the bookmobile one day, minding my own business, when Sarah Anne practically begged me to read the children a story so she could get her bearings." He shrugged. "So I did."

"You?"

"I didn't feel like I had a choice, Miriam."

She chuckled. "I would've liked to have seen that." *Nee,* actually, she would have liked to have heard about it before this moment.

His chin went up. "I did a *gut* job of reading, believe it or not. Anyway, Miles was there, and he seemed so out of sorts, my heart went out to him. We started talking about books. Then, the next time we saw each other, we talked some more. Now, I think we have the beginnings of a real relationship."

69

"So much so that Ruth is going to permit you to visit him at her house?"

"She's encouraging it. And, since she's taken in a lot of foster kids over the years, I'm going to take her advice."

"I understand."

Warmth filled his gaze. "*Danke,* Miriam. I know it's bad timing, what with us worrying about having our own family."

"It sounds as if this poor boy has had a lot of bad timing in his life already. I'm glad he's met you." She meant that sincerely. She felt sorry for Miles. She also loved Calvin and wanted him to be happy . . . even if she wasn't sure how she felt about his news.

"If my visits go all right, and Miles learns to trust me . . . Maybe you could meet him one day, too."

"Really?"

"Of course. I mean, if you wanted. You don't have to meet him if you don't want to."

"I do want that. I would love to meet Miles." She realized she wasn't just saying the words, either. She now wanted to get to know the boy who had taken her husband's heart so easily.

He wrapped an arm around her shoulders. "I'm not sure where the Lord is taking us, but I'm glad you will be by my side."

"There's nowhere else I'd rather be, Calvin." Recalling their vows, she added, "By your side is where I belong."

EIGHT

· **TIP #8** ·

A coffee shop is a good place for a
first meeting. Unless, of course, you
don't like coffee.

The day was so mild, Sarah Anne had
pulled a lawn chair outside. It was the end
of the day, and she'd already put in a full
day's work, filling out paperwork and re-
ports for much of the time. All she wanted
to do now was stretch out her legs, feel the
warm sun on her face, and read another
chapter of her book. At least until one of
her patrons showed up.

"Do they pay you to laze about like that?"

Startled, and rather offended, she jolted
her head up.

And then looked into Pete Canon's eyes.
"Pete! What a surprise! What are you doing
here?"

"I thought I'd get a book." He crossed his

arms over his chest and raised his eyebrows.

Pete's problem was that he was far too handsome. Once again, he was wearing old jeans, boots, and an untucked flannel shirt. His undershirt's collar peeked out near his Adam's apple. It seemed to accentuate his five-o'clock shadow. Or maybe it was the dark sunglasses he had on.

And . . . once again she'd been checking him out while he was just trying to check out a book. Embarrassed, she stood up.

"Sorry. It's been a long day. Go on in."

Noticing her pick up the chair, he stopped her. "You don't need to get up on my account."

"I needed to get up anyway. I only pulled this out because it's the end of the day and no one was here."

"I don't know if it's a good or bad thing that I came here, then."

"It's good." When he grinned, she felt herself blush. "I meant the bookmobile is here for patrons. I'm glad you're here."

Still gazing at her, he stuffed his hands in his pockets. "Me, too."

It was obvious that he wasn't talking about books. Sarah Anne looked away, attempting to clumsily wrangle the fold-up chair into the little bag it was stored in, but for some reason, it didn't seem to want to cooperate.

He snatched it out of her hands. "Let me give you a hand."

"That's not necessary —" But it must have been because in less than fifteen seconds he had the chair in its nylon bag and handed it back to her. "Thank you."

He grinned again before disappearing into the vehicle.

She fanned her cheeks. Goodness, but she needed to get herself together. Yes, she liked his company . . . and she found him very attractive. But he probably acted the same way around a lot of women. She needed to keep reminding herself of that.

But instead of perusing the books, Pete was picking up some wooden blocks that a preschooler had left in the corner an hour or two ago.

"You didn't need to clean, Pete."

He brushed off her protest. "It wasn't a problem. So, how are you? I haven't been in town for a while. Anything new?"

Well, she'd been wondering why she hadn't seen him. "I've been fine. Just working. What about you? Were you on vacation?"

"I got an account with a construction company over in Erie. It's been good, helping all the employees get set up with new insurance, but I've been gone a lot."

74

"You've been going out to Erie, Pennsylvania?"

"The one and only." He smiled at her. "It's a good opportunity for my firm. The business has almost a hundred employees. They had a pretty poor agent before, so I've been answering a lot of questions."

"I bet. But it's going well?"

"It is. In spite of the fact that I'm making everyone fill out new paperwork, the folks have been easy to work with. That isn't always the case, you know."

"I imagine not." Thinking about Pete working with everyone, Sarah Anne felt flooded with a warm, cozy feeling. He had a calm, easygoing way about him. She imagined that was very appreciated. Looking at him more closely, she noticed he really seemed pleased about the job. "It's gratifying work for you."

He laughed. "It is. But it has its share of headaches. Sometimes I think it would have been easier for me to help them create a whole new insurance program instead."

"They'll come around. Personal and medical insurance policies are pretty confusing things. I've always felt like the wording was like trying to maneuver a car through a giant spider's web. One wrong turn and a person can get stuck!"

He chuckled. "You're not alone." He shrugged. "Actually, I was so frustrated with the previous agent's work that I ended up asking some of the guys if I could lend a hand on a sweet lady's rundown house they're working on in the evenings. I needed to de-stress by doing something with my hands."

"You can do that?"

He nodded. "I worked construction all through five years of college. I'm not an expert or anything, but I can hold my own."

She bet he could. "So, um, how is the lady's house coming along?"

"Well enough. After they put in some new wiring and plumbing, all it really needed was a little help around the worn edges."

"Sounds like everyone my age," she said with a smile. "We've got some parts that need a bit of repair, but we make up for the flaws with a good dose of character."

"It's everyone *our* age, Sarah Anne."

That was true. A couple of weeks ago, he'd mentioned that he was sixty-three when she admitted that she had just turned sixty-one.

But he didn't look sixty-three. All in all, he seemed to be in particularly fine shape. Embarrassed that she'd even thought that, she pulled a book from the shelf closest to her. "Well, I'll, um, let you look around. I'm going to take a peek at this."

"Oh. Well, okay." His eyebrows rose, but his face went blank again.

"What?"

"Nothing. It's just that the title of the book caught me off guard."

"Really? I keep all types of books here, you know. My patrons are all ages and interests."

"Of course. I . . . You're right. Sorry."

Looking down, she noticed the title: *Animal Husbandry and How to Improve It.* Oh! Oh, for goodness' sakes.

She dropped that book on the counter like it was on the verge of bursting into flames.

Well, at least she knew one thing she'd always thought to be true was a total lie: Years ago, she'd been sure that when she was older, she would be wiser and far more sure of herself. But it turned out she was just as goofy as she'd ever been.

Maybe even more so.

"Can we forget what book I was just pretending to read?"

Pete grinned. "Not on your life. The image of you holding that book close to your heart is already cemented into my brain."

"For some reason I thought you'd say that."

"I've been accused of being a good guy

from time to time . . . but never a saint." As Sarah Anne felt her cheeks heat even more, he moved to stand right in front of her. "I think we should talk about something else, though . . . like, why you are so nervous around me."

Because he was handsome as all get-out. Because she'd never imagined being attracted to another man, and she didn't know how to handle it. Because it had been so long since she'd been on a date that she wasn't even sure people called it that anymore.

She might be a goof, but she still had her wits about her. There were some things she wasn't going to share out loud — no matter how handsome and interesting a man might be.

"I don't know," she lied.

"Sure about that?"

Maybe some truth *was* in order. "Pete, I have to say that I'm pretty rusty when it comes to anything that has to do with the opposite sex." She rolled her eyes. "And now I just managed to make an awkward conversation even more so. I'm sorry."

His grin faded. "No, I'm the one who owes you an apology. I'm pretty rusty at this, too." He rubbed a hand along his thigh then held it up. "My hands are even sweaty."

"Really?"

"You don't need to look so happy about that."

"I'm just glad I'm not the only one."

He blew out a breath. "How about I end our misery and just ask you out."

She gaped at him. "Like, on a date?"

He nodded. "Do you date?"

She was so shocked, she just nodded.

A couple of seconds passed.

"Is that a yes to dating or a yes to going out with me?"

If she chickened out now and said no, she was pretty sure he would take that rejection very politely, walk out without a book, and never come near her again. And then she would always wonder . . .

"Yes to the date. Maybe lunch?"

His eyes lit up. "How does lunch on Saturday sound?"

"Lunch on Saturday sounds good." She smiled, even though she was already having second thoughts. As much as she was thrilled about Pete's interest, she wondered if she was dishonoring Frank's memory.

"Will you give me your phone number, and I'll text you about places and times?"

"Yes." She got out her cell phone. "Let's exchange numbers before I embarrass myself anymore and you change your mind."

"There's no chance of that." He got out his phone and typed in her number when she called it out, then texted her so she'd have his, too.

Twenty minutes later, he was gone, and she was staring at her cell phone's screen. Boy, talk about surprises! She could soon be dating again . . . if she was ever able to push aside all her worries and fears and start living again.

NINE

It's helpful to set a clear ending to the
date. If you don't have a good reason to
end it, make one up. There's nothing
worse than being stuck on a bad date for
hours on end. Trust me on this.

Driving home with two books resting on
the bench seat next to him, Pete Canon
wondered again what had come over him.

He had a fairly solitary life and he was
used to it. He was sixty-three years old, with
three years to go at a company where he'd
already put in thirty years. He had his two
kids, Neal and Cassie, and an adorable
granddaughter, Aimee, whom he saw every
couple of weeks. He enjoyed hiking on
Saturdays, going to church on Sundays, and
lifting weights at the gym twice a week.

It had been that way for a while, too. He
and Alana, his ex, had divorced back when

81

their kids were in college. Though it had been relatively amicable — they'd both realized their marriage wasn't making either of them happy and they'd tried just about everything to make it better — it still had been hard on all of them.

In the end, though, they'd decided to do their best for Neal and Cassie. Alana had kept the house, he'd gotten a townhome nearby. And they'd both tried to be flexible when the kids came home from college.

About eight years after they divorced, Alana had remarried. He'd been happy for her. But when his children had begun pestering him to start dating, too, he'd simply shrugged. He just hadn't been interested in going down that path.

Until recently, he'd thought he'd always be that guy, the man who'd been married for a while, then opted to live the rest of his life on his own.

That plan had seemed to work, too. What with his children, his work, and his few activities, he hadn't felt like he'd been missing much. Even the few dates he'd gone on hadn't made him yearn for anything more.

But now things seemed different, and it was all because of Sarah Anne.

After arriving home, he got a glass of water and sat down on the couch. And thought about her some more.

Honestly, there was something about Sarah Anne Miller that made him yearn for more than he had. Whenever he visited her in that silly bookmobile, he felt as content as he did when he was out fishing or hiking. She was easy to be with, and easy to talk to. Actually, being around her simply felt right.

To his surprise, he often found himself thinking about her and wondering how her day was going, wondering if it had been long or if it had flown by the way she often said it did.

When the weather was bad, she was the first person he thought about. He'd worried about her driving that bus by herself on those lonely roads. Especially since half the time she would get little to no cell phone reception.

Sometimes, he'd been so concerned, he'd gone on the library website to see if there was an alert about the bookmobile. And, once or twice, like a stalker, he'd driven to the stop where she was supposed to be, just to make sure she was okay.

But last week, when he'd been over in Erie and hadn't been able to check on her, he'd realized that he missed her voice, missed the way she looked at life like everything was a gift. And so he'd made the decision to get her cell phone number so he could call her and chat.

Or, heaven help him, so he could at least text her. Just like a teenager.

Now, looking at his contact list, there was a very good chance they were going to have plans soon, too. Progress had been made.

His phone buzzed while he was staring at it, bringing him out of his stupor. Seeing it was Cassie, he picked up.

"Hey, Cass."

"Hi, Daddy. What's going on? Where are you?"

He'd secretly loved that she still called him *Daddy* half the time. "Nothing much. Just sitting at home."

"Oh, good. So you're not in Erie?"

"Nope. I should only be heading over there about once a month now. Why?"

She paused. "Oh, no reason. I just like knowing where you are."

"Where are you? Anything new?" When he heard her take a deep breath, he smiled to himself. His daughter might be a grown woman with a child of her own now, but in many ways, she was still the same little girl she'd always been. Cassie was a talker.

"Dad, you wouldn't believe it, but Aimee got in trouble yesterday in *preschool*!"

"What happened?"

"She was talking too much! Can you even believe that?"

He certainly could. He seemed to remember a little girl who often got the same report. "Uh-oh," he murmured.

"I talked to her, and Danny did, too, but she only said that she couldn't help herself."

Pete smiled. "Any ideas about what to do?"

"Not really. I guess it's been a problem for a while. Her teacher said it was time for us to get more involved. She isn't even in kindergarten yet!"

"Hmm."

"Dad, I know that *hmm.* What are you thinking?"

"I seem to recall another little girl who was always so sure that she had something important to say and that the rest of the world needed to listen."

She laughed. "Did I really?"

Remembering a particularly uncomfortable parent-teacher conference when she was in fourth grade, he said, "Sometimes."

"So it might be genetic."

He laughed. "I don't think there's a lot of 'might' there, Cassie. But, I do remember what finally worked."

"What?"

"Your mother and I cut back on your

weekend playdates." And, boy, had that been a pain. Every afternoon, Cassie would come home with a slip of paper that said how she behaved that day. For every "frowny face" Cassie got fifteen minutes lopped off her time outside on Saturdays. It worked like a charm but made him and Alana feel like prisoners stuck inside with a grumpy girl.

"I can't believe I forgot all about that."

"I kind of can't believe it, either. I remember it clear as day." He chuckled. "I'm sure your mother would say the same thing."

"I'll tell Danny. Aimee loves to play with her friend across the street. I bet it would work."

"Well, there you go."

"You make everything seem so easy, Daddy. Now, what's new with you?" Her voice flattened. "Still working, working out, and hiking by yourself?"

"Pretty much. Though . . . I also met someone."

" 'Someone'? Are you saying you met a woman you want to date?"

He rolled his eyes. Honestly, having adult children sometimes tried his patience. "Yes, Cassie. Her name is Sarah Anne." Why he was volunteering all this information, he didn't know.

"Where did you meet her?"

"She's a librarian. She runs the bookmobile. I went in one day, and we hit it off."

She chuckled. "Dad, I didn't even know you read that much."

"I do." Well, he did now.

"When are you two going out?"

"Maybe Saturday. We're supposed to figure it out this week. She gave me her phone number."

"Dad, this is great!" Her voice rose a bit, the way she did when she was excited about something. "Daddy, maybe you two will really hit it off and you won't be alone anymore."

"I think you're jumping ahead a little too much. But I'm hoping we hit it off, too."

"Have you told Neal yet?"

"No. You're the first person I've told."

"Thank goodness I called you. Otherwise, who knows when we would have found out."

"Does this 'we' mean you're about to call your brother?"

"Of course . . . unless you want to call him."

"I'll let you do the honors. But I'm warning you, I don't know how interested Neal is going to be in my social life."

"He's going to be really interested. I promise. Your lack of dating has worried

Neal even more than me."

Pete wasn't sure if he was more surprised that the conversation had taken place or that his busy son was interested in his dating life. "I didn't know you two found that to be worrisome."

"Well . . . Mom is so happy with Doug . . ."

"Doug is a good man. She deserves some happiness."

"You do, too, Daddy. You're handsome and strong. And nice."

"I'm not sure 'nice' is how you want to be described in the dating department."

"Oh, yes it is. 'Nice' is fantastic. Trust me on that."

"Well, if anything happens with Sarah Anne, I'll let you know."

"Don't worry. I'll be asking about her. Oops! Danny just got home from picking up Aimee. I better see how she did."

"Give my sweet baby girl a hug for me. Tell Danny hello, too."

"I will. And we'll see you soon. Bye, Daddy. Love you."

"Love you back," he replied before clicking off.

And then he saw the sweetest surprise. Sarah Anne had sent him a text message while he'd been on the phone.

It looked like he had been due for a little happiness of his own after all.

TEN

· **TIP #10** ·
If dating strangers feels too
uncomfortable, aim to start as friends. If
there's no chemistry, at least you'll know
another person to help with your
mousetraps.

Her mother's tone held more than a touch
of impatience. "Miriam, what in the world
has gotten into you?"

Looking down at the broken glass she'd
just stepped on with her bare foot, Miriam
winced. The water glass had shattered well
and good — it had to be in at least a
hundred shards all over her mother's wood
floor. "I'm sorry, Mamm. I'll clean it up
right now."

"*Halt!* You'll do no such thing. Sit there
and don't move. Thomas! Come here and
help us."

Miriam didn't dare move since she would

90

likely just make even more of a bloody mess . . . but that didn't mean she wanted to get her father involved. He didn't do well in medical emergencies. "Don't bring Daed into this, Mamm. There's no need for that."

But it was too late. Her father was rushing into the room.

"Into what? Oh, Mimi. What have you done?" As if she were a child again, he scooped her up into his arms and set her on the countertop.

Well aware of the blood that was still dripping on her mother's clean floor, she wiggled her foot. "It's nothing to fuss about, Daed. Just a cut."

Before she could stop him, he was lifting her foot and peering at it closely. "*Nee,* this is far more than just a simple cut, Mimi. You're bleeding like a stuck pig." Her father looked around, then before Miriam could stop him, wrapped an embroidered tea towel around her foot.

Her mother gasped. "Thomas, *nee!*"

"Patricia, what?"

"Daed, you're ruining Mamm's *gut* towel. She's never going to be able to get the stains out."

He shrugged. "Stains come and go. You're what I'm concerned about." He pulled his graying eyebrows down. "You're the one who's a bloody mess, child."

She bent down and winced. Blood was already seeping through the tea towel. Boy, she was regretting following her mother's strict no-shoes-inside rule.

Mamm wandered over, took another look at the blood-soaked towel, and sighed. "I fear you'll need stitches, Mimi."

"Surely not."

Mamm ignored her. "Thomas, you'd best go hitch up the buggy."

Her father didn't like going to the doctor. He was a firm believer that homemade remedies solved any and all problems, especially if it involved a bottle of witch hazel. Miriam couldn't count the number of times she'd watched him stick a bandage on a cut with hardly a word and then continue his day. So she was shocked when he walked right out the door to do as her mother bid.

Still sitting on the countertop, Miriam attempted to look like her injury was nothing but a minor inconvenience. "I don't need to go to the doctor."

"Of course you do. Your foot needs more help than either me or your father's witch hazel can provide."

She tried again and grasped at the most believable possibility. "I don't want to spend the money. Calvin —"

Mamm interrupted her. "Calvin doesn't want a wife with a bloody *foos,* I can promise you that." She pulled her broom out from the hall closet and started sweeping the glass to one side. "You're going, Mimi."

"Are you going to come, too, Mamm?" She kind of hoped so. There was a good chance her father was either going to fuss at the doctor or faint when she started getting stitched up.

"*Nee.* I'm going to walk over to your *haus* and tell my son-in-law what happened."

"*Danke.*" Calvin would want to know even if there was nothing he could do about it.

Her mother held out a hand. "Hop down on one foot. Carefully, though."

Miriam did as she asked and then hobbled over to the door with her mother's help. "I'm sorry about the floor."

"Floors are meant to be cleaned," Mamm said as she helped Miriam hop outside and sit down on the bench. "That's why the Lord invented mops. Ain't so?"

"Whatever you say, Mamm," she teased as her mother went back inside to get her things.

By the time Silver approached with her father in the buggy behind him, Miriam had put on one tennis shoe, wrapped her foot in an old dishrag, and was holding her purse in her hands.

After setting the buggy's brake, her father walked to her side. "Well, Mimi, are you ready to get this over with?"

"I am," she replied as he helped her get into the buggy. "Are you ready to visit the doctor, Daed?"

Looking a little green, he swallowed hard. "Not so much. But, I'll do my best to get through it the best I can," he said, scooting onto the bench beside her and then motioning Silver forward. "Anything for you, Miss Miriam."

"You haven't called me that in years."

"No? Well, I guess it's about time, then."

As Silver started down the driveway and then eventually turned right toward town, Miriam tried to remember the last time her father had driven just her somewhere. Try as she might, she couldn't. "As much as I hate dragging you to urgent care, it's nice to be with you, Daed."

"I was just thinking the same thing. I reckon Silver's even happy about spending some time with you as well." He chuckled. "Look at him. I think he's showing off."

Silver did look like he was prancing as he clip-clopped down the street. "I'm glad you still have this horse."

"He's getting older, but Silver is still the strongest horse around."

She chuckled. She'd announced that once, probably around the time she'd named the handsome Tennessee Walker Silver even though he had neither a silver coat nor mane. "You've had him for almost seven or eight years now."

"*Jah.* We got him just a year or two before Calvin started coming around and talking pretty to you."

"Now we've been married over four years." She held her breath. Now was when one of her parents would usually add how it was a shame she still hadn't had a baby.

Her father nodded. "Time moves on, don't it?"

She nodded in relief and finally relaxed. Her foot was starting to throb painfully. No telling how long this little accident was going to interfere with her work at home. "I *canna* believe I did such a stupid thing, Daed."

"Accidents aren't stupid," he said, pulling on Silver's reins as they edged to a stop at a light. "Stop being so hard on yourself. In a couple hours, you'll be home again with your husband, and all this will just be a memory."

"I just meant that —"

"Dear, this isn't the first time you've apologized for something that isn't your fault. People get cuts all the time. Sometimes they need stitches, too." As Silver started forward, Daed added, "And sometimes babes don't come right away." While she attempted to catch her breath, he continued, "Sometimes things just happen, and it ain't anyone's fault." He wagged a finger at her. "God is in charge, you know."

"I know."

He glanced her way. "*Jah* . . . but do you *believe* it, girl?"

She knew there was a difference between knowing and believing, but believing was always harder to do. "I want to believe it."

He grunted. "You need to have faith, girl."

"I'm trying."

"Faith is what happens when the Lord gets tired of you making silly plans."

Her father had said that at least once a month for all of her life, but for the first time she was starting to think it wasn't just a folksy saying. He was exactly right.

There was a hitching post for horses and buggies in the back of the urgent care parking lot. "I'll drop you off here at the entrance so you won't need to hobble all the way back," he said.

"*Danke,* Daed." Without waiting for him to give her a hand, she slid out and grabbed her purse. "If you want to wait outside with Silver, I won't mind."

Glancing just beyond her, he nodded. "I might take you up on that. Silver ain't too fond of these concrete parking lots, you know."

"I'll try to be quick."

"Stop worrying and go on in, girl."

When she turned to the automatic doors, she saw Calvin was standing there. "How did you get here before I did?"

"As soon as your mother told me what happened, I hopped on my bicycle and rode through three fields."

"Old Mr. Evans is gonna get mad if he finds out."

"That's a small price to pay." Wrapping an arm around her waist, he led her inside. "Let's get you into one of these exam rooms."

"We can go right in?"

"*Jah.* I already told Valerie here that you were on the way. I gave her all your information, too."

The *Englisch* receptionist looked up at her and smiled. "Your husband was quite insistent, Mrs. Gingerich. He's a keeper."

"He is."

97

After a nurse named Paige led them into a room, Calvin helped Miriam onto the exam table. "I can hardly believe you're here."

"Don't ever imagine I wouldn't be," he said.

"Mr. Gingerich, would you mind stepping out to the waiting room? These rooms aren't real big, you know." Paige wasn't exaggerating. The room was about the size of a cubicle.

"I'll be all right, Calvin," Miriam said.

"Okay, fine. I'll go check on your father," Calvin said before he walked out the door.

Miriam smiled at him as he walked back down the hall.

"Mrs. Gingerich, let's take your vitals." Paige turned on a computer screen. One by one, she asked Miriam about her age and medical history, stopping to take her temperature, pulse, and blood pressure. "Now, any chance you could be pregnant?"

The question brought her back to all the depressing days when she realized their dreams would never come true. Feeling defensive, she frowned. "Why would you ask that? I'm here for a cut foot."

"It's standard practice to ask, just in case we need to give you an X-ray or an antibiotic." Her fingers hovered over the keyboard. "So, could there be a chance?"

"I don't think I am." Then, remembering her father's words about the Lord being in charge, she added, "But I suppose there's a chance."

"We better check to be safe." After putting on a fresh bandage, she said, "I'm sorry to make you do this with a hurt foot, but let's go get a urine sample. Luckily, the bathroom is right next door."

Having to take the test felt rather rude, but she did as the nurse asked. After all, it wasn't the nurse's fault that she'd cut up her foot.

Taking the plastic container, she hobbled into the bathroom, hoping this awkward visit to urgent care would be over very, very soon.

ELEVEN

It's good form to try to be polite,
respectful, and courteous.
Rude behavior is a turnoff.

After she'd given the nurse her sample, Miriam was helped up on the examination table, and her wound was uncovered again. When she got a good look at it, her whole foot suddenly started to throb painfully. Honestly, it was like her eyes had given the rest of her body time to react.

"Ouch," she cried out when the nurse began to clean her wound.

Paige paused. "Sorry, am I being too rough?"

"*Nee.* You're fine." She grimaced. "I don't know what happened. My cut went from just hurting a little to a whole lot!"

Paige looked at Miriam sympathetically. "I know, right? It's like out of sight, out of mind. But somehow, when one is forced to confront it, the pain comes out and hits you on the head. Don't worry, you're not alone. It happens every time."

"At least I'm not the only one." She'd hate to be known as the whiny Amish lady.

"You're not by a long shot." Just as she was about to say something else, another nurse called her to the door. Peeling off her latex gloves, she put her tray of cloths and antiseptic to one side. "I'll be right back, dear. Keep that foot right there, okay?"

"I will." When Paige closed the door after her, Miriam sighed. Both Calvin and her father were waiting for her, and everything just seemed to be taking longer than it should.

When Paige returned a few minutes later, she had a bemused smile on her face . . . and the doctor was right behind her.

"Mrs. Gingerich, I'm Dr. Collins."

"It's Miriam, please."

He gestured to her foot. "Well, what happened here, Miriam?"

"It was so silly. I dropped a glass and stepped on a particularly large shard."

He put on gloves and gently ran a finger along the cut. "I'm glad you came in. Sometimes folks think things like this will heal right up, but it doesn't, especially if it's this deep. Next thing you know, infection sets in."

"So I'm going to need stitches?"

"Yep. I'm guessing about eight or so."

"Eight?"

"Oh, don't worry. We'll give you a shot to numb it first. You won't feel a thing."

"The shot's going to be the worst part," Paige said.

Miriam wasn't too happy about getting a needle stuck into the sole of her foot, but she was more anxious to get out of the room. "I'll do my best to get through."

Paige raised her eyebrows at the doctor. "We need to discuss the other matter, Dr. Collins."

"Ah, yes." He sat down. "Miriam, I'm afraid I have a surprise for you."

She looked down at her foot. What else could they have found in her foot? "Yes?"

"Sometimes patients need to be prescribed antibiotics from time to time, which is why you were asked to give that urine sample."

"Yes. Paige explained that to me."

"I'm glad we did that test, too . . . because we discovered that you are pregnant."

She gaped at him, just as her ears started ringing. "I'm sorry, uh, what did you say?"

Paige walked to Miriam's side and took her hand. "The pregnancy test came back positive, Miriam. I even did a second one to make sure. There's no doubt about it. You're going to have a baby."

"I'm with child." At last. After all the months of praying, after giving up hope, after almost resigning herself to the fact that she might never conceive again . . . it had happened. Tears pricked her eyes just as a burst of dizziness hit her hard. Feeling a little woozy, she placed her hands on the exam table to steady herself.

"Uh-oh. You've gone a little pale," Paige said.

"Hmm? Oh, I do feel a little dizzy."

"You better lie down, Mrs. Gingerich," the doctor said. "Is your husband nearby?"

"He's in the waiting room," she said as Paige helped her lie back. "Or, um, he could be out in the parking lot with my *daed* and his horse and buggy."

"Would you like me to go get him?" Paige asked. "He could hold your hand, and then you can tell him your good news."

"Nee." She needed a minute to come to terms with it. She was so shocked. She just wasn't sure what to do next.

"No?" Paige blinked. "Are you sure, Miriam? I know I said it was cramped in here, but we could make do."

Feeling both of their gazes fixed steadily

on her, she blurted, "I would like to tell my husband later. In private, if you please."

When Dr. Collins looked confused, Paige grinned. "I did the same thing with my husband, too. It's a special moment. I went out and got the cutest little bib and put it under his dinner plate!"

"I imagine that was a surprise."

"Indeed."

The doctor looked at her kindly. "Well, Mrs. Gingerich, I think it's time we got your foot tended to so you can get to your wonderful news."

"This won't take too long, Miriam," Paige said as she swabbed some alcohol on Miriam's foot. "You're going to feel a pinch, but then it will get numb almost immediately. Try to think of something else if you can."

That wasn't going to be a problem. Miriam wasn't sure if she was in a simple daze or a full-out state of shock. All she wanted to think about was the miracle that had happened . . . and wonder how she was ever going to tell Calvin.

She was going to have to see the midwife as soon as possible. If the doctors had been right and the chances of her having a successful pregnancy were very slim, then she needed to do a lot of praying about what to do.

She didn't think she could bear to tell Calvin the good news just to see his face when they lost another baby. Honestly, she didn't know if she was going to be able to survive that herself.

And then there was Miles. Surely, if the Lord did bless them, they wouldn't be able to adopt a foster child. Not if there was a chance they could have a babe of their own . . . just like they'd always wanted.

"Mrs. Gingerich?"

"Hmm?" She blinked.

Paige clasped her hand and squeezed it gently. "You can relax now."

Looking down, she noticed that the doctor was done stitching her foot and had even put on a padded bandage.

Funny, she hadn't felt a single thing.

Twenty minutes later, Miriam was carefully walking back out to the waiting room. In her purse was some information about prenatal vitamins and a list of doctors in case she didn't want to go to the Amish midwife. She was so stunned, she hardly knew what to do or think.

Calvin rushed to her side the moment he saw her. "Miriam! Careful now." He wrapped his hand around her waist. "Do you need crutches or something?"

"*Nee.* I'm going to be okay. I'll just have a sore foot for a few days."

"I tried to pay, but the receptionist said you already did."

She nodded. "The nurse said I could pay in the exam room. We're all done now."

Guiding her out the door to her father and the buggy in the parking lot, he said, "I still don't understand why I had to wait for you in the lobby the whole time. I could have held your hand while they stitched you up."

But of course she knew why. "You saw how small the rooms were. Besides, there was no need for you to be by my side. I didn't feel a thing after they numbed my foot."

A brief look of hurt flashed in his eyes before he blinked it away. "We'll take it easy this afternoon. I took the rest of the day off so I can look after you."

Calvin was a wonderful husband. But of all the times for him to be hovering over her, this was the worst indeed! All the she wanted to do was sit and think about her miracle . . . and how she would keep it from Calvin — at least until she was out of the danger zone.

If she lost this baby, she didn't know if

she was going to be able to handle the pain. But she did know that trying to comfort Calvin while dealing with her own grief and guilt was going to be very hard.

It wasn't something she was willing to put herself through again.

Just as they reached her father, he opened his eyes. He'd pulled out a folding chair, placed it next to Silver, and had taken a little nap.

He sat up like the sight hadn't been odd at all. "All better, Mimi?"

Sharing a quick smile with Calvin, she said, "*Jah,* Daed. I'm all better now."

"Then I suppose we should get on back," he said as he folded up his chair and placed it in the back of the buggy. "I'm sure your mother is going to wonder what's been taking us so long. I'll take her right to your house, Calvin."

"*Danke.*" Still looking worried, Calvin reached for her hand. "I guess I should have thought ahead and hitched up our buggy as well."

"No worries. I'm glad you rode your bicycle so you could be here right away. Plus, we'll spend the afternoon together."

"Indeed we will," he said as he helped her into the buggy. "I'm even going to make my famous chicken and noodles for ya."

It was the one edible meal he could make.

And though her insides were churning, her foot was throbbing, and all she really wanted was to spend twenty minutes alone so she could process what she just found out . . . she smiled. "You're exactly right, Calvin. It's my lucky day indeed."

TWELVE

It's easiest to date one person at a time.

Sarah Anne hadn't ended up going out with Pete on Saturday. He'd gotten called back to Erie and had been out of touch for several days. Then, the next time he'd asked her, she'd chickened out. She felt like if she said yes, she was firmly putting Frank in her past, and there were still moments when she wasn't quite ready to do that.

But, whenever she saw Pete in person, all of those doubts faded away.

Such as right that minute.

"I think it's time we actually went on a date, Sarah Anne," Pete announced.

He had walked into the bookmobile minutes after she'd pulled into the parking lot, and he wasn't even attempting to look like he was there for the books. Instead, he was being flirty. If she were younger, she'd be blushing like a red beet.

Oh, who was she kidding? She *was* blushing like a red beet! She'd just giggled, too, which was kind of embarrassing.

One of the Amish ladies who'd been perusing the shelves had given her a knowing look. Sarah Anne didn't blame her, either. She was far too old to be so flustered around a handsome man.

But, maybe her reaction was serving as a good reminder that one couldn't always control one's heart or head. Sometimes love bloomed in spite of one's best intentions.

Pete took a seat at her desk while she busied herself by helping the Amish ladies, then another ten or so people who also walked through her door. Never once did he seem annoyed that she didn't have time for him. Instead, he seemed happy to watch her work.

Then, when only a few minutes remained before it was time to prepare the bookmobile to hit the road again, she and Pete were alone.

"As much as I like books and bookmobiles, we both know the reason I'm here isn't for reading material. I mean, not anymore." He looked at her intently. "Sarah Anne, I want to spend some time with you when you aren't working. Come out with me."

Oh! She felt like she was back in high school or college. She hadn't even been so flustered when she and Frank had been dating.

He grinned. "What do you say?"

"I . . . I . . ."

His posture changed. It was subtle, a slight tightening of his shoulders. "Last I checked, it wasn't a difficult decision. Either you still want to go out with me or you don't." Eyeing her intently, he said, "Have you changed your mind? Is that why you sounded so vague the last time we talked?"

"I haven't changed my mind."

"Okay . . ."

"But dating again . . . Well, it's not that easy."

His dark brown eyes were piercing. "How come?"

"Because I'm sixty-one years old, Pete. I didn't expect to —" She stopped herself before admitting that she feared she was on the verge of falling head over heels for him. "Can we talk about this later when I'm off the clock?"

"When? Next time you stop here and I have time to drop everything to see you?"

"You could text me."

"I'm not going to text you or have this conversation over the phone."

It was time she put on her big girl panties and stopped fussing around. "Pete, if you call me, I promise I'll talk about everything with you."

"Promise?"

It felt like he was asking her to promise so much more than just to talk on the phone. But her answer was still the same. "Yes."

He exhaled. "Thank you." Just as she was about to say something witty, he leaned down and kissed her cheek. "I'll call soon."

"I'll be waiting."

A few minutes after he left, Sarah Anne got on her way to the next stop. But for the next couple of hours, all she could do was doubt everything she'd said to him . . . and wonder if he was actually going to call her.

When she found herself staring at her blank phone screen during a lull at her last stop, Sarah Anne groaned. Why, she was no better than some of her rudest customers.

"What's wrong, Miss Miller? Are you having phone trouble?"

She smiled at Natalie, one of her English teenagers she'd grown close to. "Not unless you count wondering why someone hasn't called when he said he would phone trouble."

The girl's eyes widened. "*He?* Miss Miller, are you having boy trouble?"

"No." When Natalie raised an eyebrow, Sarah Anne shrugged. "Maybe."

"Do you want to talk about it?"

Natalie was sixteen years old. Sarah Anne could have been her grandmother. They had nothing in common . . . Though there was a good chance that Natalie had dated more in the last year than she had. "I haven't dated since well before cell phones were invented," she confided. "And yes, I know that makes me sound like I grew up in the Stone Age. But do men call just any old time now that they can?"

"I think it depends on the guy."

That did make sense. "I think you're right." She groaned. "Oh, Natalie, I'm sure everything makes total sense to you, but dating right now is really confusing. Back when my husband and I were dating, he'd call my home phone, and my parents would answer and take a message."

The teen gave her a look that said she'd rather eat liver than rely on her parents to screen her calls. "Whoa. I bet that was awful."

"Not really. I mean, it was what everyone

113

did. We didn't know any different." But then, she remembered all the times her mother would accidentally forget to pass on the messages . . . all because she was upset with Sarah Anne about some chore she forgot to do or because she thought she'd been spending too much time away from home. "But, now that I think about it . . . yes, it was awful sometimes. So, should I be worried that he hasn't called?"

"Hmm. When did he say he was going to call?"

"Later on today."

"He texted you that?"

"No, he told me when I saw him earlier."

Natalie popped a hand on her hip. "Wait a sec. Are you saying you already saw this man today?"

"Yes. And his name is Pete." Noticing Natalie's amused expression, Sarah Anne covered her face with a hand. "I'm being ridiculous, aren't I?"

"Well, it is kind of early to expect a call, Miss Miller."

"I think we should just forget I ever mentioned it. Now, do you need anything?"

"Uh-huh. I think you've got some books reserved for me. The email I received said they came in."

Sure enough, Sarah Anne found Natalie's

stack wrapped up in a piece of butcher-block paper with her name neatly written on it. Those books had been sitting there waiting on Sarah Anne to get her act together. Grabbing them quickly, she handed them to Natalie.

"Here you go, dear. I'm sorry you had to wait."

Natalie hugged them to her chest like they were long lost friends. "Oh, that's okay. I'd much rather talk to you about Pete than grab my books and start walking home."

"You're sweet. I appreciate the advice. I don't want to make a fool of myself with him."

"You won't. Just take your time." She grinned. "Next time I'm here, you can tell me what happened!"

"I will. Hopefully I'll have good news. You have a good week, dear. Thanks again for the pep talk."

"No problem. I didn't even realize people your age still dated. That's cool."

Sarah Anne kept a composed expression on her face until Natalie raced out the door . . . and then she leaned her head back and laughed and laughed. Well, that put her in her place! She was old. Old and silly. In fact, she was beyond silly. Pete Canon had probably forgotten all about his promise to call already!

Five hours later, as she was watching an old movie on the couch, Sarah Anne was still telling herself the same thing.

But then, just before nine o'clock, her phone lit up with his name on it.

Nervously, she pressed Answer. "Hello?"

"Sarah Anne, hey. Is this too late to talk?"

He was giving her an out, but she wasn't taking it. "Not at all. How are you?"

"I'm good, but I really do feel terrible that I pushed you to say yes to a date . . . I feel like I keep messing things up between us."

"You haven't messed up anything."

"Does that mean you'll still give me a chance?"

"Yes, I mean, if you want one. Not because I think you need another chance."

"What are you doing Saturday night?"

She grinned. "I don't know . . . Why?"

"Because I want to get something on the calendar. There's this great Italian place over in New Philly called Scarpetti's. Have you heard of it?"

She actually had. One of her old coworkers from her days as an accountant had asked if she wanted to join her for dinner there a couple of weeks ago. "I've heard of it, but I haven't been."

"I haven't, either. Want to be a guinea pig with me?"

She chuckled. "Sure. That sounds like fun."

"Six thirty? Or is that too early? Late?"

"Six thirty is good. I can do that." She was smiling so big now her cheeks hurt.

"Great." She could almost envision him grinning, too. "Should I pick you up or meet you there?"

She wasn't quite ready to invite him to her house. "Would you mind if I met you there?" she asked hesitantly.

"Not at all. I'll see you on Saturday."

"Yep. See you then."

After she hung up, she took a deep breath. At last, it was time. Maybe even past time.

THIRTEEN

· TIP #13 ·

If you do end up dating multiple people at the same time, it would be wise to be up front about it.

Like a fool, Pete had arrived twenty minutes early. Now he was sitting in the parking lot, debating whether he would look less creepy waiting in his truck or at the table.

Luckily, his phone rang. When he realized it was his daughter, Cassie, he wasn't sure if it was lucky or not.

Answering, he made sure to sound happy and upbeat. Cassie could hear worry in a heartbeat. "Hey, Cass. What's up?"

"I have some great news. Guess what? I'm just ten minutes away!"

"From where?"

"From you, silly. I decided to stop by and surprise you tonight. We can go grab dinner or something."

He felt terrible to do this to her, but it couldn't be helped. "I'm glad you called because I'm not at home."

"Really? What are you doing? Are you at the grocery store?" she asked, once again barely taking a breath.

"As a matter of fact, I'm not. I'm sitting in my truck in the parking lot of Scarpetti's."

"Hold on, Dad." He heard her park. "Scarpetti's is that cute Italian restaurant in New Philly, right?"

"It is."

"Why are you there? You're not eating alone again, are you?"

Pete paused, weighed the pros and cons of letting his daughter know about his plans, then decided to go ahead and share the truth. At the very least, it was easier to remember. "I have a date."

"Really?"

"Really." She sounded so incredulous, he had to smile. After years and years of dodging his kids' attempts at organizing blind dates and offers to set him up on dating websites, he was finally getting out. "Isn't that something?"

"It is."

"Hey, now. Don't sound too excited. I thought you'd be thrilled."

119

"I am. I mean, I just worry about you out there in the dating world all alone."

She didn't sound nearly as encouraging now as she had been the other day.

"I'm sure she's real nice, but it's been a while and, I don't know, Daddy. This woman could be a fortune hunter or something."

"I don't think she's a fortune hunter, Cass. She's a librarian. And I don't exactly have a fortune, anyway."

"Not all librarians are perfect, Dad."

"I don't want perfection. I just want to go out to eat with her." Glancing at his watch, he breathed a sigh of relief. "Now, I better get going. We're supposed to meet in three minutes."

"Feel free to call me when you're on your way home."

"I won't be calling you, Cassie. Now, tell Danny hello, give my Aimee a big hug from PaPa, and be careful driving home," he added before she said anything else he didn't want to hear.

"Wait! Hey, Daddy?"

"Yes, Cass?" And yes, he sounded impatient.

"Have fun. I'm sorry, I should've said that first thing, huh?"

"Don't worry about it. I love you."

120

Getting out of his truck, he figured that Cassie calling had been the best thing for him. Having to defend his date reminded him that he really did want to see Sarah Anne. He hadn't just fallen into this moment. It had happened after weeks and weeks of conversations and gaining each other's trust.

Just as he approached the entrance, he spied Sarah Anne getting out of her car. When she saw him, she gave a little wave and smiled. He thought that was adorable.

He stuffed his hands in his pockets as he watched her approach.

She was wearing taupe linen slacks and a loose, light rose-colored sweater that kind of hung off her shoulders. Leather sandals were on her feet, and some bold gold hoop earrings were in her ears. She looked both younger and more attractive than she did in her usual librarian outfit — and he'd always thought she looked cute as a bug in that getup.

As she got closer, Pete couldn't help but think that, despite the change in clothes, her face looked the same it always did. Bright and happy. Those two things drew him to her like a shiny penny.

"Oh, gosh. Have you been waiting long?" she asked.

"Not at all. I just pulled in." No way was he going to let her know he'd arrived so early.

"Thank goodness. I thought I was going to be late," she said as he held the restaurant's door open and she walked right in. "Guess what I saw on my way over here?"

"I have no idea," he said before giving the hostess his name.

As they were led through the mishmash of tables, Sarah Ann continued her story. "Oh, Pete. Two sets of geese and their goslings! They were all crossing the road. Everyone was stopped while they were ushered across."

He'd never been a real big fan of geese — or stopping for geese to cross the street. But the way she described it made him feel like he ought to start. "Tell me all about them," he said as the hostess sat them at a table in the back of the dining room.

When she beamed up at him, he knew this date, which had been so long in the making, was off to a real good start.

FOURTEEN

"I was so surprised when I saw your name on my schedule, Miriam. You could have blown me away," Edna Wood said when she greeted her.

"I thank you for keeping our appointment secret like I asked." The usual way Amish women made appointments with Edna was calling her from the phone shanty and leaving a message about when she could come in. Then either Edna or her assistant, Lila, would call back and leave a message for the caller confirming the date.

All that meant that one didn't get a lot of privacy — at least until she was afforded the opportunity to speak to Edna alone. Lila was nice and helpful . . . but she had a tendency to gossip about others.

Miriam had been so worried that her need for an urgent appointment with Edna was going to fall on the wrong ears, but thankfully that hadn't been the case.

Taking a seat on the chair in the exam room, Miriam told Edna about the broken glass, her cut foot, and the eventual pregnancy test.

Edna clasped her hands in front of her. "So, you're pregnant."

"*Jah.*"

Edna pulled over the other simple-looking ladder-back chair and sat down. "How do you feel about that?"

It was questions like that that made Miriam want Edna to be in charge of her pregnancy instead of one of the fancy fertility doctors she and Calvin had seen over the years. Edna, in her plain blue dress, white apron, white *kaap,* and simple black flats, was so approachable and easy to talk to. And she wasn't even thirty-five yet, so her relatively young age and sweet personality made her even more desirable.

Taking a deep breath, Miriam tried to find the words to describe just how she felt. Instead of one single word, a wealth of them came pouring out. "I feel excited and happy and nervous and scared."

Edna's lips twitched. "Is that all?"

"*Nee.* I maybe feel angry, too," she admitted.

Instead of looking shocked, Edna nodded like that made perfect sense. "Let's take that one first. Why do you feel angry?"

"Because this . . . this pregnancy caught me unawares. If it had been up to me, I wouldn't have gone to the doctor in the first place. But there I was, having to get stitches and being forced to give a urine sample. It hardly makes sense."

"The Lord does work in mysterious ways."

"I know. But I'm mad because I had just about given up hope of ever being pregnant again. The news shocked the daylights out of me. I can tell ya that."

"I bet it did. Now, let's tackle everything else. Anything you want to say about being excited, happy, scared, and nervous?"

"*Nee.*" She already felt like she'd said too much. "Those are all normal emotions. Right? Or no?"

"Everything you're feeling is perfectly normal." Edna smiled more broadly. "Now, what did Calvin do when you told him?"

"I haven't told him yet."

The midwife's expression turned guarded. "And why is that?"

"I couldn't bear to do it." Taking a deep breath, Miriam shared the awful news. "The fertility doctor told us it was unlikely I'd ever conceive again . . . and if I did, the chances were good that I would miscarry."

"What does that have to do with not telling Calvin?"

"I don't want to upset him." Miriam shook her head. "*Nee,* that's not true . . . I don't want to have to see the look on his face when I disappoint him again." When Edna just stared, Miriam added, "You know, because I'll likely lose this baby."

The midwife shook her head. "You don't know that. And, dear, if you did, you wouldn't be disappointing Calvin. He'd be worried about you."

"I know, he'll worry. Calvin is a kind man." She took a deep breath. "To be honest, I just don't know if I can handle hurting him again."

"You wouldn't be hurting him." Reaching for her hand, Edna squeezed it. "Miriam, if you miscarried, it wouldn't be your fault."

"I know you are right, but I would still feel like it was." When she could see that Edna was about to argue, she added, "Haven't you ever felt something that didn't make sense? Haven't you ever wished you didn't feel something, but no matter how hard you tried, you felt it, anyway?"

"Well, *jah.* I suppose I have."

"Then you must understand."

"I understand what you're saying, Miriam," she said, after a hesitation. "I can even understand and appreciate why you feel the way you do. But I don't agree. I don't agree with keeping this a secret at all."

"Edna, if something happens, keeping it a secret from Calvin will be better in the long run."

"For who? Do you really think you'll feel better if you do lose the baby and you're suffering in silence? Do you really think your husband is going to be pleased that you kept him in the dark?"

"Probably not," she allowed. "But I'm still going to keep it a secret. Just for a little while longer."

"I really do feel like you're making a mistake."

"I believe it's my choice," Miriam said. "Edna, if you don't think you can honor that, please tell me now."

"I can honor it."

"Danke."

After staring at her for another long moment, Edna sighed. "Well, now that we've discussed all of that . . . Are you ready for me to examine you?"

"I am."

"Well, thank the good Lord for that!"

Pointing to the soft cloth robe, Edna said, "You know what to do. Get undressed, put on the robe, and then we'll get your weight and blood pressure and see how you and your tiny baby are doing."

"Thank you for understanding."

The midwife paused, looking as if she was going to argue, then seemed to change her mind. "You're welcome, Miriam," she said, gently patting her arm. "I care about you, is all." That statement hung in the air as she crossed the room and closed the door behind her.

Miriam breathed a sigh of relief. Her secret was hers . . . at least for a little while longer.

FIFTEEN

· TIP #15 ·
Don't compare your preferences to
everyone else's. Go out with men you
feel comfortable with, not who friends and
family think you should see.

Today was finally the day. Maybe. Calvin
Gingerich was supposed to have come by
their house to spend time with him and Mr.
Schmidt a week ago, but he'd had to cancel
it suddenly. Mrs. Schmidt had gone to great
lengths to tell him that the reason hadn't
had anything to do with Miles. Instead, it
had been because Calvin's wife had gotten
a bad cut on her foot and he'd had to take
her to urgent care.

Miles had nodded and said he didn't
mind, but there had been a part of him that
was sure the excuse was made up. After all,
he'd had plenty of cuts and never had to go
to the emergency room.

The worst part, of course, was that Ethan had teased him about getting stood up. He'd said that if Calvin really wanted to get to know him, he wouldn't have canceled. Of course, Mary had told him to hush, but the damage was done.

Well, as much damage as possible since Miles privately agreed with Ethan. It was hard being a foster kid, especially a foster kid who was almost eleven. His birthday wouldn't be as much a celebration as it was another reminder that he wasn't going to ever get adopted. Even at seven years old, Ethan understood that.

Today was supposed to be different, though. Mrs. Schmidt had taken the other five kids to the bookmobile for story time, and Mr. Schmidt had stayed home with him to wait for Calvin to finally come over.

Anxious, Miles kept sneaking glances out the window.

Mr. Schmidt noticed. "I'm sure Calvin will be here soon, Miles. He felt terrible that he had to cancel on you before."

"I remember you said that." Although Miles didn't understand Calvin's excuse — a cut seemed like a stupid reason to cancel plans — he kept reminding himself that Calvin had no reason to keep a promise to him. After all, it wasn't like they knew each other well.

Mr. Schmidt walked to his side. As usual, he had on a light green shirt. Mr. Schmidt had hazel eyes, and his wife was always sewing green shirts so the green in her husband's eyes would stand out. "Are you worried that he is going to show up or that he isn't?"

"Both," Miles said honestly. "I don't know what I'm going to talk to him about."

"What do you talk to Calvin about when you see him at the bookmobile?"

He shrugged. "All kinds of things. Books. Me." He thought some more. "Sometimes Miss Miller does a lot of talking, too."

Mr. Schmidt laughed. "She's a chatty one, for sure and for certain."

"She's real nice."

"That she is." His kind smile grew. "And here Calvin is, right on time."

Miles's gaze swung back out the window. Sure enough, there was Calvin, striding up the walkway, his blond hair covered with a straw hat like always. He was also holding a tote bag. Miles turned back to Mr. Schmidt.

Panic set in. "Mr. Schmidt, what do I do?"

"I'll go greet him and bring him in, and then we'll go from there."

Miles nodded his agreement, not that Mr. Schmidt even noticed. He was already striding to the door.

Miles sat down in an empty chair as they greeted each other.

"Calvin, I'm James Schmidt."

They shook hands. "Good to meet ya. Calvin Gingerich. Sorry again for missing my last visit. It couldn't be helped."

"I understood, but it's not me you need to be talking to. *Jah?*"

"Of course." Looking over at Miles, Calvin visibly straightened his shoulders. "Hiya, Miles. It's *gut* to see ya again."

Miles scrambled to his feet. *"Jah,"* he mumbled, then wished he could take it back and try it again. He should have said something better. Smarter sounding.

Looking at Mr. Schmidt, Calvin said, "How do you want to handle this? Should the three of us talk together?"

"It's up to Miles, but I'm thinking in this case, three's a crowd." Mr. Schmidt pointed to the picnic table where they sometimes ate dinner on Sundays. "Maybe the two of you would like to visit out there? My Ruth made some cookies and lemonade for you two."

Calvin walked toward Miles. "What do you say? Want to give the picnic table a try? Or would you rather we sit with James here? Either is fine with me. I promise."

After glancing at his foster *daed* and receiving a nod, Miles took a deep breath. "I think going outside would be good."

Calvin motioned toward the door. "Let's go on out, then. I'm excited to show you what I brought."

Reminding himself that he was ten years old and far too old to be acting like a baby, Miles led the way to the door. "We eat outside sometimes on Sundays." He hoped he sounded confident and relaxed.

"I'd eat outside all the time if I could," Calvin said. He ran a hand along the table's top. "This is a nice table."

"Mr. Schmidt built it."

Still looking at the table, Calvin added, "It would be nice to be able to build something like this, wouldn't it, to leave a real legacy?"

Miles had never thought about that. "I guess." He shifted uncomfortably. He had no idea what he was supposed to say or do.

"Oh! Before I forget, here," Calvin said, handing Miles the tote bag.

Inside was a box of saltwater taffy and a new copy of *Stuart Little*. Miles set them on the table. "Are these both for me?"

"*Jah*. I thought you might enjoy *Stuart Little*, since you seemed to like *Charlotte's Web*. I found it at the bookshop in town.

And I added a box of saltwater taffy because it's good. Do you like taffy?"

"*Nee* — I mean, I'm not sure."

"I hope you will, but it's okay if you don't." Frowning at the book, Calvin said, "Same with *Stuart Little,* too."

"*Danke.* I'm, ah, sure I'll like them both fine." Miles didn't know what else to say. He couldn't remember the last time anyone had given him a present for no reason.

A line formed between Calvin's brows. "Were the gifts too much? Too pushy?" Looking stricken, he added, "Am I making you uneasy?"

"Nee." Realizing his answer didn't sound believable at all, Miles cleared his throat. "I mean, you're not, Calvin. Not really."

Calvin raised his eyebrows. "If you're not feeling awkward, then you're doing a sight better than me. I'm a nervous wreck."

Miles couldn't help but gape at him. "For real?"

"Oh, *jah.* I don't have any *kinner* of my own, you know . . . so I'm not quite sure what to say."

"I don't know —" Miles began, then stopped himself. He was the kid. He wasn't supposed to lead the conversation . . . was he?

"What were you gonna say?"

134

"That, uh, I don't know much about you, Calvin. Other than the fact that you like books and wanted to spend time with me."

His boldness seemed to catch Calvin off guard. He looked taken aback, then slowly nodded. "You're right. I guess you haven't known what to think of me talking to you so much." His words were mumbled, almost like he was talking to himself instead of Miles. "I should've known better than to act so impulsively."

"I don't mind talking to you. I . . . Well, Mr. Schmidt told me I shouldn't get my hopes up or anything."

"About?"

Calvin looked so confused, Miles felt even more awkward. "Never mind."

"Please, I really do want to know what you're thinking. I won't know if you keep your thoughts to yourself."

"It's not important."

"Miles —" He stopped himself, then looked up at the sky, like he was seeking help from God. Then he chuckled. "Forgive me." Taking a deep breath, he said, "I'm twenty-eight years old and I've been married to my wife, Miriam, for four years."

"You didn't get married until you were twenty-four?"

"It does seem late, don't it? But you're

135

right. I didn't move to Holmes County until I was twenty-six. My Onkle David passed away suddenly, and his sons gave me the land."

"They didn't want it?"

"*Nee.* One ain't Amish no more, and the other lives up in Pennsylvania. They knew I was close to my uncle, and so they gave me the land, saying it would make their father happy to know that a family member was farming the land."

"Wow. Where did you move from?"

"Kentucky."

"Really?"

"*Jah.* I grew up in the center of the state, in Hart County." He grinned. "That's right where Mammoth Cave is. Have you heard of it?"

He shook his head.

"Well, one day I hope you'll get to see it. Mammoth Cave is a huge cavern. So big they give tours with twenty or thirty people in a group. It's real pretty there."

"Did you get to visit it a lot?"

He shrugged. "Three times is all." Leaning back on his hands, Calvin added, "I guess that's the way of the world, though. One never knows how special something is when it's right there in front of you."

Miles reckoned that was right. Ian, Jonas,

and Mary never seemed to realize just how blessed they were to have parents.

"Sorry for the wait," Mr. Schmidt called out as he approached. "I couldn't find the tray for this. Ruth said she put it out, but I couldn't find it."

Miles noticed that their "tray" was a baking sheet. "Mrs. Schmidt wanted you to use a pan?"

"Of course not. But I figured it would do in a pinch." Setting the metal pan on the table, he gave Miles a long, steady look. "How are things going?"

Mr. Schmidt was a kind man. Miles knew if he acted uncomfortable, his foster *daed* would either sit down with them or tell Calvin they were too busy for him to stay. But Miles wasn't ready to end the conversation yet. "Things are *gut*."

"I'm glad. Well, I'd best go check on the chickens." He turned and headed back to the house before either of them could say a word.

Calvin poured them both glasses of lemonade and drank half of his in two gulps. "Now, what were we talking about?"

"The cave. I mean, Mammoth Cave," Miles replied, after taking a sip of his own drink and picking up a cookie.

"Oh. Yes. Well, I only went a few times,

but that was enough, I reckon." He paused, looking reflective. "I guess it's like going to a big bookstore in the city. At least, for me. See, I like going to the bookmobile and the library to pick out a slew of books and not having to worry about not liking or not finishing them. And I like visiting with Sarah Anne when I'm there. And you. It's comfortable, but a bookstore is an experience. Growing up in the country in Kentucky, going to a town that had a real bookstore was a ways. And my parents, they liked books but were always watching their pennies. So the couple of times I went, I spent more time simply looking around and dreaming about having my own stack of books than I spent shopping."

"They never let you get any?"

"Oh, they did. Each time I went, I got to choose two."

"Do you still have any of them?"

Looking a little melancholy, Calvin shook his head. "*Nee.* I gave them to friends. But I remember the visits more than the books. I guess that's what I'm trying to say about the caves. If I went all the time, it would be nice, but it wouldn't be special." He blew out a breath. "I bet I'm sounding pretty confusing, huh?"

"*Nee.* I . . . I can understand what you

mean." It was kind of like living with the Schmidts and spending time with just Calvin. One was fine. It was what he was used to. The other? Well, it made him excited and nervous and confused . . . but it was memorable. Maybe even better because it incited so many emotions.

"Anyway, now I live here, and I'm a farmer," Calvin said. "That pretty much sums up my life."

Miles nodded, but he was sure there was more to Calvin than that. Maybe a whole lot more. He might only be ten, but he knew there was more to himself than most people saw.

Sometimes he felt that there was a whole lot more.

Sixteen

If you are using a dating app, be
prepared to take a break from swiping
from time to time.

Calvin stayed at the Schmidts' house for an
hour. Walking back home, reflecting on just
about every single word he and Miles had
exchanged, Calvin decided it had been both
the most exhilarating and most excruciating
hour of his life. The boy's eyes had been so
full of hope, yet strangely shuttered. Every
time Calvin caught sight of how Miles was
really feeling, he'd been floored.

If anyone ever doubted how much influence one person could have on another,
Calvin reckoned they should meet Miles.

Because that was how he felt now. He felt
changed.

Talking with the ten-year-old, doing nothing more than carrying on a stilted conver-

sation about caves and his childhood, Calvin had been both humbled by the boy's insight and proud that they'd accomplished even that much together.

But through it all, one phrase stood out, one phrase would haunt him. That was when Miles had blurted out that he shouldn't get his hopes up.

That one sentence, together with Miles's refusal to speak any more about it, burned in Calvin's chest. He wasn't an especially smart man, but even he knew what the boy had been referring to. That he shouldn't get his hopes up about being adopted.

From the moment he'd first met Miles, Calvin had felt a pull toward him that didn't make a lot of sense. It had felt like God had placed them in the same place at the same time and was just waiting for Calvin to do His bidding.

Calvin wanted to do it, too. He did want to adopt the boy. Even though he didn't know how to be a father and wasn't sure how to help a foster child get over his terrible past, he still wanted to give Miles his heart and his help, as imperfect as they might be.

But if he went down this path, he knew he had a chance of losing Miriam. She'd tearfully admitted more than once that she didn't want to adopt a baby. If his wife didn't want to adopt a baby, how could he try to convince her to adopt a ten-year-old boy? It wasn't fair to her.

On the other hand, if he didn't reach out to Miles, it might be far worse. Calvin didn't know if he was going to be able to live with that.

He was startled from his contemplation when he spied Miriam waiting for him on the front steps of their house. He smiled at her and gave a wave, but his insides were churning. He loved his wife. There was no doubt about that. However, right that minute, she was the last person he wanted to see. If she reacted like he feared she would about his wishes for Miles, he didn't know how he was going to be able to hold his tongue.

But he knew that not talking about this would propel their marriage into an even more difficult spot.

"Hiya, Miriam. Am I late?"

She got to her feet. "*Nee*. I was just anxious to hear how the visit went."

"It was *gut*."

"That's it?" Her smile wavered. "You were gone a long time."

"Only an hour." Realizing that wasn't quite right, he added, "I guess it was two. It

142

took me about thirty minutes to walk each way, and then I also chatted with James Schmidt when I got there and when I left."

She waited a second or two, looking at him expectantly, before folding her arms around her middle. "Do you not want to tell me about Miles, Calvin?"

"*Nee!* I mean, no, of course not. I do want to talk to you about him." But what, exactly, did he want to say?

Needing another minute or two to figure that out, he walked to her side. "Come, let's go in the house." He held the screen door open for her and led her into the hearth room. When she sat down on the couch, he sat next to her and held her hand.

"Calvin, what is it?"

"I'm not trying to be secretive. I'm just not real sure how to describe what happened."

Her blue eyes softened. "Maybe you should just start at the beginning?"

Well, he could do that. "When I first got there, I talked with both Miles and James. I think it was to make sure that Miles was comfortable."

"That makes sense." She smiled encouragingly.

So, he told her everything. About giving him the book and candy. About the cookies and lemonade and the awkwardness of it and Mammoth Cave and bookstores. Miriam listened with wide eyes, asking him questions every now and then.

As she prodded, he relaxed. Perhaps he'd been overthinking things, worrying about Miriam's reaction when he should have been giving her his trust and faith. Feeling emboldened, he finally revealed what he'd been thinking.

"The boy needs a forever home, Miriam. He's ten, and I fear there's already a part of him that feels like he won't ever be adopted. Isn't that awful?"

To his surprise, she nodded. "I feel terrible for him. Even without knowing his past, I can tell he is suffering."

"Don't get me wrong, the Schmidts are good people . . ."

"I don't really know them, of course, but they seem decent." Her lips curved up. "It's just their triplets who are difficult."

He chuckled. "Indeed."

"That would be wonderful-*gut* if they did adopt him, wouldn't it?" She brightened. "If he's as nice a child as you say, maybe they'll change their minds. Then everything will be better."

Now Calvin knew he couldn't hold it back any longer. "Miriam, I wasn't thinking about the Schmidts adopting him."

She frowned. "Then who . . . You mean *you*?"

"I mean *us,* Miriam. He'll need a mother, too."

His wife was shaking her head before he had a chance to continue. "Calvin, I don't think —"

That was all he needed to hear before he lost it.

"Miriam, as much as I understand your feelings about adoption, I'm going to tell you now that I think you're wrong. Adopting this boy could be the best thing we ever did. You need to give him a chance. He needs us."

She paled. "I'm not entirely against adoption . . ."

"Oh, you're just against adopting this little boy who is alone in the world?" Even though he was cutting her off and his voice was turning increasingly sharp, he continued, "You know what your problem is? You can sometimes be selfish."

She inhaled sharply. "That's not true."

"I think it is. I think you have gone through so much pain that you've taken to forgetting that other people go through their fair share of trials, too." He stopped and looked at her intently. "You're not the only person who has experienced pain, you know."

"I never thought I was special in that regard, Calvin. Now, if you'd just let me explain. You see, there's a re—"

"Nee." Right at that moment he felt like he'd done nothing but wait for her to come around and listen to her explain why she couldn't. How she was so sad, how hard it had been . . . all while she seemed to forget that he'd been experiencing the same losses. "I don't want to hear your excuses, Miriam."

Her expression turned carefully blank. "Then what is it that you do want to hear?"

"That you're going to do some thinking about my needs for a change. I want to help this boy, Miriam. Don't make me choose." But the minute the words were out of his mouth, he ached to pull them back. Of course he didn't mean them.

"Choose? Choose between what?" She inhaled sharply. "Are you saying that you feel like you need to make a choice between a boy you just met . . . and me?"

Of course not! He adored his wife. They were joined by God and were going to be together until death parted them.

"Nee."

She wrapped her arms around her waist,

like she was protecting herself from further hurt. "You don't sound too certain about that."

"Miriam, stop judging every word I'm saying. You're not being fair."

"I see."

Miriam looked crushed. Ending the conversation in such a way made him feel terrible. But since he couldn't take back his thoughts or words, he simply turned away, leaving the hurt and brokenness between them like an open wound, changing everything between them and embedding pain into the fabric of their memories . . . ready to be taken out and evaluated again and again for years to come.

Which, he was already sure, was going to be a very bad thing.

SEVENTEEN

· **TIP #17** ·

Keep in mind that not everyone tells the truth all the time. Beware of suitors who seem too good to be true.

Sarah Anne hadn't felt so awkward in years. Standing by the front door, wearing a pair of black slacks, a silvery-blue sweater, and silver earrings, she examined herself in the mirror in her entryway again. Did she look like she was trying too hard?

She'd completed her look with a pair of two-inch black pumps that she'd gotten for a song the last time she'd gone down I-75 and visited several of her favorite outlets. So, her feet looked good.

At least, she thought they did.

But as she turned and spied her backside in the mirror, she was starting to think that the rest of her didn't look so good at all.

Her skin was pale, her blue eyes didn't

seem as bright as they used to, she was carrying twenty-five pounds that didn't want to come off . . . and her hair was gray. So gray.

All in all, she looked like a moderately dressed-up version of her usual self. Good enough for church, but that wasn't exactly the look she wanted to achieve for a second date.

When Pete pulled his Ford truck into her drive, she peeked at him through the window, then wiped her hands on her thighs. Had her palms ever been so sweaty?

Then, at last — or maybe far too soon — he knocked on the door.

After taking a deep breath, she opened it. "Hi, Pete." He was wearing a pair of dark jeans, black cowboy boots, a black leather belt, and a cotton shirt with the sleeves rolled up. He looked like a cross between the Marlboro Man and Tom Selleck about fifteen years ago. Well, Tom Selleck without any hair.

He smiled at her. "Hi. Are you ready?"

"Hmm? Oh, sure." She grabbed her purse and pulled out her keys.

After leading her out the door, he waited for her to lock it. Then smiled at her again as they walked to his truck. "You look nice."

"Thanks. I could say the same about you.

Hey, those are some pretty fancy boots."

He chuckled. "I guess they are. I bought them a couple of months ago at my daughter's urging. I thought they might need to get out of the closet for a spell. I haven't worn them in a while."

He opened the truck's passenger door, helped her in, and then walked around the front to his side. She buckled up and silently coached herself to get a grip.

After he buckled his seat belt as well, he turned to her. "So, I did some thinking, and I thought we could try that new steak house in Walnut Creek. Oscar's, I think it's called. Have you been there?"

"No. I've seen it, but I haven't had the pleasure."

He looked relieved. "Great. We'll check it out together."

He drove with one hand on the wheel and the other on his gearshift. She liked how confident he seemed — and how relaxed he was, not making a single complaint when they got stuck behind a horse and buggy for almost a mile on a curvy road.

"So, tell me the truth. Are you glad I'm driving, or do you wish you were back behind the wheel?"

Sarah Anne appreciated how light and fun Pete was at keeping the conversation. Grinning at him, she said, "I was just thinking about how nice it is not to be driving down these hilly, curvy roads. I'm glad for the break."

"Did you have a hard time getting used to driving that big thing?"

"Yes." She grinned. "I took a two-day class and even drove with a retired driver, but I was still scared to death my first day on the road."

"I can imagine."

Encouraged by his comment, she added, "Pete, for the first month, I lived in fear of going into reverse. But then I got used to it. Now, I don't even think about how big it is." She waved a hand. "But, I think I've been at an advantage. I've always liked driving, and that has been helpful."

"The first time I met you, I kept looking around for the driver."

"What?"

"Yeah, I just couldn't wrap my head around the fact that you were out on the road by yourself."

Sarah Anne wasn't sure if he meant that as a compliment or not. And though she was 90 percent sure that he hadn't meant it as a slight against either her gender or her age, she asked, "Why is that?"

"Hmm? Oh. Well, because . . ." He glanced

her way. "Did I just offend you?"

"No. I'm just being silly. I thought maybe you thought I was too old or something."

"Hey, I'm older than you, remember? Look. We're here." He pushed the release on his seat belt, and she took his momentary distraction as a chance to sneak a peek at him. He really was aging well — he looked like he was still in his mid-fifties.

He shrugged as he reached for his door handle. "But does age even matter anymore?" As she unbuckled, he said, "I'll come around and get your door."

She was glad for the small respite. She needed to collect her thoughts. Her concern about her age had thrown her for a loop. Why was she feeling so insecure?

Opening her door, Pete helped her out. "Hey, Sarah Anne?"

"Yes?"

"I'm not sure what's going on. You seem more quiet than usual . . . and maybe unhappy with me."

"I'm sorry. I didn't mean to make you uncomfortable."

"Look, I like you, but I'm a grown man. Please, be honest. Have you changed your mind about me and you're regretting saying yes to going out with me again? If so, I'd rather just know. I promise, I can take it."

"No! Not at all."

"Are you sure?"

It was time to buck up. "Pete, I'm just nervous. And I'm afraid I've let a good dose of pride and insecurities get the best of me, too. I wasn't sure what to wear or how to act or how to date at my age . . . I promise, everything that's going on in my head has everything to do with me and nothing to do with you."

Pete stared at her. Then, after a pause, he seemed to make a decision. He placed his hands on her cheeks, leaned down slightly, and kissed her.

Kissed her! Right there in the middle of the restaurant parking lot!

Oh, it wasn't anything to be shocked about. Just a quick, firm, chaste kiss. But it was a kiss all the same.

A couple chuckled as they walked by.

When Pete dropped his hands and stepped back, he looked completely satisfied. She, on the other hand, felt as flustered as all get-out. "What in the world was that about?" she sputtered.

"I couldn't think of a better way to get you to settle down."

"So you kissed me?" She still wasn't sure if the little zing in her insides was from happiness or shock.

"Absolutely." He stuffed his hands in his pockets. "Now, tell me the truth. Did it work?"

Sarah Anne was speechless, but Pete continued, "I like you, and I'm attracted to you. I want to take you out to dinner, and I've been looking forward to this night for a while." He lowered his voice. "Sarah Anne, will you try to not overthink everything tonight?"

There was only one answer. He was right. She needed to calm down. "Yes. I'm, ah, sorry for being such a ninny."

Looking pleased, he placed a hand on the small of her back and guided her toward the restaurant's entrance. "I wouldn't have put it that way, but I'm glad you're willing to give this a shot."

"Can we start this date over?"

Pete, all six-foot-two inches of him, grinned. "If that's what you want."

"I do."

He opened the restaurant's door. "Then, Miss Miller, let's go out to eat. You ready?"

Walking into the soothing, modern dining room, she nodded. "Yes. Right now I feel as if I'm ready for anything."

And it was the truth. She might be a widow, a little over middle-aged, and rusty as all get-out in the dating world . . . but suddenly, she felt like she was ready to finally start living again. At long last.

EIGHTEEN

· **TIP #18** ·
Remember that not every good
relationship starts out like they do
in the movies.

It was raining again. Pouring, really. About two hours ago the skies had erupted in a barrage of lightning streaks and heavy thunder. Some of the lightning struck so close, the windows in the house shook.

Though the worst of the thunder and lightning had abated, heavy sheets of rain were still falling. Miriam reckoned it would last through the night.

Perhaps it was fitting. The storms seemed to match her mood.

For the first time in their marriage, Miriam was sleeping alone in her bed. It wasn't by choice. Well, not her choice. Calvin didn't want to be near her.

She hadn't known he could be so upset

with her.

Tears filled her eyes every time she recalled what he'd said before storming out of the room. Boy, that had hurt. And, as much as she would love to pretend she'd never heard those words, Miriam knew such things could never be unsaid.

Honestly, she hadn't been able to think of anything else. How could she? Calvin had called her selfish and narrow-minded. He was *embarrassed* by her feelings and couldn't understand how someone who treated everyone kindly could be so unfeeling about the plight of a little boy.

Miriam had been so taken aback by his harsh words that she hadn't said anything in her defense. She'd just stood there and taken it.

The rest of the day hadn't gotten any better. She was struggling even more now with her decision to keep the pregnancy a secret, but the last thing she wanted was to get her husband's hopes up, only to see the look of disappointment — and maybe even a hint of regret about their marriage — in his eyes when she lost yet another baby.

Though she doubted that would be any worse than how things were at the moment. Listening to the rain, plagued by doubts, Miriam had never felt more alone. Even

Paddy had trotted off after Calvin hours ago, and Miriam hadn't seen her since.

Swiping a stray tear, she realized Edna had been right that keeping this baby a secret wouldn't help either of them. Perhaps she should get up and talk to Calvin, tell him that she actually had a very good reason for not wanting to adopt a little boy right now. That she had legitimate concerns about taking care of a little boy when she wasn't even sure if she was going to be able to take care of their unborn child. And if she started having any problems at all with the pregnancy, Edna would encourage her to stay in bed and rest. That would be almost impossible if Miles was there. Little boys needed mothers to care for them, right?

However, the thought of telling all of that to Calvin made Miriam's stomach go queasy. He was going to be upset she'd been sneaking around behind his back, and that would make her feel even worse. Then she wouldn't be able to sleep, which was bad for her and her baby's health.

Rolling over on her side, Miriam kept trying to think of a way out of the situation, but she couldn't. Because another part of her felt angry, too.

Yes indeed, she was very angry with her husband. They'd been married four years and had courted a year before that. Did he really not know her at all? He had no right to call her selfish and accuse her of not thinking of other people and ignoring his pain, especially when shielding him from the eventual hurt was all she'd been trying to do!

When the door creaked open and a soft glow from a candle entered the room, she kept her back to it. First she heard Paddy's light steps as she walked to her dog bed next to Miriam's easy chair. But then, she heard Calvin.

Though she stiffened and pretended to sleep, she did listen intently to Calvin's footsteps as he approached the bed. Every nerve ending was on edge when she felt him slide under the covers next to her. But, instead of hearing him blow out the candle and encasing them darkness, he let it burn on his nightstand.

After a pause, he ran a hand down her back, playing with the ends of her long hair like he always did. "Miriam?" he whispered. "Mimi, are you awake?"

She closed her eyes but told the truth. *"Jah."*

He cleared his throat. "Look, I know our argument was bad, but I don't want us to go to sleep upset with each other. Roll over and talk to me."

His words were sweet, and they had merit as well. But she had no idea what she could say or how to defend herself while still keeping the pregnancy a secret.

"I don't want to talk about our fight right now, Calvin," she said at last. She closed her eyes again, mentally preparing for him to lash out once more.

He ran a fingertip down her spine, the way he used to do when they first married and everything about her seemed to fascinate him. "I don't want to rehash our fight again, either." When she said nothing, he sighed. "Mimi, I know I said some things I shouldn't have. They were cruel, and I'm sorry I got so worked up and hurt you because of it. You know that I would never choose anyone, or anything, over you, right? Will you forgive me?"

Even though she couldn't see his expression, she could feel so much pain in his voice. She knew he was being sincere.

Slowly, she rolled over to face him.

Sure enough, his eyes were filled with the same pain that she was feeling. Studying his face, the way his body seemed tense, Miriam realized that Calvin truly was as upset as she was. Yes, he'd made a mistake, but he felt bad about it, just as she did that she might be making one as well.

More importantly, she loved him. She loved him dearly, and no matter if they had this baby, if she never carried a child to term, or if they ended up adopting six children one day, that would never change.

Therefore, there was only one thing to say.

Reaching out, she pressed her hand to his cheek, loving the way his soft, short beard felt against her skin. Looking into his eyes in the soft glow, she murmured, "Of course I forgive you, Calvin."

His light brown eyes scanned her face. "You sure?"

"I am sure."

"I love you, you know."

She smiled slightly. "I know. And I love you, too." Feeling the worst of the tension leave them, she stretched her legs out under the blankets. Her whole body suddenly felt as if it weighed twice as much. "Let's go to sleep, Calvin."

He shifted, blew out the candle on his nightstand, and then rearranged the sheets on his side of the bed. She flipped over, lying on her side with her back to him. Just like she always did.

After a few seconds, he rolled to his side and wrapped an arm around her waist. She snuggled closer, finally feeling protected and warm.

And though her mind and heart might still be upset, her body seemed to be reassured. She relaxed against him. Just like she always had.

"I love you, Miriam. With all my heart."

She didn't reply; there was no need. But there in the dark, as she listened to the rain continue to fall, Miriam had hope for their future.

Yes, it might be scary and filled with uncertainty and pain . . . but then again, it might not.

She chose to believe that it would get better. Just like the rain, this storm would pass. And while she might not be greeted with rainbows and sunshine in the morning, it would be brighter.

For now, that was enough.

NINETEEN

· **TIP #19** ·
Make a list of must-haves in a man that
are nonnegotiable.

"Miriam! Long time, no see!" Sarah Anne
called out from somewhere in the back of
the bookmobile.

Miriam smiled in spite of herself. The
librarian had a knack for making her feel
like they were good friends instead of mere
acquaintances. It was especially notable
because Miriam didn't visit the bookmobile
nearly as much as her husband. Though she
liked to read, she often preferred to knit,
quilt, or sew. She was also a slow reader,
and it sometimes took her a whole month
to finish a book. Taking all that into account, she was amazed Sarah Anne could
call out her name after the briefest of
glances.

Feeling better already, Miriam looked

around the small cheery space . . . then looked around again. "Sarah Anne, you might see me, but I don't see you," she said. "Where are you hiding?"

Sarah Anne's head popped up to the right of a small table and chair. "I'm here in this corner." Looking sheepish, she waved a rag. "I decided to do a little bit of spring cleaning since this is usually a slow stop." Moving to a crouch, she added, "Do you need anything, dear? Don't be shy. I promise, I'd rather help you look for a book than chase more dust bunnies around here."

Here was her chance. An empty bookmobile with no risk of anyone overhearing. Summoning some gumption, Miriam replied. "As a matter of fact, I do. If you don't mind."

"Of course not." Looking delighted to be of use, Sarah Anne got to her feet and walked toward her, her rag, a bottle of cleanser, and a wad of paper towels in her hands. "Let me clean up for a minute and then I'm all yours."

"Take your time. I'm in no hurry."

Miriam glanced at the display of new fiction but couldn't seem to get excited about any of the selections. Instead, she kept glancing toward the box of toys next to the rocking chair. Which her baby might use one day if the Lord continued to provide.

"Sorry about that," Sarah Anne said as she put the cleaning supplies away. "I'm at your service now. What can I help you find?"

Hoping she didn't sound as nervous as she felt, she said, "I wondered if you had any books about pregnancy."

The librarian blinked. Her face a careful mask, she asked, "You're wanting a nonfiction book, I assume? Like *What to Expect When You're Expecting*?"

She was familiar with that book. She'd checked it out two years ago . . . just one week before she'd eventually miscarried. "*Jah*. Do you have any books here like that?"

"Well, now, let's go see." Sarah Anne turned to the reference section, which was right next to her desk. Thumbing through the titles, she mumbled to herself, then pulled out a book with a bright smile. "Success!"

Miriam took the book from her. *Nine Months of Wonder and Happiness*. The cover showed a photo of a beaming, very pregnant woman standing in front of a beautiful baby's nursery. Though she was sure the image was accurate for a lot of pregnant ladies, neither the title nor the photo seemed to reflect her at the moment. She was currently neither very happy nor filled with awe and wonder. "Um, do you know much about this book?"

"I was never blessed with children, but some of my patrons seem to like it a lot. Perhaps you'd like to take it home and I can order you some other books for next time I'm here? Some, ah, maybe a little less flowery?"

It was as if Sarah Anne had read her mind! "Thank you," she said with a smile. "That would be very helpful."

"It's no problem." She walked back to her desk, pulled out a pen and a sheet of paper, and wrote down some notes. "At least one of them should be pulled for you by the time I'm on Gardner Way next week. I'll send the books home with Calvin if he arrives before you."

"Nee!"

Sarah Anne froze. "Sorry?"

"No, I'm sorry to bark like that. What I meant to say was thank you, but I'd like you to keep those books for me and, uh, not tell Calvin about them." Realizing how panicked and shifty she sounded, Miriam attempted to smile. "If you please?"

"I'll do whatever you want, Miriam. If you'd like to keep this between us, we can certainly do that."

166

"I would. I . . ." She lowered her voice. "I mean, Calvin doesn't know about the babe yet."

If Sarah Anne thought Miriam's statement was curious, she didn't let on. "I'll order the books and keep them in my cabinet for the next time we meet. I promise I won't say a word." She held out her hand. "May I have your library card? I'll need it to place the books on hold for you. Or, would you like to look at any other titles first?"

"No, I'll just check out this one." She fished the card out of her purse and handed it to Sarah Anne.

Sarah Anne had just scanned both the book and her card when the door opened and Ruth Schmidt and six children rushed in like a mini cyclone.

Sarah Anne froze before smiling brightly at them all. "Hello, Ruth! Hello Mary, Minnie, Ethan, Jonas, Ian, and Miles! This is a real . . . surprise."

"It's been a long day, Sarah Anne," Ruth replied as two of the youngest ones raced to the picture books. "Plus, with all this rain, we need as many distractions as possible. Some of my children need a lot of activity to burn off energy, I'm afraid. Maybe more than I can provide," she added under her breath.

The children who were standing by her side nodded.

"Well, you came to right place at the right time. Miriam here was just finishing up," Sarah Anne said. "Here you go, dear." She handed Miriam her library card and book.

Miriam took care to quickly stash the book in her tote bag before Ruth could peek at the cover. "It's *gut* to see you, Ruth," she said politely.

"I'm pleased to see you, too, Miriam. It's been too long," Ruth said just as two of the younger children tugged on her apron.

"Mamm!" the boy said. "Mary stuck her tongue out at me."

It was time to leave before things got even more chaotic. "*Danke* for your help, Sarah Anne," Miriam said.

"That's what I'm here for. You take care now," she called out as she walked to the chair in the center of the room. "Who wants to hear a story?"

"Me!" a chorus of voices rang out.

Thinking that Ruth was likely hoping Sarah Anne would pick out *War and Peace,* Miriam smiled as she walked to the door.

"Is Calvin coming here today, Miss Miller?" the oldest boy asked.

Miriam stopped mid-step.

Sarah Anne quickly glanced at Miriam

168

before replying. "I don't believe so, Miles. I expect Calvin is working on his farm today."

Suddenly, it all clicked. Miriam had been so focused on keeping her book a secret and making a speedy exit that she didn't even remember Ruth was caring for the boy who had stolen her husband's heart. Feeling like a rock was lodged in her throat, she turned to look at him more closely.

The boy — Miles — stared at her as well. He was a handsome boy, a little on the thin side, but Miriam thought most boys his age were. Besides, what caught her attention was his solemn expression. He seemed to be as interested in her as she was in him. She wondered then if Calvin had mentioned her to the boy in passing.

"Ah. Here we go," Sarah Anne said as she held up a picture book with rabbits on the cover.

Realizing she was still staring, Miriam turned away and hurried out the door.

Miles was darling. And he was alone and looked so grave.

He'd also been looking for Calvin. It was obvious the boy was already fond of him. It was no wonder Calvin wanted to help him.

It was also no wonder Calvin had been so upset with her when she'd tried to tell him she couldn't even consider adoption.

Guilt and uneasiness rushed through her. Was she the one in the wrong?

As she started on the walk home, Miriam's head started to pound. Everything seemed even more mixed up and convoluted than it had last night, which was really too bad.

As a fresh wave of nausea hit her, she stopped walking and tried to will it away. Of course it didn't help.

When the rain started up again, she pulled out her umbrella, but it was pouring so much that stray droplets kept landing on her face.

She supposed it didn't matter. The raindrops mixed in with her tears just fine.

TWENTY

· **TIP #20** ·

Remember that everyone of a "certain age" has habits they're not going to easily give up. I wouldn't plan on trying to change them.

Sometimes the noise was just too much, and this was definitely one of those times. The storm last night had kept Minnie and Ethan up, which meant that Miles had been up, too. All three of them had woken up late and cranky. Things hadn't gotten better when they'd hurried downstairs and been subjected to a rare lecture from Mr. Schmidt about the rules in the house.

It had been really hard to just nod and apologize for oversleeping when all Miles had wanted to do was point out that it wasn't the foster children in the house who were so much trouble.

After the lecture, he, Minnie, and Ethan

had received small bowls of cold cereal instead of pancakes like the triplets.

And the day had only gotten worse from there. All their chores seemed to take longer than usual, and then just as they arrived at the bookmobile, it had started to rain.

But at last, perhaps, the day was going to get brighter. For once, the triplets were quietly looking at books, and Minnie and Ethan were working on a small puzzle at the back table. Sarah Anne's mood seemed to have lifted, too. She was shelving some books.

Even better, the skies were now clear, and the sun was out. Miles approached Mrs. Schmidt.

"Can I go sit outside and wait until everyone's done?"

His foster mother looked at him with concern. "You won't be able to sit down, Miles. Your clothes will get all wet. Again."

"I won't sit down. Please, may I go outside for a little bit?" He was suddenly desperate for even five minutes by himself.

"Is anything the matter?"

"*Nee.* I just don't need a book. Miss Sarah Anne already renewed the one I checked out last week."

After eyeing him for another moment, she nodded. "All right then. But don't go far."

"I won't." He walked out the door before she could change her mind.

Once outside, he felt the humidity soak into his skin and heard the fierce hum of crickets and other insects in the air. Both reminded him of his real home, the home he used to have before his parents died and he was moved into the foster care system.

Five years ago, he'd lived with his parents . . . well, his grandparents. His real mother had jumped the fence when she was just fourteen and gotten into a mess of trouble. When he was three years old, she'd died of a drug overdose and he'd been sent to live with his grandparents.

Though he'd been very small, Miles did remember that he'd had a difficult time at first. He wasn't used to living on a farm or being Amish. He'd struggled to learn Pennsylvania Dutch and struggled even more to gain friends in his one-room schoolhouse.

But he had, and everything had been pretty good. His grandparents were older and strict, but loving. And, as time went on, they seemed to relax a bit. He'd loved to bake with Mommi and work in the barn with Dawdi. But an illness that swept through the region put them both in the hospital, and they died within days of each other. After that, he'd gone to one foster home after another, eventually ending up with the Schmidts, and he was more aware than ever that his time in the house was going to be a temporary arrangement. His social worker, Amanda, had told him he would probably only be at the Schmidts' for a year at the very most.

When the door to the bookmobile opened behind him, he turned, half expecting to see one of the triplets coming out to keep him company. Instead, it was Mrs. Schmidt herself.

"Do I need to come inside now?" he asked.

She shook her head. "I thought you had a good idea to get a few minutes of peace and quiet. Do you mind some company?"

"*Nee,* but is Miss Sarah Anne gonna be all right in there?"

"I hope so." She winked. "I guess I should feel guilty, leaving the five of them in there, but for the life of me, I don't feel too terrible. Sometimes it's nice to take a five-minute break."

"*Jah.*" That, of course, was why he'd stepped outside in the first place.

She stepped closer. "Is that what you're doing?" she asked in a gentle way. "Are you taking a five-minute break?"

"I guess." He looked down at his feet.

"Is something wrong?"

"Not really." When she raised an eyebrow, he shrugged. "It's not like we've got time to talk now anyway."

"It might not seem like it, but I always have time for you. I take my time as your foster mother seriously. But more than that, I take our relationship to heart, Miles. No matter what happens during the rest of your days, you'll always have me."

What was he supposed to say to that?

"Danke."

"Nee, don't thank me." She smoothed the end of one of her *kaap*'s ties before letting go of it. "Now, please. Talk to me. What is going on today? Are you upset over my husband's lecture about oversleeping?"

He shook his head. "I was just thinking that I don't know where I'll be next."

"Uncertainty is hard, isn't it?"

He nodded. He felt like he had lived his whole life being uncertain. "Some days I get upset that nobody in my life stuck around. Not my father or my mother or my grandparents." He hung his head. "And I know I sound mean, since they all died."

"Actually, I think you sound honest." She folded her hands across her chest. "And it is an honest statement to say that you've had a worse time of it than most."

He felt like he had, too. And what was going to happen to him next, since so far no one had wanted to adopt him? "I don't know what I did wrong," he admitted.

"You didn't do anything wrong. It's a mystery why the Lord decided you needed to lose so much at such a young age. But it's not your fault. And He's not doing it to make you upset. I'm sure of that."

"You believe that?"

"I do. I believe it with all my heart. *Got* loves you and He has a plan for you. One day you'll understand what it all means." She pressed a hand to her heart. "I promise you that."

"Okay."

A new shadow filled her eyes. "Miles, I wish James and I could keep you with us for years and years, but I honestly don't feel that we're the right permanent home for you. Everything is too unsettled and chaotic." She smiled slightly. "And as much as I love my triplets, even I realize that they can be, um . . . exhausting to be around."

"But what if the next place I'm sent to is bad?"

"We'll just have to make sure that it's not."

"Is that even possible? How can you do that?"

"I'll ask your social worker to tell me who

176

you're going to. Chances are good that I'll know the family. James and I have been foster parents for a long time, remember."

Miles didn't think that was much of a guarantee, but he was learning there weren't too many guarantees in life anyway. "All right."

"Don't forget, Amanda is a *gut* social worker, too. She cares about you, Miles. She won't let you go someplace bad."

He nodded.

She wrapped an arm around his shoulders. "Do you feel better at all?"

He didn't. What he wanted was to have his grandparents back. Or to get to stay with the Schmidts, as chaotic as life with them was. At least Ruth and James were nice people. However, he was starting to realize that just because someone hoped something would happen didn't mean it actually would. Life didn't work out that way.

He needed to focus on what he had instead of what used to be or what could be. He needed to start being grateful instead of telling the Lord what he wanted.

"I do, Ruth." He tried to look happier.

It didn't look like she was fooled for a second, though. "Are you sure about that? Because it's okay if you don't feel better. All of us have bad days from time to time."

"I'm not having a bad day. I'll go inside now."

Mrs. Schmidt's eyes looked as sad as his heart felt. "You know, you can always talk to me, Miles."

"I know. *Danke,*" he said as he entered the bookmobile again.

There was nothing left to say, since he and Ruth knew the truth. One day soon, he wouldn't be at her house. He wouldn't see her. He might never see her again. She was not always going to always be there for him. She wasn't even going to be there for him next year.

He now knew that "always" didn't mean too much. And sometimes? Well, sometimes "always" didn't mean anything at all.

TWENTY-ONE

When the last child had left and Ruth Schmidt had carefully closed the door after them, Sarah Anne collapsed into her rocking chair. She was exhausted.

Goodness, but what a roller coaster of a day it had been. First, the tourist traffic had been so bad coming out of the parking lot, she'd feared she was going to be hopelessly late for her first stop. Then old Mr. Troyer had yelled at her because the books he'd requested hadn't come in. Soon after, she'd realized that she'd forgotten her lunch. But, because of the traffic, she'd had no time to stop to grab anything to eat.

The cherry on the top of her very long day had been this stop on Gardner Way. She knew Miriam Gingerich's business wasn't any of hers, but Sarah Anne could practi-

179

cally see the pain and worry etched into the young woman's face.

But Miriam's worry had nothing on poor Miles's expression. The boy had looked like he had a terrible headache. But, who could blame him, with the triplets in fine form?

She'd been so worried about Miles when he stepped outside that she hadn't even minded when Ruth walked out to join him. Thankfully, the triplets had taken pity on her and quietly looked at books for the few minutes Ruth was out of the bus.

Continuing to lazily rock back and forth, Sarah Anne frowned at the state of the bookmobile. All the commotion and the continuing problems had left a real mess of things, no doubt about that. When she got back to the library parking lot, it was going to take a bit of time to put everything back together, which of course meant that her stomach was going to have to growl a little while longer.

She glanced at her watch. Nothing was going to get done if she didn't stand up and get going. Sarah Anne folded the rocking chair and stored it, then did a quick run-through of the area, locking bookshelves into place and securing the door.

At last, she got into the driver's seat and started the engine.

It was pouring down rain again. The drive back was going to be a tough one, without a doubt. The streets in Berlin and the surrounding areas were at times narrow and windy, with a couple of good hills every now and again. Slick roads made the drive even more stressful than usual.

After realizing her shoulders were tense and she'd been clenching her jaw, Sarah Anne forced herself to relax. She was a sixty-one-year-old woman, by golly. She'd had a career at a prestigious accounting firm and had survived both chauvinistic bosses and weeks of sixteen-hour workdays during tax seasons. If she could get through all that, she could certainly survive a rough day in the bookmobile!

With that little boost in her mind, she continued to navigate the roads, hardly saying a peep when a motorcycle passed her on a curve.

And then, not ten minutes later, she caught sight of a buggy parked off to the side of the road, an Amish man holding the reins of an agitated horse. Two teenagers stood next to a car in the ditch . . . and there was that motorcyclist she'd seen earlier. He was now lying on the ground with another teenager kneeling next to him.

When they saw her approach, the teen

kneeling on the ground jumped to his feet and waved his arms.

Sarah Anne slammed on the brakes, felt the old tires on the bookmobile screech and slide on the slick pavement . . . and then at last she came to a halt ten feet from the accident. Praying with all her might as she picked up her cell phone and ran down the stairs, Sarah Anne entered the fray.

"Has anyone called 911 yet?" she called out as she rushed forward.

One of the teens held up his phone. "I did. The lady who answered said someone would be here soon."

"That's real good. What happened?"

"We were trying to go around that horse and buggy when this guy came flying down the road. We tried to get out of the way, the horse got spooked, and the biker here lost control. He went down hard."

"How is he?" she asked as she knelt down beside him.

"I'm not sure," the teen said, gesturing toward his helmet. "I was going to take it off, but everyone seemed to think we shouldn't touch it."

"I felt his neck for a pulse," the girl said. "I'm not sure, but I don't think he's alive," she said. "Chris and I and that man over there checked."

Sarah Anne looked again at the Amish man — and realized it was Calvin Gingerich. "Calvin, I can't believe you're here. Are you okay?"

"Well enough." He patted his horse's neck. "Windy here has been as steady as she goes." His expression turned solemn again. "But this accident, well, it don't look good," he said. "Since the ambulance is supposed to be on its way, we decided to leave him be."

Since she was no medical professional, everything they said made perfect sense, but it was still hard to stand around and do nothing.

She decided to crouch next to the man and hold his hand. If he was still alive, there was a chance he would register human contact.

Resting her knees on the pavement, she took hold of his hand. It was still warm and pliable, though she didn't know if that was a good sign or again her inexperience at play.

"Sir, my name is Sarah Anne," she whispered as she heard the sound of sirens approaching. "You were in an accident. But the ambulance is on its way, and we're all going to stay here with you."

She thought she might have felt the smallest of movements, though it was surely her imagination. However, she wrapped her other hand over his. "Don't give up. Please, don't give up." She wondered if she was speaking to herself as much as to him.

An ambulance, followed by a sheriff's car, screeched to a stop just a few feet away. EMTs seemed to pour out of the vehicle. "Ma'am? What's going on?"

"I just got here myself." After briefly sharing what she knew, Sarah Anne added, "None of us know if he's okay or not. I sure hope he is." She hurried to her feet and backed away so the medical team could get to work.

"There's a lot of blood," one of the teens said. "I think he's hurt bad."

One of the paramedics called out to the others, and the sheriff motioned for everyone else to back up. "Let's head over here," the sheriff said. "All of you stand here a minute and don't go anywhere. I need to call for assistance."

They all listened as he started talking on the radio attached to his vest. Then, he turned back to them. "I need to know who was directly involved." Turning to Calvin, the sheriff said, "Were you?"

"*Jah.* I was."

When it was obvious that Calvin didn't

want to leave his horse, Sarah Anne walked to the mare. "I can hold her reins if you'd like."

"*Danke,*" Calvin said before he started telling his story to the officer.

Things got crazier then. Two cars pulled over, the drivers obviously trying to help, and one of the deputies started directing traffic. Every couple of minutes, other vehicles approached and slowed down, and then eventually turned around and went back the way they came.

The rain slowed to a drizzle. When the teenage girl started to cry, one of the boys wrapped his arm around her shoulders and whispered to her.

But overshadowing all of it was the scene on the ground. It was obvious that the paramedics were doing everything they could to save the motorcyclist.

Then, when the doors opened again and a stretcher was carried out, they collectively held their breath. By this time the cyclist's helmet was off and an IV had been inserted into his arm.

"He's still alive," the boy who had been kneeling on the ground murmured.

Sarah Anne smiled encouragingly at him. "He sure is."

"That's a miracle," Calvin said.

Sarah Anne liked the sound of that. "It is indeed."

TWENTY-TWO

· TIP #22 ·

Consider this . . . if you can't count on
your date to show up on time, can you
count on him to show up in an
emergency?

"Hey, Pete, you don't head down SR-39 on
your way home, do you?" Dane asked.

Pete looked up from his laptop. He and
Dane had decided to meet at a McDonald's
so they could compare notes about a couple
of their clients' term life policies. "I was
planning on it. Why?"

"My wife just texted me. There's a big accident over there. She said there's a couple
of sheriff cruisers, an ambulance, and a fire
truck blocking the road."

"Wow. I hope everyone's okay."

"Me, too." Dane whistled as he looked
down at his phone's screen again. "*Whoa.*
Get this — there's also a horse and buggy, a

sedan, and a bookmobile."

Every nerve ending in him froze. "Say again?"

"Looks like an Amish horse and buggy were involved. I hate to hear that, don't you? Horses and buggies don't stand a chance next to trucks or SUVs."

"Wait . . . Did you say there was a bookmobile there, too?"

He nodded. "Go figure, huh? I didn't even know those were still around."

Pete got to his feet. "I've gotta go."

Dane looked at him in alarm. "What? Why?"

"I know someone who might be there," he said as he disconnected the power cord from his computer and stuffed it into his backpack.

"Who? Do I know him?"

Pete ignored him and strode to the door, even as Dane tried to keep up.

"Pete, come on. Who do you know?"

"I've gotta go," he said again, this time with a lot more force. "I'll talk to you later."

He didn't hear what else Dane said as he got into his truck and dialed Sarah Anne's number.

After it rang three times and went directly to voice mail, his pulse went up right as his heart seemed to lodge in his throat.

When a car blared its horn at him, making him realize he'd been stopped at the edge of the parking lot and was blocking traffic, he realized he had to get it together. He was getting himself all worked up, and there was nothing he could do about it. He didn't even know if Sarah Anne was involved. He was taking two and two and getting seven.

He said a prayer for everyone who was involved in the accident, and fifteen minutes later, he pulled up behind a police cruiser, a sedan, and the bookmobile. There wasn't an ambulance in sight, but he did see the remains of a motorcycle.

When he got out of his truck, one of the deputies in uniform looked his way. "You got a reason to be here, buddy?"

"Yeah. I'm looking for Sarah Anne Miller." He pointed to the bookmobile. "She drives that."

After giving him a good long look, the deputy pointed to a shaded area a few feet away. "She's over there."

It took him a minute, but he did see her, sitting on the grass with a teenage boy. She looked calm and at peace, pretty much the complete opposite of the way he was feeling.

Confused, he thanked the deputy and

189

walked over to her.

She was talking with the boy, but she drew to an abrupt stop when she noticed him. "Pete, what are you doing here?"

When she moved to get to her feet, he said, "No, no. Stay put." After giving her a reassuring smile, which probably didn't fool her for a minute, he added, "My buddy Dane got a text from his wife, saying that a bookmobile had been involved in an accident. I knew it had to be you."

"I'm okay."

"Sure?" As he spoke, his gaze drifted from her eyes all the way down to her toes, looking for bruises and cuts, any sign that she was hurt.

She frowned but ignored his brusque tone, as well as his statement. "Pete, this is Carson. He and I decided to take a breather before his father arrives," she said, sounding much like the two of them had just happened to meet in the middle of the field. "It's been quite a busy couple of hours."

The teenager didn't say a word, just merely looked up at him.

That's when Pete noticed some of his clothes were stained in blood. "Are you okay?" he asked. "I mean, do you need assistance?"

Carson shrugged. "I'm all right, I guess.

The EMTs checked me out and said I was fine. I didn't need to go to the hospital or anything."

"What happened?"

"A lot," Carson said. "It was really bad."

When the teen didn't add anything more, Pete raised his eyebrows at Sarah Anne.

Sarah Anne's soothing tone came to the rescue again. "Pete, Carson here is a senior over at West Holmes High in Millersburg. He was driving around my friend Calvin, who's Amish and drives a horse and buggy. Anyway, right then, a motorcycle came out of nowhere, skidded, and then lost control."

Feeling awkward standing over them, Pete joined them on the grass. To his surprise, the ground was wet. Now the seat of his pants was soaked. Shifting, he frowned.

Sarah Anne noticed his movement and grinned. "Oops."

"Do you know something I don't? Are your clothes not soaked through?"

Sarah Anne shifted slightly, enough to show a square plastic mat. "I've had these in the bookmobile. I decided they'd work in a pinch."

"I guess so." He shifted uncomfortably, wishing he could go back in time five minutes.

"Would you like me to go get one for you, Pete?"

"Thanks, but I'm good. There's nothing to do about it now." He shifted until his legs were half stretched out in front of him.

Amazingly, that action seemed to amuse the boy and break up some of the tension. He grinned.

"Hey, there are worse things to happen. So, is the motorcyclist going to be okay?"

"We don't know," Sarah Anne answered, her expression grave again. "At least he was alive, which is saying something."

"He was that bad, huh?"

Carson nodded. "When it all first happened, I thought he was dead. I tried to find a pulse, but I couldn't." Lowering his voice, he added, "There was blood everywhere."

"Was he wearing a helmet?"

"Yeah, but I don't know if it mattered. One of the paramedics said he was pretty cut up and he probably broke his arm, maybe hurt his leg or hip, too."

"Poor guy. But you're okay?"

"Yeah. The paramedic said I might have some bruises from my seat belt, but at least my friends and I were all wearing them. It's good the Amish guy was fine, too."

Sarah Anne smiled at the high schooler. "There's your silver lining, I suppose. All of you are okay, and you got to meet my friend Calvin and his horse."

Carson's lips curved up. "His horse was cool."

She chuckled. "She is, though I happen to think Calvin is pretty cool as well."

Pete felt like he was entering the twilight zone. She and this boy were sitting on plastic mats in a field after watching a motorcyclist almost die. And what were they talking about? An Amish man and his horse, whom she just happened to be friends with.

He cleared his throat. "Sarah Anne, I don't understand how you came to be in the middle of all of this."

"I was driving past about five minutes after it happened. Someone needed to help."

So she decided it should be her. "That sounds like you."

"I just happened to be in the right place at the right time. There was no way I was going to simply drive on."

A lot of people would have seen the wreck and turned around or just called 911 to report the accident. "And now? Do the police need to talk to you?"

Carson answered. "Nah. They already did that. But since I was the driver and I'm only seventeen, they want to speak to a parent, too. My dad has to come from work, and that's about an hour away."

Sarah Anne smiled at Pete. "I didn't want him to sit by himself." Looking over his shoulder, she brightened. "Hey, is that your father, Carson?"

"Yeah." He got to his feet and hurried to the man getting out of a white sedan.

"Thank goodness," Sarah Anne murmured. "That poor boy is as rattled as can be."

"It's good of you to stay with him."

She shrugged. "I don't have any kids, but if I did, I'd want someone to sit with them, too."

"Back when mine were in high school, an accident like this would have freaked them out. No way could they have just sat with a deputy while they waited for me to show up."

"Looks like Carson is close to his dad."

Pete turned and saw the boy's dad had his arm around his son's shoulders and was talking to him quietly, seemingly oblivious to the deputy who was obviously waiting to speak with him. "He's blessed."

"Indeed."

"Now, how are you doing?"

"Me?" She smiled softly. "Pete, I told you, I came after the fact. I'm fine."

"You've taken a lot on." And acted incredibly, too, he silently added.

She waved his comment off with a hand. "Don't make me into someone better than I am, Pete. This . . . Well, it's just life, right?"

"I guess so." Before he could make any other meaningful comments, Carson and his father approached.

Sarah Anne hopped right up and straightened her cotton shirt that was still neatly tucked into her jeans. As Pete stood up, he felt like he was taking about a cup of water with him. His jeans felt that soaked. At least he wasn't wearing khakis.

"Miss Miller, this is my dad, Doug. Dad, this is Miss Miller and, uh, Pete."

"I'm pleased to meet you, Miss Miller," he said, shaking her hand.

"It's Sarah Anne, and I'm pleased to meet you as well."

"Carson told me a little about how kind you've been, talking with all the kids and their parents. And now you've been sitting here when I'm sure you have other things to do. Thank you."

"You're very welcome, but it was really nothing. I was just on my way to return the bookmobile. My day was done."

"But still, thanks."

She smiled at Carson. "I would say anytime, but I really hope there isn't another one of these days for a long time."

"No kidding."

"You work for the library?" Carson asked.

"I do." Pointing to her vehicle, she added, "I usually drive the bookmobile, but every once in a blue moon I help out at one of the branches. Who knows? Maybe one day we'll see each other again sometime."

"Maybe." Carson looked up at his dad. "Can we go home now?"

"You bet." Doug squeezed his son's shoulder. "I'm sure your mother is going crazy. I texted her from the car and told her that you looked okay but not to call. We better go ease her mind."

After they said goodbye and Carson thanked Sarah Anne again, the sheriff and deputy said goodbye as well and drove off.

Then it was just the two of them in the field. Pete noticed that, now that everyone else had left, Sarah Anne looked a little wilted. It was obvious — to him, anyway — that she'd given all she had to the whole group and now she had next to nothing left. He needed to take her home.

But she was also independent, so he weighed his words carefully. "So, what are you going to do now? I mean, after you take the bookmobile back to the main library."

"I'm going to go home and probably collapse. What about you?"

"I was hoping we could spend some time together."

"Like, go out?" She sounded incredulous. "Oh, Pete. I'm afraid I'm not dressed for that. I need a shower. Plus, the rest of my day wasn't all that great to begin with. All I want to do is sit on the couch."

"I was thinking of something more along the lines of ordering a pizza and then watching a movie or something on your couch. That is, if you don't already have plans for dinner."

"You know what? That sounds great. I think it would be nice to have some company for the next few hours." She waved a hand at the street. "This whole thing was pretty stressful."

He was relieved to hear her say that. Part of him was pretty sure his pulse was still racing. "How about I follow you back to the library and then head home and change. I'll come to your house in about an hour. That will give you time to take a shower and change, too."

"You don't need to follow me to the library, Pete. I'm not rattled or anything."

"I know you're capable and have nerves of steel, Sarah Anne," he teased. "However, I'd still like to make sure you get back there safe. I mean, I'd like to if you'll let me."

She blinked, and then her face got the sweetest, softest look. "Then I'll let you."

He leaned toward her and kissed her lightly on the lips. "Thanks." When he took her hand and walked her to the bookmobile, she smiled up at him.

He wouldn't have changed that moment for the world.

TWENTY-THREE

Not every date needs to be fancy or
expensive. Some of my favorite outings
were just long walks in a park.

Had there ever been a longer day? Guiding
Windy down the driveway, Calvin's amazing mare picked up speed. It seemed she,
too, was very ready to relax at home.

"Almost there, Windy," Calvin murmured,
letting her have her way as she hurried to
the barn. "As soon as I get you unhitched,
I'll give you a good brushing and some oats.
You deserve a *gut* break after the last two
hours, for sure and for certain."

Their barn was a good fifty yards from
the house. They'd planned it that way, both
to give Miriam a little distance from the
work in the barn and to provide a small
measure of safety in case of a fire. As he
passed the house, he saw Miriam watching

him with her arms folded over her chest. He didn't need to be a mind reader to know she wasn't happy with him for being so late.

When he raised his hand in greeting but she didn't move a muscle, his suspicion was confirmed. Miriam was not happy with him. Yet again.

Realizing he was now going to have to soothe his wife's worries, he stifled a sigh. He was getting so very tired of having to convince her he wasn't doing anything wrong.

"Maybe I'll stay with you out in the barn for a while longer, Windy. I've a feeling that you'll be a more sympathetic companion right now."

Of course, he felt terrible for saying such a thing. Miriam was his wife — and a good woman. He loved her and had promised to care for her as long as he lived. He knew she was fighting her own battles with infertility, and she was having difficulty coming to grips with his desire to adopt a ten-year-old.

He needed to be patient with her and try to be more understanding. However, right at that moment, all he wanted to do was worry about himself and Windy for a spell.

After he set the brake and gave in to a few minutes of self-pity, he got busy taking care of his horse.

As he unhooked the traces and ran a hand along her flank, Windy shivered with happiness.

"I know, girl. You've been attached to this contraption a long time today. I'll give you a break tomorrow and ride my bicycle if I need to go somewhere."

Though Windy didn't do anything more than gaze at him with her pretty brown eyes, he felt as if she was grateful for his promise. Getting out the curry comb and brush, he carefully smoothed her coat and gently rubbed her sides. Windy never fought getting hitched, but he knew enough about horses to know that pulling a buggy down a street with a two-hundred-pound man in it wasn't a comfortable combination.

After removing the bit and reins, he led her into the comfort of the barn. Like a pleased puppy, she walked right into her stall. Then, it took no time at all to give her fresh water, hay, and a good helping of oats.

With a cursory look to the henhouse and a quick peek at Mabel, their cow, Calvin knew he had no option but to go greet his wife. He closed the barn doors and headed to the house, but Miriam was no longer waiting on the porch for him. He hadn't expected her to, but he couldn't deny that he wished she was still there, anxious to see him, or, better yet, had even walked to the barn to greet him like she used to.

Of course, that had been four years ago, back when they were newlyweds and everything about married life was fresh and new. Things were different now. Instead of wishing for what wasn't, he needed to figure out how to tell Miriam about the accident without worrying her.

He found her in the kitchen, frowning as she cut up a chicken. "We're having fried chicken for supper?"

Her hands stilled. "*Nee.* I thought I'd bake it instead. Is that all right with you?"

"You know it is. I would never tell you what to cook for supper."

Still not looking at him, she nodded. "It should be ready in about an hour." Her voice sounded wooden.

Walking to the sink, he turned the faucet on. "Since I came home so late, how about I help you?"

"There's no need for that. Working in the kitchen is my job."

Miriam still hadn't looked his way. "I'm sorry I got home so late," he said. "Were you worried?" Perhaps this was the opening he needed to tell her about the motorcycle wreck.

202

"Of course I was." She chopped off the chicken's wing with a bit more force than necessary. The blade hit the wooden chopping block with a solid *thunk*.

He grimaced. Obviously, he needed to discuss what had happened sooner rather than later. "Miriam, put the knife down and come sit with me, will ya?"

"Supper is already late. If I don't get this chicken in the oven, you'll have nothing to eat but peanut butter sandwiches."

When she chopped off another section of the poor bird, Calvin raised his voice. "I'm fine with peanut butter. But, Miriam, please. Stop. You're chopping that bird with so much force, I'm afraid you're going to hurt yourself."

At last she placed the knife on the cutting board and turned to him. Her blue eyes were full of fire. "What do you have to say that *canna* wait, Calvin?"

He was just tired enough to blurt "nothing" and walk off, but he forced himself to remember the way she'd looked standing on the front porch. She'd been so alone.

And that accident had made him realize that she could have been that way forever.

"Windy and me were almost hit on the road today."

Her face went slack. "When?"

"A couple of hours ago. We were on SR-39 when a car of teenagers passed us and then a motorcycle came out of nowhere. It was *verra* bad."

"How bad? Was anyone hurt?" She looked concerned . . . and perhaps a little bit eased? As if she was relieved to know he hadn't been avoiding her on purpose.

He nodded. "The man on the motorcycle." Remembering the blood staining the road, he added, "At first, everyone thought he was dead."

"Oh my word! But he lived?"

"I think so. The ambulance took him away."

"The ambulance," she murmured to herself. After a second's pause, Miriam seemed to wrap her head around his news. "You were just in an accident. That's why you were late." She exhaled.

"*Jah.* Oh, Miriam. You wouldn't have believed it all! Minutes after it happened, none other than Sarah Anne Miller came upon us in her bookmobile. She went right down to the man's side and tried to help. Then the ambulance, a fire truck, a sheriff, and a deputy came. There were vehicles everywhere."

"It must have been scary."

"It was a bit, but we were mostly waiting

around a lot. See, everyone had to talk to the sheriff and deputy. We had to wait for our turns."

"Even you."

"Oh, yes." Calvin ran a hand over his face, taking comfort in the motion. "I think the sheriff kind of figured Windy and me were a big part of it. After all, we were on the road."

"How did Windy do with all the noise and commotion?"

"You know what a good horse she is. She was uneasy but minded her manners. I was proud of her."

"I am, too." Gazing up at him, she blinked several times, then began to cry. "Oh, Calvin. I had thought . . . I feared . . ." She looked up at him. "I am ashamed of the things that crossed my mind."

"Nothing to be ashamed about." It did hurt that she still didn't trust him, but he supposed he'd have to settle with earning it back a little at a time.

When he reached for her, she jumped back. "You *canna* touch me. Look at my hands! Chicken."

Right then and there, he started laughing. "You certainly do have some chicken hands, *frau.* Why don't you wash them and I'll finish cutting up the chicken?"

"You don't mind?"

205

"Not at all. I, um, would much rather handle the sharp objects tonight. You looked rather frightening with a cleaver in your hands."

She walked to the sink. "I fear that I rather did seem to be taking out my frustrations on helpless poultry."

"It was quite a sight." Eying all the pieces stacked on the cutting board, he said, "What do you do now? Put the pieces on a baking sheet with some salt and pepper?"

As he'd secretly hoped, fire lit her eyes. Scrubbing her hands with soap, she declared, "Baked chicken is more than salt and pepper. Get out an egg, some flour, and a box of cornflakes."

"Cornflakes? Like the cereal?"

"*Jah,* just like the cereal." She giggled.

As soon as she turned off the faucet, he pulled her close and kissed her. Miriam melted against him like she always did.

"What was that for?"

Because he was glad he hadn't been the person who'd been rushed to the hospital today.

Because he was mighty relieved she was no longer mad.

And because he was glad Miriam was his.

Most of all, he was glad he was alive and there to argue with and kiss her. "It was for everything," he said at last.

Pressing her hands on his chest, she smiled. "In that case, you'd best kiss me again."

He didn't hesitate to oblige. Supper could definitely wait a bit longer.

Twenty-Four

· **TIP #24** ·

If you're determined to date more than one man at a time, you might want to take notes so you don't ask about the wrong hobby or job.

Looking at herself objectively in the mirror, Sarah Anne analyzed her outfit. She was wearing a violet jogging set and a pair of white Keds that she'd bedazzled with rhinestones on a whim several weeks ago. She'd put on mascara and pale pink lip gloss, and on impulse, she'd heated up her hot rollers and rolled her hair. They were on her head now, working their magic. The heat would calm her somewhat wiry hair and give it a little extra bounce that blow-drying alone couldn't accomplish.

Looking back at her reflection, she nodded. She would do. It wasn't a first-date-worthy effort, but all things considered, she thought she looked pretty good. Good enough to share a delivery pizza with Pete.

And certainly better than the state of her living room!

It was a mess! She had an awful habit of taking off her socks and shoes in front of the television at the end of a long day. Sometimes, she took off all her jewelry and placed it on a side table as well. And, on occasion, she would leave the glass or cup from whatever she had been drinking there, too. And wrappers from candy. Forgotten tissues. Magazines she'd read but hadn't put away. Mail she'd sorted through but had forgotten about.

It was more than a mess. It was a disaster!

There was no way she was going to let Pete see all of that.

More quickly than she thought was possible to move after the day she'd had, Sarah Anne scurried around the house, picking up everything in handfuls and depositing them in the trash, the dishwasher, and the cabinets. Two squirts of furniture polish and a damp rag removed the worst of the dust.

Right after she'd sprayed air freshener throughout the entire living room, the doorbell rang. She quickly deposited the spray bottle in her media cabinet, then opened the door to Pete.

His polite smile turned into a full-fledged grin when he saw her. "I'm flattered."

"Why is that?" She led him into her living room, quickly scanning the entryway as she did so. Everything looked good and smelled even better. The room was reasonably neat, too. No stray socks or — heaven help her — undergarments that had fallen when she'd raced to put the clothes sitting on the top of her dryer into the basket in her closet.

Looking as if he was trying his hardest not to burst into laughter, he pointed to her hair. "Your curlers."

Though she could already feel them, Sarah Anne still reached up to touch them. Just in case he was making it up.

But, of course, he wasn't.

She. Still. Had. Hot. Rollers. In. Her. Hair.

She closed her eyes in mortification. "I'll be right back."

He chuckled. "Take your time." Pulling out his cell phone, he said, "I'll order the pizza. What kind do you want?"

"Anything is fine."

" 'Anything'? Are you sure?"

She nodded. "I like anything but sausage, ham, peppers, or pineapple." And yes, she now realized how ditzy she sounded.

He grinned again. "Glad I asked."

In another life, she would have traded

some quick, clever little remark. Unfortunately, her cleverness had left her right about the time she'd answered the door to her first gentleman guest in years — with curlers in her hair.

"Make yourself at home," she murmured before striding to her bedroom and closing the door.

When she caught sight of herself in the mirror, she had to laugh. Not only was her hair up in rollers, but those curlers had drooped and twisted, leaving a great number of stray hairs sticking out. She looked like Medusa with her finger in the light socket, all because she felt the need to frantically clean in order to make herself look better in Pete's eyes.

The whole situation had been just what she needed.

Sarah Anne paused to give thanks. "This was exactly what I needed, Lord," she whispered to herself. "Thank you for reminding me of the dangers of pride . . . and to remember that laughter and smiles really are worth more than perfection."

After she put her hair to rights and added a touch of hair spray, Sarah Anne walked into the living room again.

Pete was wandering around the space, inspecting her paintings, bright quilts, and bookshelves.

"I'm sorry about that," she said.

He glanced her way and smiled warmly. "It was no problem. You gave me time to order two pizzas and inspect your living room without being watched." Turning to her, he said, "You've got a lovely house, Sarah Anne. And, if you don't mind me saying so, I think your hair looks pretty, too."

"That moment is going to go down in history as one of my most embarrassing!"

"Hardly that."

She shrugged. "How about this then . . . It was a good reminder for me not to take myself too seriously."

"Oh?"

"You probably wouldn't have cared if I opened the door in old sweats and air-dried hair."

"I wouldn't have, but I appreciate this version of you, too." He stepped closer. "Don't get mad, but you gave my ego a much-needed boost. It's been a long time since anyone tried so hard to look nice for me."

Noticing that his cheeks looked freshly shaven and he smelled like soap and cologne, she reached for his hand. "I won't get mad."

"Good." He leaned down and pressed a kiss to her forehead. "Now, tell me about these quilts. Did you make any of them?"

"Oh, no. I tried my hand at quilting years ago and realized very quickly that I don't have the temperament for it."

"I didn't realize there was a certain quilting temperament."

"I didn't realize that at first, either! And then, there I was, chatting while cutting pieces, mismeasuring others, and then sewing squares together all lopsided." She looked up at him as she tried to keep a straight face. "All of that contributed to a round-the-world quilt that looked a whole lot like a world that was off-kilter."

His eyes lit up. "Do you still have that quilt?"

"I do. And no, you may not see it. I might not be trying to look perfect all the time, but that quilt is pure embarrassment." Running a hand down her favorite quilt, a star quilt composed of various shades of pink, she said, "I got this one in downtown Berlin four years ago. It's pieced together by a Mennonite woman in Cincinnati and hand quilted by an Amish lady in Sugarcreek."

"And then sold in Berlin."

She nodded. "Not only is this quilt quite beautiful, but every time I see it, I think about all of the hours those ladies spent on this piece."

"It looks too nice to use."

"And you wouldn't know it to see it, but I've already washed it several times."

"Well, I like it. I like everything in here. It all looks like you."

She smiled up at him, warmed by his sweet words. "I guess it all is like me. I love these quilts, the photos are of people I hold dear in my heart, and my books feel like old friends. It all makes me happy to be home." Feeling a bit self-conscious for going on and on about herself, she met his eyes again. "Just as I'm sure your house reflects everything about you."

"I wish it did, but I'm afraid when you come over to my place, all you're going to think is that I need a trip to the furniture store."

"You don't have any furniture?"

"Oh, I have it. It's just decorated like an old-man bachelor pad."

"I haven't heard of that style," she teased. "What's it like?"

"Oh, it's something real special." He waved a hand across the room, like a used-car salesman. "Picture a brown velour recliner, a lumpy couch I inherited from my sister, and a pair of scarred and scuffed-up end tables, circa 1992."

"And on the walls?"

"Old movie posters pinned up with thumbtacks."

"I don't know whether I should be intrigued or very afraid."

"Be intrigued, of course." When they heard the doorbell chime, he grinned. "And . . . I've just been saved by pizza." Walking to the door, he called out, "I'll get this. You get the plates."

Sarah Anne smiled to herself as she heard Pete joke with the pizza deliveryman while he paid.

She kept it to herself, but right at that moment, she knew Pete didn't have a thing to worry about. She was definitely intrigued. In fact, the only thing she was afraid of, as far as he was concerned, was that she'd already given him her heart.

TWENTY-FIVE

· TIP #25 ·
Wear comfortable shoes.

Miles wasn't the only foster child in the Schmidt house, but he was the oldest and had been there the longest. Perhaps that was why Amanda, his social worker, and Mr. Schmidt had called the meeting with him.

Ethan and Minnie were off on an errand with Mrs. Schmidt and the triplets, and it felt strange being the only kid in the house. Scary, too, especially because Mr. Schmidt seemed a lot more uptight than he usually was.

The three of them were sitting in the dining room, at one end of the large oak table that Mr. Schmidt had built himself the day he and Mrs. Schmidt had decided to become foster parents. The big table was scarred and full of nicks and dents and even a few stubborn crayon and marker marks that no amount of cleanser seemed to be able to erase.

Ruth had told him once that she reckoned the table was a fitting symbol of the way she and her husband tried to run their life together. It was imperfect but sturdy and useful. Miles liked how whenever he ran his hand over the smooth surface it felt sleek and warm. Right at the moment, however, it only felt too big and empty.

But maybe that was just how he was feeling inside.

Steeling himself for what could only be bad news, Miles took care to keep his face expressionless and his body still. Showing too much emotion was never a good thing. It sure didn't make life easier.

So, he sat there with his hands clenched in his lap as he watched Amanda fuss with her laptop, glasses, file folders, and cell phone, just like she always did. Once she got all organized, Amanda was super efficient. But Miles had learned that it always took her a while to get settled, and that it didn't do any good to try to rush her.

Obviously noticing the way he was watching her, Amanda grinned. "Miles, every time I see you watch me so patiently, I want to cover my face and say that I'm trying to do better."

On another day, he might have joked around, too, but he was too nervous. "I don't think you need to do anything better."

Her eyes softened. "You really are a gem."

Mr. Schmidt looked amused. "He is at that. Well, Miles is a gem when he's not waiting in line for the shower."

Miles knew Mr. Schmidt was only joking. "I only grumble when Mary's in there," he said. Mary took double the time that she was supposed to take. Always.

"I've told her mother more than once that Mary lollygags, but Ruth doesn't seem to listen to my complaints." He folded his hands together on the table. "I mean, she listens but pays me no mind."

Amanda smiled as she clicked onto a new screen on her laptop. "I'm ready at last. I tell you what, some days, I wish I could go back to printed forms and file folders. It seemed easier."

"Well, let's get to it," Mr. Schmidt said.

"Right." Looking serious, Amanda said, "Miles, Mr. and Mrs. Schmidt contacted me last week with some news."

News? Suddenly, all he could think about was Calvin Gingerich. Maybe he wanted to adopt him? Sitting up a little straighter, Miles said, "What news?"

Her expression turned shadowed. "Well, you see . . . I mean, what I'm trying to say is that the Schmidts have a surprise."

"A surprise?" His worry eased even more. All surprises were good. At least he thought so.

"Yes." Amanda adjusted her glasses again and glanced at James.

James nodded. "Miles, Amanda's trying to tell ya that Mrs. Schmidt is in the family way again."

Miles thought she already was in a family way. Six children sounded like a family to him. Then, realizing that neither adult seemed to look all that happy, Miles blurted, "I don't understand."

"What we're trying to tell you is that Mrs. Schmidt is pregnant, Miles," Amanda said. "She is going to have another baby."

Mr. Schmidt frowned. "Maybe two."

"Oh." Since they were both looking at him expectantly, he attempted to say the right words. "Congratulations?"

"*Danke,* but we aren't quite at the celebratory stage yet, I'm afraid," Mr. Schmidt said. "She's been having a difficult time of it."

Miles wasn't sure why they were telling only him this. Since there didn't seem to be anything else to say, he sat still and waited.

After sharing yet another look with Mr. Schmidt, Amanda said, "I'm sorry, Miles, but there's no easy way to say this." She took a deep breath. "I'm going to need to find you a new home placement."

"Oh." Everything inside of him clenched. He felt like he was going to either throw up or cry, or both. Worse, he should have known this was coming. After all, he'd been through this process before.

"I'm real sorry, Miles," Mr. Schmidt said. "Ruth and I have loved having you here, but she needs to make her life a little easier, you know."

So, James and Ruth thought their lives would be easier without him in it.

That hurt.

He'd tried to do everything right. He tried to not complain or be difficult. He tried to do his chores and get along with everyone. But it still wasn't enough.

"When am I going to leave?" he finally asked.

"I've been looking at your options, but so far I'm not thrilled with any of them," Amanda said. "I want to find a good fit for you." When he continued to stare at her, his body tense, she finally answered his question. "Within two weeks."

Two weeks at the most. Thinking back to

his other moves, Miles realized he'd never been given any notice. Amanda had just shown up and said he needed to gather his things. He wasn't sure if this way was better or not. On one hand, he wasn't caught off guard, but now on the other, he was going to have to wonder what was going to happen for the next fourteen days.

"Is there anything else you need to tell me?"

Amanda shared a look with Mr. Schmidt again. "Not really. Unless you'd like to talk about things?"

What could they talk about? That the Schmidts didn't want to adopt him or even keep him as a foster child? That it was looking more and more like he was never going to get adopted? *"Nee."*

"I'm really sorry about this, Miles," Mr. Schmidt said. "Ruth and I have come to really care for ya. If we didn't have a babe or two on the way, we could keep you longer." Looking aggrieved, he lightly hit the top of the table with his hand before standing up. "I'm going to leave the two of you alone for a spell and go, ah, check on the chickens."

"I'll come find you before I leave, James."

"You take your time." Turning to Miles, he said, "When you're finished, you can come on out to the back garden or go on up to your room if you want. The choice is yours."

"All right."

When they were alone, Amanda put the papers back in her tote, disconnected her computer, and then packed it up, too. Finally, with a sigh, she took off her glasses. "Miles, we've known each other a long time. Please, talk to me. Tell me what you're feeling."

"I'm fine."

"We both know you aren't fine. I'm sure not."

That surprised him. "How come you aren't?"

She raised her eyebrows, like she was taken aback by the question. "Because I feel like I'm failing you. I feel like we've had too many of these conversations over the last five years, and it's not fair to you."

He didn't think it was fair, either. He'd met plenty of other fosters who had real parents now. He wasn't sure why prospective couples never chose him, but they didn't.

"Everything isn't supposed to be fair, Amanda. You've told me that before."

She pursed her lips. "We talked years ago about you maybe going to an English family, but we both agreed that wasn't the best option."

"I remember that."

"What do you think now? Do you want to try going to an English family, maybe in Columbus? I've worked with some really nice families in the foster system there. It might be a good change."

"I don't want to go to Columbus." That just sounded scary. As hard as it was going to lots of different Amish houses, at least most everything was still the same. What would he do with a bunch of city kids?

"All right." She crossed her legs. "There is one other option. I'm going to throw it out to see what you think."

"What is that?"

"There's a group home down in Ashland."

"A group home?"

She smiled, but it didn't reach her eyes. "I know it sounds strange, but hear me out for a sec. There are some teenagers there. Some Amish, some former Amish, some Mennonite. The couple running it are good people. Very caring."

Amanda didn't seem too enthusiastic about it, though. "What's wrong with it?"

"Nothing's wrong with it. It's just . . ." She paused. "Miles, I talked to the couple, and they'd be willing to take you. But I fear it might be a hard transition for you."

She seemed to be talking in riddles. "Miss Amanda, just tell me the truth."

"You're right. The truth is always the best." She sighed. "The truth is that some of the kids are troublemakers, and you would be the youngest. And this home in Ashland, while it is nice and all, it's kind of a last stop."

He knew what she meant now. "Until I'm eighteen."

"Yes. You'd be there until you turned eighteen, and then you'd be on your own."

"So I'd be there for eight years."

Amanda pursed her lips. "Yes."

Eight years was a long time, especially if he was going to be stuck in a group home with a bunch of other kids no one wanted. It sounded like a prison sentence. "It sounds pretty bad."

"It's not horrible, Miles. I've placed two children there and I visit them often."

"Not horrible" didn't sound very good at all. "Do they like living there?"

She swallowed. "They're older and have faced a lot of difficult situations over the years. It was a good place for them."

"But do they like it?"

"I don't know if they would say that. But

they haven't liked any of the other places, either."

He was going to have to learn to live with these people.

Suddenly, everything sounded worse than horrible. And like a dam bursting, he covered his face with his hands and cried.

"Oh, Miles, I'm so sorry," Amanda said as she rushed to his side and threw her arms around him. Even though he was too big, he leaned his face on her shoulder and let go. "You cry all you want. If anyone deserves to have a few tears, it's you."

He hiccupped. "I met a man, and he's come over here three times. When I saw you here, I almost got happy. I . . . I knew I shouldn't have, but I started to hope."

She rubbed his back. "James told me about that man. His name is Calvin, yes?"

"*Jah.* He was real nice. I thought he might have wanted me."

Amanda pulled back to look him in the eyes. "You know what? I'm going to talk to him."

"It won't do any good. Ruth said he didn't want to foster me or adopt me."

"He might, now that he knows you. Don't give up hope."

"Amanda, no one wants me."

"That's not true. I just haven't found the

right people yet." She hugged him tighter. "Listen, I love you. I am not going to give up on you. I swear I'm going to find a place where you will feel happy and loved."

He hugged her back. But though her words were probably meant as a balm, they were anything but. After all, he was old enough to know that not everyone got to have a loving family.

Some kids had to go to group homes in Ashland for eight years and simply wait to grow up.

TWENTY-SIX

· **TIP #26** ·

Limit the amount of personal baggage
you unload on those first few dates. If
you've got a lot, it might be
overwhelming!

It was getting harder for Miriam to keep
her secret and even harder to remember
why she'd wanted to in the first place. Her
reasons felt so selfish and silly now. Disappointment and tragedies came along for
everyone. The motorcycle accident that
Calvin had witnessed was proof of that.

And then there was Miles. Ever since
she'd seen that little boy, she'd felt torn up.
There he'd been, actively looking for Calvin
and trying so hard to hide his disappointment when he'd learned that Calvin
wouldn't be at the bookmobile. His silent
acceptance had broken her heart and served
to remind her once again that she was not

the only person in Berlin to know heartache.

She was also discovering that her pregnancy was a mighty difficult secret to keep.

Of course, part of the problem was that her morning sickness was actually an all-day sort of thing. It would be one thing if she was merely a little queasy when she first woke up — Calvin was always up and out in the barn milking the cow, gathering eggs, and tending to Windy anyway. Miriam had honestly thought she'd wake up after him, tackle a touch of morning sickness, then head to the kitchen and make him a hearty breakfast. But it wasn't going like that, exactly. For the last three days, she was running to the bathroom, vomiting, willing herself to get dressed, then doing what she could as the day progressed. Most of the time, it wasn't much at all.

Yesterday she hadn't been able to make Calvin his usual eggs and bacon. Both smelled so awful she almost left the house when he was eating his runny fried eggs.

Today had been worse. She'd barely been able to hold anything down and more than anything she wished she could call her *mamm* or her sister for advice.

Calvin knew something was wrong, too. He kept looking at her in concern and had already asked her twice if she was ill. He'd even gone so far as to wash all the dishes after supper. Though he'd done it without complaint, she felt guilty. After all, he had worked in the fields all day. Doing dishes was her job.

All that was why everything came to a head shortly after seven o'clock that evening.

Standing in the center of the kitchen, Calvin folded his arms across his chest. "Miriam, I think tomorrow I had better take you to the *doktah.*" His expression was as serious and as somber as his tone. "I fear that something is very wrong with you."

"I'm fine. I promise." But of course, she wasn't fine at all. She was queasy, exhausted, and currently a liar.

He shook his head. "*Nee,* I don't think so. I've never seen you so pale. You are sick."

"I'm not sick."

He kept studying her. "Miriam, I know you don't care for the doctor, but I think you're being stubborn." Folding his hands over his chest, he added, "Maybe you have the flu."

"I don't, Calvin. I'm fine."

Once again, he ignored her protests. Suddenly looking stricken, he blurted, "Maybe it's something worse. Mimi, you might have some stomach ailment. Those things don't show up right away, you know. Not until it's too late."

Knowing that he was no doubt thinking of his great uncle who'd died of stomach cancer, Miriam knew she had to put Calvin out of his misery. It seemed it didn't matter if she was ready or not. For his sake and maybe for hers, too, it was time to tell him the truth. "Calvin, I know what is wrong with my stomach."

He strode forward and took her hands. "You do? How? Did you go to the doctor and I didn't know about it?"

Oh, what a pickle. "Kind of," she hedged.

His voice deepened. "Miriam —"

She could not have this conversation standing up. "Please, Calvin. Come sit down with me."

She led the way into their living room. When she entered the space, everything seemed a little brighter. It always did.

She loved how it faced the front driveway and got the best morning sunlight. She also loved the pale yellow paint on the walls, her brightly painted clay pots filled with herbs and ivy, and the sampler her grandmother had stitched for their wedding day.

Just last year, they'd splurged and bought a new couch and easy chair. The couch was a blue plaid, and the easy chair was covered

230

in faded denim fabric. Her mother had hated it on sight, but she'd always loved it. Plus, the denim fabric ensured that it wouldn't be ruined easily. Calvin loved it, too. He said it was comfortable and didn't make him feel like he was living in a doll's house. That chair was manly, he'd said.

To her surprise, instead of sitting in that chair, he sat down next to her and took hold of one of her hands again. Rubbing his thumb over her knuckles, his voice softened. "Talk to me, Miriam. What is wrong with you?"

But how did one begin this tale? Oh, she wished she'd prepared for this moment better. She'd been so foolish not to. She could have made a tiny bib or embroidered something adorable.

But, like with everything else of late, she was woefully unprepared.

She supposed there really was nothing else to say but the truth. "Nothing is wrong, Calvin. I . . . I'm pregnant."

He gaped at her. "Say again?"

Clasping his hand with both of hers, she raised it to her lips and kissed it. "We're going to have a baby, Calvin," she said in a stronger tone. "Most likely around Christmas."

"Christmas?"

"*Jah*. Isn't that a miracle?" She tried to smile.

But her husband still seemed like he was having a difficult time putting two and two together. He swallowed. "Wait a minute. Miriam, how do you know about the due date? How do you know all of this?"

Feeling like she was the worst wife ever, she blurted, "Calvin, the truth is that I've known for a few weeks now. I, uh, learned I was pregnant at urgent care."

He pulled his hand from hers. "You found out when you cut your foot?"

"*Jah*. They, I mean, the nurse had to take a pregnancy test in case they did X-rays or had to give me antibiotics. The doctor came in and told me the news."

"Why didn't you tell me then?"

There was so much hurt in his eyes, it was almost impossible to look at him. "I didn't want to disappoint you."

"Miriam . . ." He stopped and sighed. "You are making no sense. Of course I would be pleased about this." He got to his feet, like he needed some space from her. "We've always wanted a family."

"I was afraid you'd be upset with me when I lost our babe," Miriam blurted. When he stilled, she pushed forward. "I knew you would be so happy but then so sad when

232

my body couldn't keep it. Like you were last time."

"You thought you were going to miscarry?"

She nodded. "Even though the doctors and nurses said it wasn't my fault, I felt that it was." Looking into his brown eyes, she told the rest of it. "I've felt guilty about my inability to conceive . . . and for losing our babies."

He shook his head. *"Nee."*

"It's true. I've felt that way for years, Calvin."

" 'For years'?"

Glad he was hearing her, Miriam nodded. "I knew something was wrong with me and that you probably regretted marrying me."

"You know that ain't true. I've told you time and again that I've never blamed you." He waved a hand as he strode back to her side. "Miriam, you know how fond I am of that little boy Miles. You know I want to adopt him. If we couldn't have children on our own, I wanted to adopt them. I wouldn't have felt like we were settling or giving anything up."

She had messed up so much. All of her fears had gotten the best of her and instead of overcoming them she'd allowed them to rule her life, and it made things worse.

When he sat down by her side, she spoke again. "I realize now that I shouldn't have kept everything a secret. I should've trusted you. *Nee,* I mean, I should've trusted us. And God." Feeling even more weary, she murmured, "I'm sorry, Calvin. I should've been better."

He pulled her into his arms. "Stop that, Miriam. Stop overthinking and worrying so much."

"I hate that I turned our amazing news into yet another source of contention."

"You didn't." Pulling away, he ran a finger down her cheek. "Now, please tell me everything."

"What do you want to know?"

He kissed her lightly on the lips. "Just what I said. Everything!" Grinning, he declared, "Tell me how you are feeling, what they said at the urgent care, what the midwife said. I want to know it all."

"That might take a bit."

"I don't care. We can talk all night! Today is special."

Yes, it was. It was a special moment. She felt lighter and almost like her regular self. No, she felt like she had just lifted the heaviest load off her shoulders.

This shouldn't have been a surprise, either. If she'd had more faith, they could have started each morning like this. In this expecting-a-baby bliss.

"Miriam?"

"I'm sorry." She chuckled. "My sister told me once that losing track of one's mind is a side effect of pregnancy."

After kissing her again, he grinned. "If that's what's happening, then indeed it's a wonderful thing. If anyone needed to stop worrying so much, it's you."

Miriam rolled her eyes, but she had a feeling he was right. Worrying and doubting and second-guessing both her husband and God's plans for their child had only made her miserable and sick.

It was time to finally relax and let other people help her. After all, they had a baby on the way.

TWENTY-SEVEN

· **TIP #27** ·
Consider talking about church and plans
for traveling, work, and even finances by
the fifth or sixth date. It's not very
romantic but will help you in the long run.

When he woke the following morning,
Calvin didn't know if he'd ever been happier. Even his wedding day hadn't been
filled with the gravity of this moment.

Honestly, there were so many emotions
spinning inside his head, he doubted it
would be possible to catalog them all. Not
only had Miriam relieved all his worries
about her health, but she'd also shared the
most amazing news. At long last, Miriam
was going to have their baby.

That knowledge had carried him through
his morning chores. But as he finished the
milking and headed back into the house for
breakfast, he started worrying again, new

worries this time. Worries of another miscarriage, though with this pregnancy he could already tell things were going to be far different. Miriam was weepy but hopeful, and hope could do wonders for one's outlook.

When Miriam had miscarried before, she'd been hurting right away. She'd felt so awful she could hardly get out of bed. And though Edna, the midwife, had tried to sound as optimistic as she could, it had been apparent that there hadn't been much hope for the pregnancy. The loss of that child had plunged both him and Miriam into a deep depression.

Looking at her now as they finished the breakfast dishes, he couldn't help but be thankful for how far they'd come.

He was also incredibly thankful to no longer be worried sick about the state of their marriage. All the differences, the small arguments, the feeling that she'd been keeping secrets from him . . . it all made sense now.

"Calvin?" she murmured. "Are we going to be okay?"

She'd had a simple breakfast. Dry toast for her, a quick plate of fried eggs and toast for him. Then, after declaring that the rest of his chores could wait a little longer, he had walked with her back to the living room and held her hands. "We're going to *have* to be okay, don't you think, Miriam? I mean, we're a family now."

Her cheeks turned pink, and she rested a hand on her stomach. "*Jah*. We are almost a family."

"*Nee*, as far as I'm concerned, we're already a family of three. I love our baby."

"Me, too." She smiled brightly. "I know you might feel like you have no reason to trust me, but you do, Calvin. I really wasn't trying to be deceitful, I just didn't want to hurt you any more than I already have."

"You haven't hurt me, Mimi." He pressed his lips to her brow. "Of course I trust you." Just as he was about to try to explain his feelings, their doorbell chimed. He got to his feet. "Are you expecting anyone?"

"*Nee*. But maybe a package came."

Figuring that could be true, he opened the door to an English woman, about forty years old, in dark jeans, black loafers, a white button-down blouse, and a blue checked blazer. She had on glasses and was holding a backpack.

"Yes?" he asked.

"Are you Calvin Gingerich, by chance?"

"Yes. May I help you?"

"My name is Amanda Brown." Still looking at him intently, she added, "Calvin, I'm

Miles Bishop's social worker."

Miriam walked up to join them. "I'm Miriam, Calvin's wife," she said. "Are you referring to the Miles the Schmidts are caring for?"

"Yes." Looking at them both, Amanda said, "I know we don't have an appointment and that you may be busy, but can we please talk? It's important. Very important."

"Yes. Yes, of course," Miriam said as she stepped back. "Please come into the living room."

"Thank you," Amanda said.

Calvin let Amanda follow Miriam and waited a moment, needing that time to come to terms with the fact that this social worker had sought him out about Miles. He wasn't sure what to think about that, except that she couldn't have come at a worse time. Just as he and Miriam were finally reconnecting.

But the Lord had a plan and maybe a sense of humor, too.

"Calvin?" Miriam called out. "Are you coming?"

"Of course. Sorry." He closed the door and strode forward, hoping neither woman noticed his hands were practically shaking. He wasn't sure what was about to happen, but in a way, it felt just as important as Miriam's news.

Sitting down in his chair, he noticed Amanda had already taken the least comfortable chair and had set her backpack down at her feet.

Miriam, to his relief, didn't look upset by their visitor, mainly curious. She was sitting back on the couch with her hands clasped loosely in her lap.

As soon as he sat down, Amanda said, "I decided to take a chance coming here because I've been Miles's caseworker for several years now, and I've never seen him look both so lost by his current situation and so moved by the friendship the two of you have recently struck up." She sighed. "Calvin, to put it bluntly, you've been able to form a relationship with a boy who doesn't form relationships easily. I'm grateful for it, and also a little scared."

"Why?" Miriam asked.

"I recently discovered that the Schmidts are expecting another baby. Because of that, they don't feel they can foster three children anymore. Since Miles has been there the longest, they asked that I find a new home for him." Amanda stared at them both. "I need you to find it in your hearts to take this boy in." Amanda turned her head slightly. She was now staring directly at

Calvin. "You know how sweet Miles is. How special he is."

"He is special. That is true." Calvin shifted uncomfortably, feeling the heat of both women's gazes resting on him. More than anything, he wished he had clear direction about what he should say. He felt for Miles and wanted to give the boy a home. But he couldn't deny that he and Miriam were at a very fragile point in their marriage. After years of trying to have a baby, their wishes had been granted. This should be a special time for them. He wanted to focus on her and the baby.

Miriam deserved that.

But didn't Miles deserve a chance, too?

"Miriam, what do you think?" he asked, wanting, needing her opinion.

Miriam wrung her hands. "I feel mighty bad for this boy, but we are expecting our own baby. I don't think bringing an older child into the home is a *gut* idea. It's too much. I mean, it's too much right now."

"I'm happy for you and for your pregnancy," Amanda said. "I truly am. But this child needs a safe place. Every child deserves a loving home. Especially Miles. I think he'd have that here with the two of you."

Amanda looked down at her file folder,

241

paused, then took a deep breath. "Miriam and Calvin, won't you please at least think about this? Give it a week?" Before either of them could answer, she rushed on, "You see, the only other alternative is to place Miles in a group home. It's run by well-meaning folks, but some of the boys there are much older and pretty rough. It's not going to be easy."

Calvin glanced at Miriam and saw the tears in her eyes before she looked away.

Every protective instinct he possessed was fighting against Amanda's pushy attitude. "This isn't being fair, Amanda. You're essentially saying that if we don't change our minds, Miles will suffer."

"No, what's not fair is that a little boy lost all of his family at too young an age and has been subjected to a stressful, unsettled life for years. What's not fair is that if he goes into this group home, it will change him. I know it will." Her voice turned ragged and strained. "He'll have to change in order to survive the next eight years."

"Eight years?" Miriam asked.

"Eighteen is when they are no longer wards of the state, Mrs. Gingerich. They age out of the system. That's when Miles will have to find his own way in life." Amanda's expression hardened. "Don't you

242

see? We're not talking about an anonymous child in the paper. We're talking about Miles."

Each word stung, and Calvin knew he'd likely hear each of them late into the night, over and over, hurting his heart. But he didn't have a choice. Not if Miriam opposed the idea.

He said, "We appreciate you coming over, and I'll pray for both you and the child. I hope he finds a home soon."

His words hung in the air like poison darts, pointed and painful. They weren't just aimed at Amanda, but all of them. He didn't like sounding so unfeeling. He didn't like wishing someone else would step up. But sometimes a man had to do what was best for his family.

Looking stiff, Amanda picked up the folder and slipped it back into her tote bag. Calvin and Miriam watched her zip it up, straighten the glasses on her nose, then stand up. "Thank you for your time."

"Wait!" Miriam jumped to her feet.

Amanda stopped. "Yes?"

"We'll think about it," Miriam said. "We'll let you know our decision in a few days."

Calvin frowned at her. "Miriam, we don't have to do that," he said softly.

"Nee," she said. "I think we do, Calvin."

243

Slowly, Amanda nodded. "I'll stop by midmorning on Friday. But, ah, take this," she said, fishing in her pocket. "This is one of my business cards. My phone number is on it. If you have any questions or make up your mind before then, give me a call."

Miriam took the card, carefully read it, then set it on the table. "Thank you."

Calvin walked Amanda the short way to the front door. "We'll be in touch."

"Thank you. Thank you both. I'll see you Friday."

After she walked away, Calvin hurried to his wife's side. "Miriam, I know it's hard, but you don't have to feel pressured to do this."

"This may sound strange, but I think I *need* to feel pressured. I want to do as she asked. I don't want to simply dwell on my fears . . . I want to think of this boy."

"Are you sure? Miriam, I promise, I won't be upset if we both decide that saying no is the right thing to do."

"I'm sure. I'm not thinking about you and me anymore, Calvin. At long last, I'm think-ing about somebody else . . . Perhaps I could go with you next time you see Miles?"

"You're serious, aren't you?"

She lifted her gaze to meet his straight on. "I don't know what to think or what is going to happen, but I am serious."

"Then yes, of course. Let's go tomorrow."

The smile she gave him was beautiful. Almost as beautiful as the feel of her in his arms as he held her close.

At long last.

TWENTY-EIGHT

· **TIP #28** ·

It's okay if your new relationship isn't
anything like a previous one. That might
even be a good thing.

Miles had just finished cleaning the chicken
coop, one of his least favorite chores, when
Ruth walked toward him wearing a bright
smile. "Miles, guess what?"

"What?"

"You have two visitors today. Calvin and
his wife, Miriam."

Calvin had come with his wife? A week
ago, he might have gotten excited, but now
he only felt resentful they were pretending
to show interest in him. "What do they
want?"

Ruth shrugged. "I couldn't tell ya. The
moment they arrived, Calvin asked to see
you right away. I was so surprised, I left
them inside with Mary, Jonas, and Minnie.

No telling what is going on," she teased.

Miles had a pretty good idea. Mary and Jonas would be either arguing with each other or vying for their attention. Minnie would probably be trying to keep them in line . . . if she hadn't already lost interest. "I finished cleaning the coop," he said. "I *canna* meet Calvin's wife like this."

"No?" Looking over at him, her eyebrows pulled together. "Ack! You are right, child." Looking around, she said, "I have an idea. Go to the spigot by the barn and wash your face and hands, then go around to the back of the house and come in through the laundry room. I'll have out a fresh shirt for ya."

"You'd do that?"

"Of course I will, silly. Don't ever doubt that." She clapped her hands. "Now, hurry, and I'll hurry, too. I need to rescue them before Jonas starts poking Mrs. Gingerich or something worse."

She walked away before Miles could comment on that, which was probably a good thing. He never knew if her quips were serious or not. He decided not to worry about it and hurried to the spigot by the barn and crouched in front of it.

The water was chilly and felt perfect when he ran his hands over it and splashed his face. It dripped in rivulets down his neck and into the collar of his shirt.

When he stood up at last, his hair was partly wet, and his shirt was really wet. But at least he didn't smell like bird poop.

Hoping Mrs. Schmidt really had remembered to place a shirt out for him, he quietly opened the laundry room door and closed it behind him.

He had to blink his eyes several times to adjust to the dim light. And then, just as she'd promised, he spied his brand-new, dark blue short-sleeved shirt laid out for him. Ruth had somehow managed to make it for him last week and had given it to him before they went to church on Sunday.

Quickly, he pulled off his soggy shirt, hastily dabbed the remaining water droplets off his face with a dish towel that was lying on the counter, pulled on the new shirt, and buttoned it up.

Finally, he was ready. He just hoped he wasn't going through so much trouble just to hear Calvin and his wife say they didn't ever want to see him again.

"Here he is!" Ruth called out merrily. She was standing in front of Ian and Jonas, almost like she was shielding his guests from them.

Or maybe she was shielding them from

Mary, who was coloring on some pages at the kitchen table, or Minnie and Ethan, who were glaring at Calvin like he'd done something wrong.

Calvin and Miriam were perched on the edge of the sofa. Calvin looked relaxed. But Miriam's eyes were open really wide, and she looked kind of scared by the chaos.

He would've thought it was pretty funny if he wasn't so nervous.

The moment Calvin spied him, he got to his feet. "Hiya, Miles. I brought Miriam with me today. She wanted to meet you."

Miriam, who was really pretty, smiled at him. "Hello, Miles."

"Hiya." Looking into her dark blue eyes, he suddenly felt shy.

Calvin took a step closer. "So, it's been a week since we've seen each other. How are you?"

He had gotten terrible news from Amanda. He wasn't sleeping and had even started crying the other night when he was in the shower. So, he wasn't good at all. But he knew better than to share any of that. No one ever wanted to know how he truly felt. "I'm *gut.* I was, uh, just cleaning the coop."

"That's a big job," Miriam said.

And a dirty one. Realizing that she might

not want to get near him, he gestured to his damp hair. "You don't have to worry. I cleaned up in the barn."

"That's why he's all wet," Jonas said. "The hens don't like visitors much."

Miriam, to his surprise, giggled. "You don't have to explain chicken coop cleaning to me. I've done that many a time." She wrinkled her nose. "Paddy, our *hund*, always runs the other way after I've been inside the henhouse for any length of time."

"I didn't know you had a *hund.*"

Calvin shrugged. "Paddy is *mei frau's hund.* We adopted her together, but she loves Miriam. She follows her around all day long."

"It's not quite that bad. But she is a good dog." Miriam brightened. "Maybe one day you can meet her."

That sounded like they weren't going to tell him goodbye forever. "*Jah.* Maybe so." Not sure what to do, he looked at Ruth.

She didn't disappoint. Clearing her throat, she said, "You know what? It's a mighty nice day out. Maybe you'd like to take Calvin and Miriam for a walk?"

Calvin grinned. "How about we walk down to the ice cream store? We'll get some cones and bring back a couple of pints for everyone else?"

After seeing Ruth nod, Miles said, "Sure. Is it okay if I go barefoot?"

"It's good with me," Calvin said.

"Go on your way, Miles," Ruth said. "And, Calvin, that is mighty kind of ya, but there's no need to bring back ice cream."

For once, all of the triplets kept their mouths shut.

"Of course we will," Calvin said. "It's only the right thing to do."

Within minutes they were off, Miles walking by Miriam's side and Calvin taking the lead.

Miles thought Miriam smelled like flowers. Part of him wanted to simply enjoy the scent, but the other part wanted to cover his face, he was so embarrassed for even noticing. Afraid she'd see him looking at her or somehow be able to read his mind, he kept his eyes on his bare feet.

"I used to do that, too," she said.

"Do what?"

"I used to stare at the ground when I walked, even when I was with other people."

He lifted his chin. "Sorry."

Her blue eyes softened. "Miles, I didn't mean anything against you. I . . . Well, I guess I was awkwardly trying to make conversation." Smirking a bit, she said,

"Obviously I'm not too good at it . . . which is why I probably looked at my feet so much."

"I don't usually stare at my feet. I, uh, just don't want to step on a rock."

She nodded like that stupid comment made perfect sense. "That's smart. There are a lot of rocks to worry about. You need to watch out for *shlangs*, too."

"*Shlangs?* Do you really think there are snakes around here?"

Miriam nodded. "Oh, *jah. Mei bruder,* Eli, once stepped on a sleeping snake."

He wasn't sure if she was teasing him or not . . . but he was interested. "What happened?"

She winked. "Why, he woke it up, of course."

"Miriam, if you're gonna tell that story to Miles, you need to tell it right," Calvin chided.

Her eyes shone. "Wouldja like to hear my tale, Miles? It's not very long."

He shrugged, doing his best to act like every word she was saying didn't matter to him. "All right."

Miriam smiled like he'd made her day. "So, Eli is two years younger than me but acted like he was always right. When we were little, we used to go fishing and camping with our *daed* at a lake in the summer. It was a bit of a challenge for me, you see, because my older sister, Lavinia, would stay home with Mamm, so it would be me and the boys."

"Were you good at fishing?"

She lifted her chin. "Kind of."

"Don't pay no mind to her modesty, Miles. Miriam here could catch a three-pound bass with her eyes closed."

"What about Eli?" Miles asked.

"I was older and therefore better, but he didn't like to believe that." She chuckled. "So one morning, *mei* and Eli were following our father from our campsite to the lake. Daed was walking real fast, probably because he was carrying almost all of our gear and a cooler of food. Eli and I were following . . . and arguing."

Miles grinned. "What were you arguing about?"

"I couldn't even tell you now, though I have a feeling it was most likely about how he kicked in his sleep." She cast another look at Miles. "We had to share a tent, you know.

"Anyway, there we were, arguing, when our father told us to be quiet. So then we made a game of being as silent and stealth-like as could be in our bare feet . . . when all of a sudden, Eli stepped right in the middle of a curled-up copperhead!"

"Did he get bit?"

"Well, the snake hissed and moved, but Eli moved faster!"

"The snake had been fast asleep, remember," Calvin interjected, though his tone was kind of sarcastic.

"Unfortunately, Eli moved so fast, he knocked into me. Next thing we knew, he was squealing, I was squealing, and we were both scared to death that the snake was going to come after us!"

"Like, chase you?" Miles blurted.

Miriam nodded. "Oh, *jah.*"

They were stopped now, and Calvin had come around to his side. Resting a hand on his shoulder, he said, "It's hard to believe, but it seems Eli and my wife were absolutely sure that the snake would rather attack them than slither to safety."

Slither to safety? Before Miles could stop himself, he started laughing. Maybe Miriam had just been telling him a tall tale after all. Wanting to respond the way he should, Miles peeked at Miriam.

Catching his eye, her lips twitched, but she said nothing. It seemed it was obvious she knew her story was silly, too.

"Well, what happened?" he asked.

254

"Our father dropped all the fishing gear and came running to our sides. After we told him what was going on, he started yelling at us."

That sure didn't seem fair. "Your father got mad even though nothing was your fault?"

"He was yelling because he was scared, Miles," Miriam said gently. "Sometimes people react in a way that doesn't make sense, but they *canna* help it."

"Oh."

Calvin smiled. "I hear he calmed down as soon as he didn't see any blood."

"But what about when Eli told him the story?"

"Well, believe it or not, I don't think our father ever actually did believe our story. He said that he never heard of a person stepping on a sleeping snake." Looking off into the distance, she murmured, "Our father has always relied on facts and common sense, you see."

"But you believed your brother?"

"For sure I did. Why would he lie about a thing like that?"

Miles was silent for a moment before looking up at Calvin again. "I don't know," he said at last. "I never had a brother."

It was the truth, of course, but when he

noticed a look of sadness fill Miriam's eyes, he wished he would've kept his mouth shut. No one wanted to be around a kid who was always feeling sorry for himself, did they?

Hoping to make things better, he blurted, "I'll be on the lookout for snakes from now on."

Laugh lines appeared around Calvin's eyes. "*Gut.* That will save us both a lot of trouble and needless running around. Ain't so?"

Miles nodded. But already he was thinking that soon he would be gone, in the group home in the city.

He doubted he would have to worry about snakes there. At least, not any snakes resting in the grass.

TWENTY-NINE

· **TIP #29** ·
I've found it helpful to take a break from
dating from time to time. It can be
stressful!

Their walk ended way too soon. They went
to get ice cream and sat on the red leather
stools at the ice cream parlor and each had
a cone. Miriam had orange sherbet, Calvin
had rocky road, and Miles, after much
debating, had ultimately chosen one scoop
of strawberry and one scoop of chocolate
chip.

After Calvin glanced at the time on his
pocket watch, he'd said Ruth was going to
start worrying if they didn't head back. He
purchased several pints for the rest of the
kids at the Schmidts', then ushered them
outside.

"We're going to have to walk back a lot
quicker or the ice cream will all melt," he

declared.

Miriam believed that to be true, but it didn't make it any easier . . . or help her heart. Soon after she'd begun her awkward conversation with Miles, she'd known he was special. In some ways, he reminded her of Eli. In other ways, there was a sweetness and a seriousness about him that was so very Calvin.

He was also, well . . . Miles. A good boy. No, a wonderful-*gut* boy.

Gazing at him, thinking about his uncertain future, Miriam would have given just about anything to have God give her a sign about what she should do.

That was the problem Calvin had been wrestling with, she now realized. There wasn't one "right" way to act. One couldn't even rely on facts or a pros-and-cons list for something like this.

When they reached the foot of the Schmidts' driveway, Miriam started walking even slower by Miles's side. He noticed.

"Is something wrong?" he asked.

What was the right answer? She didn't know. "I guess I didn't want our afternoon to end," she admitted. "I enjoyed spending time with you."

He blinked, seemed to hesitate, then blurted, "I did, too."

She glanced toward her husband. His footsteps had slowed as well, but he wasn't exactly walking with them. No, it looked like he was giving her space so she could get to know Miles better. However, she was so torn up, she wasn't sure if that made things better or worse.

No, she was sure. It made things worse. She felt sick inside.

Up ahead, Miriam could see a girl sitting on the front porch. She had a bowl of green beans in her lap and she was snapping the ends off. She was a pretty child, perhaps around eight or nine years of age. She was wearing a pink dress and white *kapp* and had dark brown eyes and brown hair. When she noticed them, she smiled before going back to the beans.

"Who is that, Miles?" Miriam asked.

"That's Minnie."

"Is she one of the Schmidts' *kinner*?"

"*Nee.* She's just a foster child."

The "just" part of his statement hurt to hear. "Is she nice?"

He shrugged. "She's all right, I guess. She's eight."

"So, there are altogether six of you *kinner* here."

"Yes." He opened his mouth to add something but shut it quickly.

After debating whether to press or not, she decided to give Miles a nudge. They weren't going to be able to be friends if she had no idea what was on his mind. "What were you going to say?"

"Nothing."

"Please, won't you tell me?" she coaxed. "I'm trying to get to know you."

He looked back down at his feet. "It doesn't matter. I was just going to say that I was going to have to leave soon, but you already know that."

"*Jah.* Amanda came by our house and told us."

He glanced at the front door again and seemed to steel himself. "I had better go. Mr. Schmidt has some more chores for me. I'll need to do my part."

Miriam ached to point out that he'd already cleaned out the chicken coop. Surely that meant he could spend a few more minutes with them. While Miriam tried to get a grip on herself, Calvin stepped forward. "Have a good afternoon, Miles. Pass this ice cream on to Ruth, all right?"

"I will. Um, *danke* for the ice cream. I liked it a lot."

"I did, too," Calvin said.

Just as Miles turned away, Miriam reached for him. She caught the tips of his fingers.

"Miles, wait, if you please."

"Jah?"

"Would you mind if . . . Would you mind if I gave you a hug?"

"Why?"

She didn't want to think about why. At least, she sure didn't want to share that. "I guess because I like hugs. And because I will soon be a mother, and it feels like the right way to end our day." Seeing how blank his expression was, she backtracked quickly. "Or, we don't have to do that, of course. I'm sorry. I didn't want to make you uncomfortable."

A muscle worked in his cheek. Then, just as she thought he was going to turn away, he blurted, "You can give me a hug."

She didn't allow another second to go by. No time for regrets. Instead, she carefully wrapped her arms around him and held him close. He was thin but not spindly. He smelled like cut grass and dirt and fresh laundry and little boy.

When he wrapped his arms around her and leaned in slightly, she felt like her heart was growing.

"Goodbye, Miles," she said softly before stepping backward.

Their eyes met for a moment. Something flickered there, then it vanished again.

He turned around, walked to the door, and stepped inside.

When he was out of sight, Miriam felt like she'd missed something important. Like she'd missed too much.

Calvin pressed a hand around her waist. "We'd better get home. Paddy will be wondering what has happened to us."

Miriam knew Calvin had brought up her dog in order to make her happy. She pretended it did the trick. "Oh, *jah.* I bet she is looking out the window very impatiently right about now. We should hurry home."

"That *hund* better not have climbed up on our window seat."

"Oh, I'm sure she didn't," Miriam lied. Because of course she always did.

They stayed quiet most of the way home, each of them deep in thought. Miriam thought about the baby and their house and all of her plans. And then she thought of Paddy and how much that dog had come to mean to her. It had been a surprise.

Almost a bit like how much this afternoon with Miles had meant to her. She'd been prepared to get to know him, to understand how Calvin had been feeling, to maybe even have felt torn.

But she hadn't expected to lose her heart.

When their house was in sight, Calvin

pressed a kiss to her brow. "I'm sure you're tired after all our walking, Mimi. Why don't you go lie down for a spell? I'll tend to Paddy and the animals."

"I am tired. But, Calvin, I think we need to discuss something."

"What is that?"

Could she do it? Yes. Yes, she could. Some things were more important than lying down or tending to the animals — or her old ideas of what their family should look like. "I think we need to take in Miles as our foster child," she announced.

But instead of looking relieved, her husband looked upset. "Miriam, you *canna* be serious."

"I am. I . . . I can't bear for him to be on his own. It's all I can think about."

"I know Amanda painted a sad picture, but I have to believe that the group homes aren't all that bad. She wouldn't place him someplace that was dangerous."

"I don't think it matters how bad or good the home will be. The fact of the matter is that he has already grown attached to you. Plus, we have a home, a home right here."

"And you?"

"I . . . I guess I've suddenly become attached to him, too. That means something, don't you think?"

But instead of looking pleased, her husband only looked more wary. "We need to think hard about this, Miriam." His voice was firm. "I don't want you to regret anything."

"I'm not asking to adopt him right now, just to foster him. That's all."

"*Jah,* but things might change," he countered. "I don't want you to get hurt or upset. My priority is you, you know. You and our babe."

She knew that. Which was why she knew her mind was made up. "I'll wait until tomorrow to discuss it again, but I think we both know what we need to do, Calvin." She smiled softly. "Or, maybe I've simply just caught up to you and have come to the right state of mind."

When he turned around without saying a word, she felt let down. But then she remembered that both Calvin and the Lord had been waiting for her to come around.

She could wait a bit, too. She was good at waiting.

After all, she'd already waited four years for this babe.

THIRTY

Be warned, sometimes double-dating with
longtime friends can be difficult . . .
especially if they were friends with your
former husband.

Sarah Anne's boss, Ron Holiday, had encouraged her to take a week off. Though
she'd fussed that she didn't need any time
at all, he'd held firm. To her amazement,
though, she'd ended up being extremely
glad to have had that little break from work.

The fact was, some days she found being
in charge of the bookmobile to be very
stressful. It was hard work, driving along
the windy roads surrounding Berlin all by
herself, not to mention ordering the books,
making sure they'd been pulled, cleaning
the bookmobile, constantly making sure she
stayed on schedule. And none of that even
took into account all of her interactions with

the public.

Her patrons were wonderful people, and she'd become good friends with many. But they were still people, each with his or her own needs and idiosyncrasies. It was simply a fact of life that some folks were easier than others.

And on top of it all, she had a new relationship with Pete. He'd been so caring and attentive after the accident. Now, they were very much together. Yes, she had a boyfriend!

Sometimes even thinking that made her blush. After Frank passed on, she'd gone through a lot of phases, from thinking she'd never want to be in a relationship, to being sure she'd never want to fall in love, to sometimes wondering if she could be so blessed.

Now, here she was, practically head over heels with a handsome new man. Even more surprising was that he seemed just as smitten as she was.

For whatever reason, Sarah Anne had begun to think she wasn't "good enough" for anyone else. She'd honestly thought that a handsome, successful, good man like Pete wouldn't be attracted to someone her age, or with gray hair and a good twenty pounds to lose.

Sarah Anne realized that one day soon she was going to need to sit down and really think about why she'd come to this conclusion. Had she privately thought that older women weren't allowed to be romantically involved? Or, had her confidence slipped somewhere along the way? That made her disappointed in herself.

All of those deep questions were going to have to wait, however, because she was at her first stop, on Gardner Way, and Miriam Gingerich was sitting on a bench at the side of the parking lot waiting for her. After parking, Sarah Anne opened the wide side door and walked out to greet her.

"Hi, Miriam!" she called out. "I'm so sorry you've been waiting. Give me another two minutes, and I'll be ready for you to come on in."

Miriam walked closer. "You're not late, I'm early." She held out her hands and smiled. "I also have two perfectly good hands. What may I help you with?"

"Nothing at all. Since the weather is so nice, I'm going to set up a display outside. But since everything has its own special place, I'm afraid it's easier if I take care of it on my own," Sarah Anne said as she unlatched a cupboard and pulled out an expandable metal bookshelf.

After watching for several more minutes, Miriam frowned at her. "Are you sure I *canna* help? I feel funny just watching you work."

"As much as I would welcome your hands, I'm afraid I can't allow you to cart these crates around." She *umphed* as she brought some books outside. "Liability, you know."

"Ah." Miriam looked down at her feet, almost like she was lost.

Sarah Anne realized right then and there that the younger woman might have come for a book, but she was likely in need of some other things, too. Maybe even some conversation. Pretending to weigh the idea, she added, "You know, I don't think it would hurt anyone if I got a little bit of help. So, if you'd like, you could put these books on the cart over here."

Miriam's expression lightened right up. "I'll be glad to do that." Immediately, she started pulling out books and neatly displaying them on the shelves.

After pulling out another crate and walking through the bookshelves inside to make sure everything was in order, Sarah Anne walked outside to join her. "This is really nice of you. Thanks. I mean, *danke.*"

Miriam smiled at her. "Very good. Are you learning *Deutsch,* Sarah Anne?"

"No. But I thought it might be fun to learn a couple of words. What do you think?"

"I think that was a fine thank-you." She paused, looking like she was about to bring up something but looked down at the book she was holding instead.

It was a popular cookbook — one-dish meals using a Crock-Pot.

Sarah Anne knew Miriam likely didn't have such an appliance in her Amish home. "Do you ever wish you could use electricity?"

"Why do you ask?"

She pointed to the cover of the cookbook. "I was thinking that a Crock-Pot might come in handy on the farm from time to time."

Miriam looked amused. "I actually know someone who was able to get a Crock-Pot converted to being battery operated. We Amish can be pretty resourceful, you know."

Sarah Anne chuckled at the quip. "Truly? How does she like it?"

"She likes it fine." Miriam put the book on the shelf. "I've never thought about using one, though. Regular cooking suits me well enough."

"Me, too. Actually, the truth is that I'm not a great cook. I can only make about five things well. I'd be afraid to try them out in a different contraption."

"I feel the same way. Plus, it's only been me and Calvin for so long . . ." Her voice drifted off as she seemed to catch herself.

"But not now, right?"

Miriam's smile practically lit up the parking lot. "Right."

"How is your pregnancy going? Did you come here to order more books? I can help you with that."

"I did not. I actually came here for another reason." After looking around, Miriam seemed to come to a decision. "Sarah Anne, I came to ask you about Calvin and Miles."

Alarm bells went off in Sarah Anne's head. Fearing she might tread into something that was obviously touchy territory, she murmured, "Calvin and Miles? What about them?"

"It's okay. I now know that Calvin has been meeting the boy here from time to time."

He'd come to see Miles almost every week for two months. Did Miriam know that? It kind of sounded doubtful. "What is your question?"

"You see, we got to spend the afternoon with Miles on Saturday."

"The three of you together?"

270

"*Jah.* We went for a walk and got ice cream and got to know each other better." She blushed. "I mean, I got to know Miles."

"He's a sweet boy."

She nodded. "He has such a sad story, too. I'm not sure why the Lord felt he needed to have such a rough go of it, but I feel sorry for him."

Sarah Anne wasn't sure what to say. She also felt for the little boy, but she didn't want to inadvertently speak against Ruth or even Calvin. "I'm sorry, Miriam, but what is your question?"

"You're right. I guess I have been beating around the bush, haven't I?" She drew in a breath. "Sarah Anne, yesterday I saw my husband and Miles together for the first time. But I'm thinking that you've observed them several times now. What have you noticed?"

Plain and simple, it looked to her like Calvin had needed that little boy as much as Miles had needed him. But how could she say that? "The two of them seem to get along well."

"I'm not trying to spy. I'm just trying to make sure that what I observed was really happening."

"What did you see?"

Miriam paused, then said, "I saw two

people who were brought together by the Lord. I feel certain about that. Sarah Anne, I think Calvin and Miles were meant to be father and son."

"I saw the same thing," Sarah Anne admitted.

"You're telling me the truth, aren't you?"

"I wouldn't lie about that, Miriam. Not when a child's future is at stake."

She exhaled. "*Danke* for being so truthful."

"I don't know if I helped, though . . ."

"You did. You helped more than you know." As two families approached, Miriam added, "I'm going to look at the books right quick before I leave."

Watching her dart inside, Sarah Anne decided that not only were Calvin and Miles meant to be together, but it seemed that Calvin and Miriam were, too.

Now, she supposed, it was up to God to decide if the three of them should be together as well.

THIRTY-ONE

· TIP #31 ·

When you get involved with a new person of a certain age, you're getting involved with that person's children, grandchildren, and friends, too. That's something to consider.

Miriam had been so flustered by her conversation with Sarah Anne that she'd only spent five minutes looking at books. She'd gone directly to the new addition section and picked up a book on pregnancy and a novel — a sweet romance about two friends meeting at the shore on Siesta Key.

After quickly scanning her library card and her books, she'd thanked Sarah Anne and headed on her way home. It was only a short twenty-minute walk, but it could have taken half that time for as much as she'd been concentrating on the route. All she really wanted to think about were the changes taking place in her life at lightning speed now.

Today Calvin was going to call Amanda. Given the heartfelt way the social worker had discussed Miles at their house, her husband thought it would be an easy call. He reckoned that Amanda would be interested in their suggestion and would probably stop by their house that very evening.

Miriam hoped things would go that smoothly.

Tomorrow, she had another scheduled appointment with Edna, but this time Calvin would be accompanying her. Even when she'd murmured that there was no need for him to give up another morning of work, he'd declared that nothing could keep him from the appointment. Of course that had delighted her.

So, yes, after years of waiting and multiple disappointments, their lives had suddenly become extremely blessed. There was a very good chance that they were not only going to have a baby; a ten-year-old might be on the way, too.

Stopping to admire a clump of bright orange daffodils that had mysteriously grown on the side of the road, Miriam allowed herself to think of all she had almost lost. She'd been so focused on her own feelings of inadequacy — even though both Calvin and the special doctors had taken great pains to let her know she had done nothing to feel guilty about — that she'd let her mind play tricks on her. She'd been so sure that she'd become so undesirable that Calvin's eyes had drifted to another woman. Then, to make matters worse, she'd even pushed all thoughts of adoption away . . . just because she hadn't been willing to face the truth.

Yes, she'd been so afraid of not achieving her goals that she'd pushed so many other blessings away. That was hard to admit.

But, like this little batch of blooming flowers, the Lord had provided. He'd ignored her wishes and fears, the doctors' reasons, and even her family's advice. Instead, He'd sent miracles where none had seemed possible.

"*Danke, Got,*" she whispered out loud. "Thank You for showing me once again that I don't always know what is best. Thank You for helping me open my eyes to possibilities instead of roadblocks. Thank You for helping me see opportunities for blooming instead of reminders of my faults." After closing her eyes and adding more prayers, this time for Miles and Calvin, their baby, and their families, Miriam uttered a fervent

"Amen."

When she opened her eyes again, the little daffodils were fluttering in the slight breeze that had just popped up. Taking a good look at the blooms, her practiced eye discerned that the flowers only had a day or two before they would wither and die.

For a moment, she considered pulling them and taking them home. The three jaunty flowers would brighten her kitchen, and she could enjoy them for days.

But she left them where they were. The Lord had placed them there for a purpose, and she had a hunch that she wasn't the only person in the area who might need to see them and be reminded of His glory.

So, with a smile, she walked on, taking pleasure in the knowledge that she'd had a moment to enjoy their beauty at all.

Paddy was waiting for her on the front porch. When the dog spied her approaching, she scampered down the steps and barked exuberantly.

"Hello to you, too!" Miriam called out, bracing herself for her silly dog's signature greeting.

Paddy didn't disappoint. Like always, she barreled forward, looking for all intents and purposes like she was seconds from jumping on Miriam with enough doggy enthusiasm to knock her down to the ground. Then, at the very last second, the spaniel drew to a stop and sat sweetly at her feet, her tongue half hanging out after the burst of energy.

Also, just like always, Paddy's antics made her laugh. Chuckling softly, she knelt down on one knee, kissed the dog's nose, and gave her several pets. "You're a *gut hund,*" she said as she got back to her feet.

"I tell ya, every time she does that, my heart goes into my throat," Calvin called out. "I wish you wouldn't encourage her."

Miriam straightened. "Oh, she's just being Paddy. She's fine."

Calvin shook his head as he walked closer. Miriam allowed herself to simply stand and admire her handsome, brawny husband. His blond hair under his straw hat glinted in the sun. His bare forearms were lightly tanned — in another month or two, they would be a dark brown from all the hours he spent in the fields. He had on his work boots, dark pants, and the pale blue short-sleeved shirt she'd made for him the first year they were married. The fabric was thin and faded from weekly washings, and the uneven seam on the left side seemed to mock her as it always did.

Walking to face him, she fussed. "One day you're going to have to let me put that old shirt in the rag pile, Calvin. It's a sorry sight."

"Never. It's my favorite."

She ran a hand along his front, trying to find a way to get the garment to hang a little better. "It's uneven."

"It still fits." Pressing a palm over her hand, he added, "Besides, if I let you get rid of this shirt, you wouldn't run your hand over me in the morning sun anymore. You know that's one of my favorite habits of yours."

She pretended to be shocked. "Calvin Gingerich. The things you say!"

"Only to make you blush, Mimi. You know I *canna* help doing that."

Calvin's sweet words combined with his warm gaze made her feel almost as giddy and attractive as it had when they'd first started dating. She supposed that made sense. At the moment, every part of her felt renewed. It was as if now that they were finally talking to each other and no longer keeping secrets, the fierce love they shared was alive and well again.

Suddenly wondering why he was standing in the front lawn at all, she said, "Calvin, what are you doing out here?"

"I do live here, you know."

"To be sure. But, well, I'm surprised to see you in from the fields so early. I won't have lunch ready for another hour yet." Already jumping to conclusions, she added, "Oh, are you starving? If so, I could make you something right away. It's no trouble."

"I didn't come here for food." He smiled. "I came here to tell ya I already talked to Amanda."

"Already? What did she say?"

His smile broadened into a bright grin. "That she is looking forward to visiting with us this afternoon."

"This afternoon? She is really coming?"

"Just as I thought she would, Mimi."

"What time?"

"Three o'clock."

She pressed a hand to her chest. "My word! That's in three hours."

He reached for her hand as she started to turn away. "Hold on, now. There's more."

"What else?" She was almost dreading to hear what it was.

"Don't look so panicked. This is good." A line formed in between his brows. "I mean, I think it is."

"Calvin, what?"

"If our talk goes well, Amanda is going to go to the Schmidts' *haus,* speak with Miles,

279

then bring him over here."

"Tonight? Calvin, that is too soon. I *canna* start mothering a boy in three hours."

"Calm down and let me finish." He squeezed her hand slightly, just to get her attention. "Amanda is only bringing Miles over for a brief visit, and she'll be staying the whole time."

"What does she want us to do?"

"About what you'd expect, sweetheart," he said easily. "We can show Miles around the farm, introduce him to Paddy, maybe even show him where he'll sleep." Smiling, he said, "I told Amanda we could have dessert."

Miriam nodded before she quite realized what she was doing. She now had three hours to prepare Calvin's noon meal, clean the kitchen, clean the house, make a dessert, fix a bedroom, and mentally prepare to be observed and questioned by a social worker . . . all before attempting to put her best foot forward for Miles.

She suddenly felt a little sick. Loosening her hand from Calvin's grip, she mumbled, "I better go inside."

"Miriam, wait!"

"Don't worry, Calvin. I'll have your lunch ready soon. I made a meatloaf this morning. I can make you a meatloaf sandwich."

"Miriam."

Even though he had spoken, she talked right over him. "*Jah,* I know, it ain't your favorite, but you like it all right. Do you think Miles likes apple turnovers? I have one jar left of the apple pie filling I put up in the fall."

"Miriam!"

She turned. "What?"

"Hold out your hand."

When she did that, he slipped his hand around hers and closed his fingers easily. Looking down at their linked fingers, she said, "Now what is that for?"

"I'm holding your hand, silly."

"Calvin, we don't have time to hold hands! I've got a dozen things to do! I need to —"

"Halt!"

Paddy barked, as if she was eager to lend Calvin a hand.

That finally got Miriam's attention. She turned to her husband. "What?"

"Miriam, look." With his spare hand, he pointed to their linked fingers. "I'm holding your hand so you'll know that I'm going inside with ya. I'm going to help you this afternoon. My pregnant wife does not need to do all of that on her own."

"You're sure?"

"Very much so."

As they started walking again, Paddy scampered about their feet. "What about the corn? And the other crops?"

"They can wait. Everything else that we're working on? Well, it can't. Not at all."

Since she couldn't disagree, she smiled up at him as they walked inside the house. With Calvin's support and the Lord's guidance, she was ready for anything.

She believed that in her heart.

THIRTY-TWO

· **TIP #32** ·

Remember, your dating life is your business. You don't have to tell everyone *everything* that happens with your new beau.

Amanda sometimes said things that didn't make a whole lot of sense. Like, when she said that rainy days made sunny ones better. Miles had never agreed with that motto at all.

She also liked to tell him that her dogs were barking, which was her way of saying her feet hurt after wearing her black pumps for more than six hours at a time. The first time Amanda had uttered that, he'd had no idea what a "pump" on her foot was, or where the dogs were that were supposedly raising such a ruckus.

Boy, when he'd told her that, Amanda had laughed and laughed. When she finally calmed down, she'd explained that the saying was from her grandmother back in West Virginia, who'd said it all the time.

Just a few minutes ago, however, she'd ended up spouting a whopper of a phrase that he was still struggling with. She'd looked him straight in the eye after she'd started the car and said that this visit didn't mean anything.

He was pretty sure she was wrong about that.

After all, as far as he could tell, she'd gone to the Schmidts' house, had a serious talk with Ruth and James about Calvin and Miriam Gingerich, then told him she was going to take him over to their house for a visit.

Just to see if he liked their house.

Now, it seemed if he did like the Gingeriches' house, and they liked him there, then he was going to get to move in with them instead of going over to Ashland to the group home.

However — and there was a real chance of this — he wouldn't have to go to Miriam and Calvin's house if he decided he didn't like it.

Like that was going to happen.

But Amanda kept talking and acting like he suddenly had a lot of say in his future. She was essentially giving him a choice when he didn't really want one at all. Miles didn't want to go to the group home. Ever. He'd even rather stay at the Schmidts' house for eight more years. Even though the triplets were loud and crazy and Ruth was kind of flighty, at least everyone was nice. It didn't sound like that was going to be the case at the group home at all.

That said, if he really did get to choose where he lived next, Miles knew he wanted to move in with Calvin and Miriam, and he didn't think he needed to see their house in order to know that.

But Amanda was acting like he needed to think on it for a while.

"Do you understand what I'm saying, Miles?"

"Kind of."

She smiled and adjusted her glasses. "I'm trying to make sure you understand that you have as much say as they do. If you don't think you'll be happy at their house, you can tell me privately, after we leave. Or if you change your mind, you can even go down to your phone shanty and give me a call. We've done that before, right?"

He nodded. It was true. Over the years, they had come up with all kinds of ways to communicate. Because of things like that, he knew he was really lucky to have

285

Amanda. Minnie and Ethan had a different social worker. She was nice, but a lot older and a lot more standoffish. Minnie and Ethan never complained — at least not to him — but once he heard Ruth tell James that she thought their Mrs. Wallace should be a lot more like Amanda.

"I also want you to remember they haven't brought up adoption. They'll still just be your foster parents."

"I remember." He was used to being a foster kid. But if he was going to have to go to a group home until he was eighteen, then Miles figured he might as well stay with Calvin and Miriam at least for a little while.

"All right then, let's get on our way." Shuffling all of her things around again, Amanda stood up. "We're already going to be a little late."

Just as they headed to the front door, Ian called out to him. "Where are you going, Miles?"

"Ah, somewhere out with Amanda."

"How come?" He crunched up his freckled nose, the way he often did when he was thinking hard.

"Because I was invited."

"Wanna take me?" His light brown eyes looked up at him hopefully.

"Sorry, I can't." Turning to Amanda, he

gave her a silent look.

"Miles will be back later, Ian," Amanda said. Her voice was kind but firm. "Bye, now."

"But . . ."

"Come along, son," James said. "We have a book to read."

Watching Ian beam and abruptly change course, scampering to his father, Miles sighed in relief. That, right there, was one of the reasons why being at the Schmidt house was so hard.

They were kind to him. He had his own bed and dresser, too, which was nice. But he was always aware that Jonas, Ian, and Mary were their real children. It didn't matter what he did. Even if he got to stay for eight more years, James was never going to call him son.

Amanda didn't say much as she drove down the windy road, turned left at a stop sign, and then made another left when that road came to a dead end.

Then, over a bend, they arrived at a big farm with a bright white house on the rise. The house had a dark green metal roof that matched the barn's and a wide front porch that wrapped around to one of its sides. It was surrounded by lots of flowers and some maple and hickory trees, too.

"Wow," he murmured before he could stop himself.

Amanda smiled at him. "I know, right? Every time I come over here, I think I'm stepping onto a movie set. I think this is one of the prettiest farms I've ever seen."

Miles agreed. Looking out at the dark dirt with what looked like cornstalks, sunflowers, and maybe alfalfa growing, he said, "Calvin told me he was a farmer. I guess he's a good one."

"It sure looks like it."

The moment Amanda put the car in park, the front door opened and Miriam and Calvin came out. Calvin was wearing a big smile. Miriam looked a little more unsure. She was wearing a raspberry-colored dress with short sleeves, her white *kapp,* of course, and bare feet. But what really caught his eye was the dog standing next to her. Its tail was wagging, and it looked really cute, almost like it had brown freckles all over its nose.

"I'd forgotten they had a *hund.*"

"Her name is Paddy. She's really sweet."

Miles waited until Amanda got her purse and tote bag before getting out of the car. She looked at him and smiled. "I'll be right there. Go on ahead, if you want."

He was still debating what to do when the

dog scampered out to see him. She came bounding toward him, emitting such loud, happy barks that Miles laughed. But then he had to take a quick step backward because he was sure the dog was about to jump right on top of him.

"It's okay, Miles! Don't worry! Paddy won't —" Miriam called out just as the dog landed on all four of her feet before promptly sitting directly in front of him.

It was all was so comical, he laughed again. "Hiya, *hund*," he murmured. "Does she bite, Miriam?"

"*Nee*. Never," Calvin said as he walked toward them. "That run and screeching halt move is of her own making, I'm sorry to say."

"I've never seen anything like it," Amanda said as she walked toward them. "For a minute, I thought poor Miles was going to get run down."

As if Paddy knew they were talking about her, she looked at Calvin, then tucked her head as if she was in trouble. Miles knelt down on one knee. "It's okay, Paddy. I'm not mad. Don't be sad."

Paddy perked up her ears and wagged her tail, then leaned into him when he started to rub her soft ears.

"You've made a friend for life, Miles,"

Miriam said as she joined them. "I am sorry she scared ya. That game of hers is my fault. I'm afraid I've encouraged it over the years."

"I don't mind. I *wasna* scared." When he caught sight of Calvin's eyes, he amended his words. "I mean, not too much."

"Now that you've been properly greeted, let's take you inside," Calvin said. "Do you like chocolate pie?"

"Jah."

"And you, Amanda?"

"Absolutely. Did you go to Der Dutchman and pick up a pie?"

"Of course not. I made one," Miriam said as they entered the spacious entryway. "I made an apple one, too."

"You made two pies?" Miles asked.

"Well, *jah.* I hope you like dessert, Miles."

"I do. I really like pie," he said, though his mind wasn't really on the treat. Instead, he was looking around the inside of the house. It was really pretty. The walls were painted a pale gray. The baseboards and doors were all white, and the wood floor was a really dark shade. It was all clean and neat and silent. The complete opposite of the Schmidts' home. "Your *haus* is *shay.*"

"Danke," Miriam said. "I think it's pretty, too. Calvin here designed most of it when we were engaged. But the sunroom out by

290

the kitchen was all me."

"What is that?"

"Come, I'll show you." She started forward, her bare feet practically gliding along the wood floor.

Hesitantly, he looked at Amanda, who didn't follow. "Is that okay?"

"Of course. You're here to see the house and get to know Calvin and Miriam and Paddy. I'm not going to leave, but I'm going to stay out of the way."

"Oh."

"You'd better go, boy," Calvin said with a grin. "My Miriam has been running around for the last hour, hoping to make everything perfect for your visit."

Miles hurried to join Miriam in the big room right off the kitchen. Two of the walls were made of mesh. "It's a big screened porch."

"It is. The first summer after we married, it was so hot. I wanted a room that would always feel the breeze. I sit in here a lot and sew and read."

"I would, too."

"Paddy likes to sit in here as well," Miriam said.

Her mention of the dog made him take another look around. "Look at all those dog toys!"

"I know. I fear Paddy runs the house. She's a mighty spoiled dog. But she's good company, just as I hope you will be, Miles."

He tried to bite back a grin as he could feel a blush creeping up to his ears.

"Would you like some pie now or to see the rest of the house? Maybe you'd like to see the room I've prepared for you?"

"I'd like that."

He followed her back to the kitchen, through a big dining room with a wedding sampler on the wall, and finally to the stairs, where Calvin and Amanda had been talking quietly.

"Would you two like to join us?" Miriam asked. "We're going to go see Miles's bedroom."

"Of course," Calvin said.

"I would love to see it, too," Amanda chimed in.

As they walked up the stairs, Miles noticed that Calvin had moved to his wife's side and was whispering something to her. When they arrived at the landing, he saw that there was a big sitting room of sorts directly in front of the stairs, then a pretty long hallway leading to another two rooms.

"Your room will be the first one on the right," Miriam said.

He led the way, Paddy on his heels, but

then drew to a stop. Inside was a double bed with a green log cabin quilt on top. Next to it was an oak bedside table, a flashlight, kerosene lamp, and a battery-operated clock. On the floor was a brightly colored rag rug.

The walls were pale blue, and there were seven or eight pegs lining one wall so he could hang his clothes. There was also a desk with a chair and a short chest of drawers with a stack of books on top of it. It was the nicest room he'd ever seen, even nicer than the one he'd had with his grandparents.

"You know, there isn't a thing in here that we can't change," Miriam said. "If you don't like blue or want a different —"

"I like it," he said quickly. "I don't want anything different." Emotion overcame him as he thought about all the rooms he'd had over the years. In most houses, he'd shared a room with at least one other boy. In his first foster home, he'd had to share a space with two girls.

He'd never had bigger than a twin bed, and usually that bed was another child's hand-me-down. Though nothing was ever too bad, the rooms usually looked kind of tired and worn and smelled like the kids who had been there before.

Amanda stepped to his side. "I think my favorite part of this room is your desk, Miles. You won't have to do your schoolwork in the kitchen."

"I like the big chair."

"That's my old reading chair. I fear it's a bit worn," Calvin said.

"It looks new."

"I made a slipcover for it," Miriam said. "I surely didn't want to make you sit in his old chair."

"When did you make it?"

"This afternoon."

"You made it this afternoon?" Amanda asked.

"Well, I altered one I had on another chair," Miriam said. "It didn't take long."

"Miriam's been as excited for your visit as a child on Christmas morning," Calvin said.

Miles felt tears form in his eyes even though he tried real hard not to let them show.

Amanda wrapped her arm around his shoulders. "Ah, may we have a moment?"

"Of course," Calvin said. "Miriam, let's go slice those pies."

It didn't look like she wanted to leave, but after a pause, she backed out. "Um, the bathroom is down the hall. If you want to see that."

"I'll show him," Amanda said. After Calvin and Miriam walked out, she closed the door. "This is a lot, isn't it?"

He was so glad that she wasn't making him explain how he was feeling. *"Jah."*

"When I visited folks and talked to them about the Gingeriches, everyone said they were this way with everything," Amanda said. "They're caring, kind people."

Miles perched on the edge of the cushy chair. "It's just so different from how it usually is, you know," he mumbled, hoping Amanda would take the lead.

She pulled out the desk chair, sat down, and crossed her legs, just as if they were about to have a long conversation in her office. "Oh, I do," she said. "I know the usual pattern very well. You arrive in a house filled with kids, a leftover bed, and two experienced foster parents. Most times, they're nice enough, but there's a distance there."

He swallowed. "Half the time, the first thing we talk about are the rules I'm supposed to follow." He'd actually come to think that wasn't even a bad thing. Not really. It was a lot easier to know what he could and couldn't do instead of guessing. "The first thing I would do was figure out how to fit in. But this . . ." His voice drifted off again. He didn't trust himself to say what he was thinking.

Once again, Amanda seemed to read his mind. "Here it's the opposite, isn't it?" Running a hand down the glossy sheen on the desk, she said, "I'm fairly sure Miriam has been running around like a madwoman, trying to get everything just right."

"Calvin, too."

"Yep. They've gone to a lot of trouble to make sure you feel at home."

"And I'm not even spending the night tonight, Amanda. They did all this just for a foster kid."

"But that's where you're wrong, Miles. They didn't do this for just any foster kid. Calvin and Miriam did all of this for you."

"Same difference."

"No, it isn't. A lot of adults are interested in fostering kids for a lot of reasons. I am grateful for them, and the system desperately needs people willing to do that. But this isn't the case with the Gingeriches. They don't want any old foster kid to live here. They want you." She turned her body so they were facing each other. "I know this is different, Miles. I can't promise anything, even that it'll be easy once you move in. But I can tell you that I don't think you'll ever regret being here."

He didn't think so, either. Oh, it was going to hurt really bad when Amanda stopped by and told him that Miriam and Calvin didn't want him to live with them anymore. But he'd been through worse. "Would you tell them I can use the phone shanty from time to time? I want to be able to call you if I need to."

She smiled. "I have an even better idea. Let's tell them that you and I are used to talking every Tuesday morning. Then, you'll be able to talk to me without giving them a reason."

"That's better."

"I think so, too. And if for some reason I can't answer my phone, you can just leave a message like you do now."

Miles nodded. "I like that plan."

"Then let's go downstairs and eat some pie. Poor Calvin and Miriam are probably downstairs worried sick about you."

Though it wasn't really appropriate, Miles grinned. "Wouldn't that be something?"

Luckily, Amanda just opened the door and gestured for him to lead the way.

And so he did. He led the way downstairs to Miriam and Calvin. To his newest set of foster parents.

THIRTY-THREE

· TIP #33 ·
Be prepared to pay for your meals. The men you date might be older, but that doesn't mean they haven't adopted some new ways of thinking.

Two days had passed since Miles and Amanda had come by for dessert. Two days filled with nervousness, excitement, trips to multiple stores, and many, many long conversations about the pregnancy, Miles, and what the next few months might look like.

Calvin had walked a tightrope of emotions. He figured every one of them was to be expected, but the sudden onslaught of anxiousness, excitement, uncertainty, and fear had been hard to deal with. He liked to think of himself as a very steady, even-keeled man. That person was currently nowhere to be found, though, since they were going over to Miriam's parents' house so he and Miriam could tell their families their news all at the same time.

Calvin was looking forward to seeing the expression on their parents' faces when he told them about the baby. He was not eager to answer a lot of questions about Miles, though.

"I'm not sure why we thought this was necessary," Miriam said as she eyed the array of appetizers with a critical eye. "I feel like we could have just told my mother and she could have told everyone else."

Patricia, Miriam's mother, did have a special skill for spreading gossip and news.

"She could have . . . But then my parents would have gotten their feelings hurt, or one of our siblings might have had an exaggerated response."

Miriam sighed. "Which is a nice way of saying they would have stirred up trouble where there isn't any."

"Next thing we know, Preacher Paul would have been at our door, saying he heard I had a deadly disease that we were dealing with by raising a hooligan."

As he'd hoped, Miriam chuckled. "I can see it now. Everyone would come charging into our living room, bearing both chicken soup and child-rearing books!"

Wrapping an arm around her shoulders,

he pressed a kiss to her temple. "I wouldn't want to do this with anyone else. So, are we agreed? We'll tell the family about the baby and Miles, all at the same time?"

"Do we have to share our baby news, too?"

"I'm afraid so." He knew she loved that it was their special secret . . . just as he knew that no secret stayed suppressed for long. "I don't see how we have a choice, Mimi. It's better to get things out in the open. Ain't so?"

"It is . . . Honestly, you would've thought I would have learned my lesson by now."

"Don't fret. Everyone's going to be happy."

She smiled, but it looked pasted on. "All right then. Let's go share some news."

"Wait a moment." When she paused, he cupped her chin and kissed her lightly on the lips. "It will be all right. I'm sure of it."

After he helped her out of the buggy, Paddy on her heels, he carried the fresh strawberry cake she'd baked and frosted that morning to the front door.

Miriam took a deep breath, then opened the door. "Hello! We're here!"

Just like always, a chorus of voices floated through from the back of the house.

"You're here!" Bethy, Eli's wife, appeared first. "Look at that cake! I'll take that. No cake for you, Paddy," she added with a laugh.

Of course, her husband and their two children almost ran into her as they passed through the hall. "Careful, Bethy."

"I'll be careful with the cake. You mind the *kinner.*"

"Hiya, Mimi," Miriam's brother said as he bent down and placed a light kiss on her cheek. "I'm sorry I wasn't home when you stopped by the other day."

"Me, too, but no worries. I got to have a good *coze* with Mamm and Lavinia."

"I bet." His eyes sparkled as they shared a silent look that said they were both thinking the same thing. Holding out his hand to Calvin, he said, "Come on out to the back with me. We're grilling chicken." Giving Paddy a pet, he added, "You come, too, girl. Mamm will fuss if you get in the way in the kitchen."

Calvin watched Miriam hug Eli's children, Sam and Lilly. His heart felt full, thinking that the next time they had a family gathering, Miles would be with them. "Miriam, I'll be in the backyard."

"I heard," Miriam said with a smile.

Eli slapped a hand on Calvin's shoulder as they walked out. "Are you okay, man? You're acting a bit strange, fussing over my

301

sister like you're afraid she *canna* hold her own. I promise, she can."

Calvin chuckled. "Oh, I know she can. She puts me in my place often enough."

"I heard that," Miriam said.

"You were supposed to," he teased as he followed Eli through the kitchen to say hello to his mother-in-law and Lavinia.

When he got outside, his father-in-law, Thomas, was at the grill and Roland, Lavinia's husband, was holding John.

"Hiya, Calvin," Thomas said as he held out a hand. "How are ya?"

"I'm *gut.*"

"Your mother said you and Miriam were sitting in your buggy for a spell before you came in."

It was amazing that anyone could keep a secret in this family. He thought quickly. "Miriam was worried her cake was lopsided. You know how that goes."

As he'd hoped, Thomas chuckled. "That sounds like my Mimi. Always so worried about the smallest things." He winked. "I'll be sure to let her know her cake is as good as always."

"I'm sure she'll appreciate it," Calvin replied, though he was pretty sure that in an hour's time, the last thing anyone was going to be talking about was a strawberry

302

layer cake.

Looking up, he smiled at the sight of his parents. They were more than ten years older than Miriam's parents and far more quiet. They'd also moved out of the county, so he didn't get to see them all that often, which was a shame because he loved them dearly.

"Mamm, Daed! I'm sorry, I meant to be at the front door when you arrived."

His mother reached up and kissed his cheek. "Don't worry, Calvin. The minute Miriam's mother and Lavinia saw us, it was as if only six days, not of six months, had passed us by."

Though their two families weren't exactly close, they were a far cry from strangers. Everyone got along just fine . . . and they all seemed to be excited to have a reason to get together.

Now all he and Miriam had to do was hope and pray the day would end as well as it began.

THIRTY-FOUR

· **TIP #34** ·

Don't give up. Every relationship takes work. Even at your age.

When they all sat down at her family's large dinner table, Miriam's heart was racing, she was so excited. She was so pleased that Calvin was sitting right next to her and had squeezed her hand when they'd all bent their heads for silent prayers.

When everyone started passing food around the table, she knew it was the perfect time to announce their news. She cleared her throat. "So —"

Lavinia interrupted. "Hold on, Mimi. Pass the potato salad, wouldja?"

"Hmm? Oh, *jah.*" She picked up the bowl and dutifully passed it to the right. "Here you go."

"*Danke.*"

With an encouraging nod from Calvin,

she tried again. "Everyone, I have —"

"Do you have the pickles down by you, Calvin?" her *daed* called out. "I can't find them anywhere."

"That's because I left them in the kitchen," Mamm said. "I'll be right back."

"*Nee,* you stay. I'll go," Daed said.

Then Calvin's father, Hank, stood up. "Sorry, everyone, but, uh, nature calls."

When Hank trotted off, Calvin leaned toward her. "I know. My father has never met a bathroom he couldn't use. Eat a bite, Miriam. It might be a while."

She picked up her fork but only played with the cold mound of potatoes on her plate. There was no way she was going to be able to stomach anything until she made her announcement. So she pretended to be interested in the conversation around her, though no one was talking about much besides how hot the weather was.

Eventually, her father returned from the kitchen, and Calvin's *daed* wandered back in as well.

Under the table, Calvin squeezed her knee. It was time. She felt butterflies in her stomach and wished she'd prepared better.

"Hey, Mimi, what's going on with you?" Eli asked. "I've never seen you look so worried."

"She doesn't look that worried, Eli," Lavinia said. "Remember when she was thirteen and got the chicken pox?"

That was all the incentive she needed! After clearing her throat, she raised her voice. "Eli, I am worried, but it's not about the chicken pox. This time it's such good news that Calvin and I wanted to share it with everyone at the same time."

"Hold on, Miriam. I don't see Lilly. Where's Lilly?"

"She ran into the kitchen to get me some lemonade," Annie, Calvin's mother, said. "Lilly, where are you?" she called.

"In the kitchen. Trying to find the lemonade."

Miriam's mother jumped up from her chair. "Oh, I'll help you. I think I put it in the cooler." Turning to Miriam, she playfully waved a finger. "Don't say a word. I'll be right back."

Sam, Eli and Bethy's five-year-old, sighed. "I don't see why everyone but me can get up."

"I'm here, too, Sam. So is John," Eli said, then raised his voice. "Mamm, grab the lemonade and bring Lilly back in here."

"Come on, Patricia and Lilly," her father yelled. "Get a glass of water if there's no lemonade."

"Sorry for the trouble, Calvin," his *mamm* said.

Calvin shrugged and glanced at Miriam. "Are you okay?"

"I will be," she said with a laugh.

At last everyone was back at the table, Lilly holding two glass Mason jars of lemonade.

"Miriam," Bethy said, sending an apologetic smile her way. "Whatever you have to announce, do it quick!"

Reaching for Calvin's hand, Miriam forged ahead. "We actually have two wonderful-*gut* bits of news to share."

"Did you get a good price on the alfalfa?" Eli asked.

"Nee," Calvin said. "The first bit is that we are going to be fostering a boy soon."

"Miles is coming the day after tomorrow," Miriam added.

Everyone at the table stared at the two of them in shock.

"How come you're taking in a boy?" Eli asked.

"I met Miles at the bookmobile several weeks ago, and we struck up a friendship. He's had a hard time of it ever since his parents passed away several years ago. He's currently living with another family in the area."

"Is he an English boy? What is an English boy going to do with an Amish couple?" Mamm asked.

"I expect he'd do what any other boy would do. He'd live with us, get three meals a day, feel like he's a part of our family . . ." Calvin smiled. "But since he *is* Amish, I don't guess our home will feel much different than the home he is in now."

"Except that it will be quieter," Miriam said.

Her father nodded. "I see."

"I don't," Lavinia said. "I've never heard of an Amish child being put into the foster care system." Sounding full of herself, she added, "If this boy is Amish, then someone in his extended family would've taken him in. That's how it's done."

Eli rolled his eyes. "Lavinia, don't you think you're being a bit too opinionated? I mean, it ain't like you've ever had a foster child."

Eager to prevent an argument, Miriam spoke up. "From what I understand from the social worker, Miles didn't have any family to take him. But it's all good now, because we are going to."

"How old is he?"

"Ten," Calvin said. "You will all like him, I promise. He's a mighty nice boy."

Annie looked worried. "I'm sure he's nice . . . but what if he robs you or something?"

"Don't talk like that," Calvin said sharply. "He is a wonderful child, and Miriam and I are blessed to get to have him live with us."

"Do you want him forever?" her mother asked.

"We're going to see how it goes," Miriam said guardedly. "But that is a possibility."

"Well, I for one, am very excited about Miles," Eli said. "What do you need for him?"

"That's right," Lavinia said. "Miriam, I want to help you. Do you need some clothes? I could probably make him a pair of pants and a shirt in two days."

"We have a nice set of pillows and a blanket," Calvin's mother said. "Oh! And a bookshelf, too."

"Hold on," Miriam said, already knowing that if she didn't put a stop to the discussion now, another twenty minutes would pass before she could share the rest of her news. "We have something else to tell you."

Miriam's *mamm* folded her arms across her chest. "Well, all right, but I *canna* imagine anything could compare to that."

Miriam smiled softly. "I'm pregnant. Calvin and I are going to have a baby."

Calvin wrapped his arm around her shoulders as the whole room erupted into a mixture of gasps, cheers, and cries of joy. Every person in the room rushed to their sides and pulled Miriam to her feet. She laughed and hugged them all back.

When it was her mother's turn, she kissed Miriam on the cheek. "I guess I stand corrected, you darling girl. This is big news indeed."

"It's wonderful-*gut* for sure," her *daed* murmured as he pulled her into his arms.

When her father gazed down at her with tears in his eyes, Miriam knew she'd never been happier about Miles, the baby, Calvin, or . . . well, anything.

THIRTY-FIVE

· TIP #35 ·
I would say don't kiss on the first date,
but I have to admit that there are
exceptions to that.

"Are you nervous about tomorrow, Miles?"
Ruth asked as they followed James, Minnie,
Ethan, and the triplets down the shady,
windy road toward the bookmobile.

Mr. Schmidt had announced over breakfast that he was staying home from work so
he could spend some time with all of them
and help Miles get prepared for his move to
the Gingeriches' home the next day. That
announcement had brought a lot of questions as well, since both Mr. and Mrs.
Schmidt and Miles had elected not to tell
the other children about his move until the
last minute.

To be honest, Miles'd been surprised by
how the other children reacted to his com-

ing departure. The triplets had hugged him tight, and Mary had even started crying. Minnie and Ethan had looked disappointed as well.

As for himself, Miles had mixed feelings. He was excited about going to Calvin and Miriam's house, but he was also wary. He'd been in enough homes to know that everything wasn't always how it seemed when the social worker was there.

With that in mind, he finally answered Ruth. *"Jah,"* he said simply.

"How can I help?"

That was Ruth to a *T*. She was a mess of contradictions. Kind yet unaware, disorganized but attentive, loving but also a little distant. Now he realized that much of her actions served to guard her heart. It wasn't easy to take in foster children just to let them go again. He realized that now.

"There's nothing you can do," he replied. "I'll be fine."

Her expression softened. "I know you will. You're that type of person, Miles."

"What kind of person is that?"

"The kind of young man who somehow makes the best of any situation. And, perhaps, the kind of young man who has figured out a way to make himself happy even when his circumstances don't always make him thrilled."

He'd never thought that, but maybe she was right.

"Books do make me happy," he said, grinning at her and hoping she would realize he was kind of joking. Books hadn't made every home he'd been in wonderful, but they had been a constant source of comfort. He couldn't deny that.

She chuckled softly. "I *canna* deny that a good story helps one escape from the world, but I was also talking about your agreeableness. Or, maybe you have just been biding your time. After all, I think there are only so many weeks one can take Jonas, Ian, and Mary."

"They're not so bad," he said as they started walking across the parking lot to where the bookmobile was parked in the distance. "I . . . I've grown to be fond of them." That was the truth, too. They really were like a trio of rambunctious puppies. They were destructive and a mess, but they had their moments from time to time.

"We've all grown to be fond of you, Miles," Ruth said. "Me, especially. I'm going to miss you."

"I'll miss you, too," Miles admitted, glad James was granting them a few minutes of privacy while he took the other children into the bookmobile.

"I'm hoping that maybe Calvin or Miriam might bring you by our house sometimes, or we could even meet here at the book-mobile from time to time. That way we could at least stay in touch."

"I'd like that."

"I would, too. I'll ask Amanda if she can ask Calvin about that when she takes you to their house tomorrow. I'd ask him myself, but I think I'd better stick to the rules."

"If Calvin asks me what I think, I'll say I'd like to see all of you, too."

Stopping just short of the stairs leading up to the bookmobile's door, Ruth hugged him. "You will always have a friend in me, dear boy. Don't forget."

He had a lump in his throat as he entered the bookmobile . . . right before he stepped into chaos. Ian was holding a book up in the air too high for Mary to reach, Minnie was holding four books and trying to ask Miss Sarah Anne about them, James was looking at the new books with Ethan . . . and Jonas was calling for his *daed* at the top of his lungs.

Ruth gaped at it all like it was a big surprise. "Oh, dear," she muttered. "Every single time I think things will be different, they never are. It's always more of the same." With a groan, she sent Miles an apologetic look. "Don't forget you can get three books this time, and Calvin has promised to bring you back here when they are due."

"I won't forget."

She patted his back. "*Nee,* I bet you won't, you dear boy."

"Mamm!" Jonas yelled. "Lookit!"

"Ruth, a hand if you please," James said, sounding very aggrieved.

"I'm sorry, Miles. I think I'd better go help James."

"*Jah.* I think that might be best." He smiled as she darted over to Jonas, whispered something in his ear, then pulled the book from Ian's hands and pointed to a corner across the room. "Sit."

Miles tried his best to keep his expression blank. However, when he caught sight of Sarah Anne looking like a mouse in a houseful of cats, he grinned from ear to ear.

Ruth was right. Some things never changed, but in this case, he was glad about that.

Five minutes later, the bookmobile was relatively quiet again. Two English ladies had come in, spoken to Sarah Anne in whispered voices, picked up two DVDs, then headed out. And, after reassuring all the children that she would read a story very soon, Sarah Anne walked over to Miles.

"Miles, you are a breath of fresh air."

"I'm guessing that's *gut*?"

"You don't know how good." She smiled at him. "I heard through the grapevine that you're soon going to be living with Calvin and Miriam Gingerich."

He nodded. "I'm going over there tomorrow." Realizing he was holding two of his three book choices, he added, "Ruth told me it was okay if I got three books today because Calvin would bring me back here to return them."

"I know all about that. He told me you would be joining him on his visits soon."

He nodded again, not sure what else to say.

But Sarah Anne, on the other hand, seemed to have a good idea. "Miles, I've been thinking about you, and I wanted to get you something."

"Really?"

She motioned for him to follow her to her compact desk and pulled out a plastic sack. "I'm sorry it's not wrapped. But, pretend it is and open it up, okay?"

"All right." Feeling awkward, he opened the sack, then pulled out two pens, a note-

316

book with a leather cover, and a navy canvas backpack. "What's all this for?"

"Well, I got to thinking about you and how you've been so many places. I started thinking that maybe it was hard, you know, always having to pick up and move to someplace unfamiliar. So I wanted you to have a backpack to carry some of your favorite things. The journal and the pens are in case you might ever want to write some things down."

"Like in a diary?"

"Yes, but it doesn't have to be all personal. Not if you don't want it to be. Maybe all you want to do is write a sentence or two about what you're doing every day. Or books you've been reading that you liked." She laughed. "Or, goodness. You could simply draw in it. It's yours for whatever you want."

"*Danke.* I mean, thank you." He didn't know how to put into words what her gift meant to him. A lot of people didn't realize foster kids didn't have a lot of belongings. "I'm going to use the notebook to write down books I really like."

"I think that's a grand idea."

"Miles, what did you get?" Mary asked.

"I'll show you later."

Sarah Anne seemed to collect herself.

317

"He's going to have to show you later, Mary, because it's story time. Are you ready?"

Little Mary nodded somberly. "My *daed* said I've been a *gut* triplet today."

Sarah Anne winked at Miles. "In that case, you may sit next to me and help me turn the pages, little one."

Miles had planned on looking for more books while she read, but all of a sudden, he thought he would rather sit with the rest of the Schmidts one last time.

If he was the type of person who wrote down memories, he knew he would want to write this one down. He had a feeling that as long as he lived, he was never going to see another group of kids like them.

Joining the Schmidt clan, he placed his two library books on top of his sack and took a seat next to Jonas.

Jonas looked at him and smiled.

It made Miles realize that everything was going to be okay.

THIRTY-SIX

· **TIP #36** ·
Even if you're a whiz at social media,
don't knock good, old-fashioned
face-to-face conversation. It's amazing
what is revealed when you look someone
in the eyes.

Sarah Anne was in a quandary. Lately, she'd had answers for everyone, or at least she'd known where to find the answers. But, like the cobbler who didn't have shoes for his kids, she couldn't seem to figure out her own issues.

All she knew for sure was that she couldn't pretend everything was okay with her and Pete. It wasn't.

Actually, everything between the two of them had been rather odd.

Oh, he called her every night. He texted her back when she sent him a cute photo of some baby goats playing in a field. And, they hadn't had a fight or anything . . . But something was different with him.

Sitting in her living room, still exhausted from the Schmidt triplets, she put her feet up and suddenly felt more alone than she had in years. After living by herself and finding comfort in friends and work for so long, she had finally let herself want more. And shame on her, she'd begun dreaming of a future with Pete.

Now she was feeling rather silly. There was a good chance he'd lost interest in her but maybe couldn't figure out a way to tell her to her face. That was the thing, she realized. All the stuff that was so hard when one was twenty or thirty didn't get any easier as one got older.

After debating for a while, Sarah Anne decided the only way she was going to be able to sleep was if she called Pete. Before she could talk herself out of it, she clicked on his name, which she'd conveniently added to her contacts. Luckily, he answered on the third ring.

"Hey, Sarah Anne. What's up?"

She blinked. Boy, she'd kind of hoped he was going to sound a lot more eager to talk to her. Pushing back her doubts — honestly, had she really thought he'd sound like Prince Charming when she called him out of the blue? — she said, "Oh, I got home a while ago and finally put my feet up. What about you?"

"Me? Well, I, uh, I'm doing about the same."

"How was your day?"

"Fine."

So far, this wasn't much of an improvement. It seemed like he couldn't wait to get her off the phone. She decided to stop being so wishy-washy and get to the point. If he didn't like her bringing up his lack of interest, then so be it. "Pete, I called because I've been feeling like something has changed with us over the last week."

"We've only seen each other once this week, Sarah Anne."

"I realize that, but well, I just have a feeling that maybe you have changed your mind about us."

He didn't say a word for several seconds. Then she heard him clear his throat. "Excuse me?"

She closed her eyes. Why was all this relationship stuff still so hard in her sixties? Things were supposed to get easier! "You see, this is what I'm talking about. When you first started calling me, we talked a long time. And easily. Now? Now, it feels like you can't wait to get off the phone."

His sigh was as filled with a chauvinistic, ill-concealed impatience that reminded her of Jerry, her old boss at Pricewaterhouse. She'd hated working for him.

Before he could say a word, Sarah Anne said, "If you don't want us to see each other anymore, just say so."

"What? I haven't thought anything of the sort."

"Are you insinuating that I've imagined all of this?" And yes, she sounded peeved.

He paused again. "No."

"So?" She didn't really want to press him, but Pete was speaking in riddles — that is, he was speaking in riddles by not actually saying anything at all — and she was too old for that game.

"Sarah Anne, I know I've been difficult to deal with this past week, but I need you to hear me out."

"All right."

After yet another lengthy pause, he spoke in a quiet voice. "So, I've been experiencing some issues — some health issues. I've been tired. Losing weight. I wasn't sure what was wrong. So I went to the doctor."

On the other side of the line, Sarah Anne felt like the bottom had just fallen out from under her. Her ears were ringing, and she was having a difficult time concentrating on what Pete had to say. In a way, it was just like when Frank had gotten his cancer diagnosis. Sarah Anne shook her head, reminding herself that Pete was not Frank.

"Did he run some tests?" she asked when she finally got her voice back.

"The doctor was a she, and yes she did."

"And?" Her voice was trembling now.

"And . . . on Monday I received the results."

She had broken out in a cold sweat . . . and she hadn't even heard the results yet. Lord have mercy, but this was worse than getting a tooth pulled! "What did she find out, Pete?"

"I have COPD."

She blinked. "I . . . I've heard of that, but I'm not sure what it is."

"It stands for chronic obstructive pulmonary disease. It's a lung ailment." He cleared his throat. "I mean, it's a lung disease."

That sounded bad. "What does that mean?"

"Basically that my lungs are in bad shape and I'm going to have to make some changes."

"Pete, that doesn't tell me much." Of course, as soon as they got off the phone, she was going to do some research, but she wanted to hear his prognosis from him.

323

"That's because I still don't know much, Sarah Anne. I mean, I know I've had a cough and that sometimes I've had some problems with asthma, but I didn't expect this."

"What can you do? I mean, you said you had to make some changes. Changes mean you are going to be okay, right?" Her hand started shaking.

"I'm on some drugs, and they are asking that I slow down my work schedule for a while. Walk more. Work with a therapist."

"So . . . so you are going to get better?"

"Well, not exactly." As her heart leapt into her throat, he added, "I'm going to have this for the rest of my life. And I'm not going to sugarcoat it, Sarah Anne. There's a good chance I'm not going to live a real long time."

Tears sprang to her eyes. "Pete! I'm sorry! I . . . I can't believe this."

"I couldn't believe it, either. It was pretty hard to hear. I'm still having a hard time with it . . . which is why I haven't wanted to talk to you all that much. I didn't know how to tell you."

There were so many things that worried her about his statement that she wasn't sure where to begin. But she decided to begin with the easiest. "Why? Did you think I would not be sympathetic?"

"Of course you would be. Anyone who has talked to you for five minutes would know you would be sympathetic." Sounding even more torn up, he continued, "Sarah Anne, I didn't want to put you through this. Not again."

"Don't do that. Don't talk about dying."

"I don't want to die, and I'm going to try my hardest to get better. But I'm being honest here, Sarah Anne."

"Yes, but —"

His voice softened, turning as comforting as a soft blanket. "Listen, we've talked a lot about you and Frank and my divorce. No matter what happens, it's not easy to lose someone. You've already fallen in love and lost your man once. Now, listen. I'm not saying we're at that point yet, but I didn't want to make you go through it again."

Tears filled her eyes. She felt helpless and upset with herself for being so snippy. "Pete . . ."

"Listen. I'm sorry, Sarah Anne. I know you'd love for us to talk about it, but I'm already feeling out of breath, and I don't want to do this over the phone."

She leapt on that. "When can we see each other next?" Deciding to not let him decide, she threw out an option. "How about tomorrow night?"

"I need more time than that, Sarah Anne."

"Okay. Then the night after that? That gives you another forty-eight hours."

He chuckled. "You're not going to give up, are you?"

For the first time since their phone call started, she smiled. "No. No, I am not going to give up. You might as well give in, Pete. I can be a pretty determined woman, you know."

"I'm starting to get that idea," he said dryly. "All right. Fine."

"Fine? So . . . when?"

"I'll see you in two nights."

"Good. Come over for supper. Six o'clock."

"All right then. And, Sarah Anne?"

"Yes?"

"Thanks for being a tough old bird and not giving up."

She wasn't sure if she'd ever heard a sweeter compliment. "Anytime, Pete. Anytime at all."

THIRTY-SEVEN

· TIP #37 ·
The rules for dating after "a certain age"
are that there aren't any.

Sarah Anne took a personal day the following morning. Ron Holiday wasn't exactly thrilled about the late notice, but he didn't give her too much trouble. She wasn't sure if she would have cared all that much if he had — she needed time to really think about not only her relationship with Pete but also Frank.

Being married twenty years to someone was a long time. She had fallen in love with Frank from practically their first date. And while their marriage hadn't been perfect — no marriage was — it had been good. But then he'd gotten his cancer diagnosis, and her life had changed dramatically.

Frank's bout with liver cancer had been hard. Not just for him, but for her, too. In an instant, her world shifted, and everything that seemed so important just days before, like going to the grocery store, took a backseat to a hundred other things that mattered so much more.

It had been like a sudden, dark shadow had fallen on their usually sunny days. Their conversations about vacations and work were replaced with conversations about treatments, statistics, and doctors' appointments. And the insurance claims! She had always considered herself to be fairly bright, but that paperwork had almost driven her insane.

Frank's disease had progressed quickly, too. In a matter of eight weeks, very little about their usual daily patterns was the same. He was no longer bringing her coffee in bed like he had for the majority of their marriage. Instead, she was monitoring his medicines. He began sleeping a lot and, when he woke up, didn't have much energy except to watch television. And even then, he tired easily.

She had to cut back on her hours at work but couldn't take a full leave of absence because she wanted to be sure she had enough days for when he'd be really sick. And that future had always weighed on her mind.

So, she hired someone to check up on him while she worked and ran errands at the end of the day. Then she spent her evenings cooking, doing laundry, and caring for her sweet husband who wasn't all that sweet anymore. It hadn't been easy.

Frank hadn't enjoyed being a patient, and that was an understatement. He snapped at her and complained and generally made sure she knew he was miserable. Which meant that, within just a few months, she was miserable, too.

As time wore on and they both came to the realization that he wasn't ever going to win his battle with cancer, they'd come to an uneasy acceptance. She'd grieved and cried in private but tried to be strong for him. She'd later learned that he'd done the same for her.

It had all been awful. She'd even told herself that if she ever did fall in love again — not that she thought she actually would — she'd do her best to not become another man's nurse.

It wasn't something she was proud about, but she was human.

Now, what had happened but she'd gone and fallen in love with Pete . . . and he'd almost broken up with her because he had gotten a tough prognosis and feared she wouldn't want to go through it again.

Philosophically, she didn't. But, on the other hand, Sarah Anne knew she didn't have a choice. She'd fallen in love. But, was that love going to be enough for them both? She and Pete wouldn't have twenty years of marriage to lean on.

Compared to that, a few months of friendship followed by a few weeks of dating was nothing.

But she didn't know if she could walk away, either.

And that was the problem. She had no idea what she was supposed to do.

Sarah Anne was still dwelling on that the next morning when she went out for a long walk and ran into Miriam Gingerich and her dog, Paddy.

"Miriam, what a nice surprise to see you here. I thought you'd be rushing around your house getting everything ready for Miles."

"Oh, my goodness! Sarah Anne, that was my day yesterday! But now, we're as ready as we're going to ever be, I think." Looking down at her dog, she said, "After watching the clock's minute hand hardly move, I decided to take a little walk. Me and Paddy needed to stretch our legs for a spell."

Sarah Anne absolutely loved how everything was working out for the couple. "How is Calvin doing?"

"Oh, he's eager, and nervous, too." She chuckled. "We're quite the pair, I tell ya."

"You two are a wonderful pair, if you don't mind my saying so. Miles is blessed to be in your life."

"Thank you, Sarah Anne. We talked to Amanda about him last night, about foster care and adoption and some of the things that we'd been feeling."

"Did she give you any tips?"

"I think so." Looking a little chagrined, Miriam said, "She told us to expect the unexpected."

Sarah Anne chuckled. "That isn't all that helpful, is it?"

"*Nee*, but after praying about it, I think Amanda had a good point." Patting her belly with her free hand, she said, "I never would have believed that I would get pregnant — and especially that I'd have a relatively easy pregnancy. But here I am."

Miriam's words struck a chord with her. "You know, I've been kind of dealing with something unexpected, too. It's caught me off guard." Chuckling softly, she said, "Miriam, I was even thinking that it was a shame I couldn't go find a book to solve all my

331

problems. But I'm starting to think that a book isn't going to help much this time."

"Do you want to talk about it?"

Did she? "It has to do with, um, a relationship."

"Oh? With whom?"

"A man. I seem to have fallen in love with a man I recently met."

Miriam's pretty face lit up with a bright smile. "Sarah Anne, that's *wonderbaar!*"

"It is, but it's also scary. I never thought this would happen to me again. Certainly not at sixty-one years of age."

"That's why we need to keep the Lord in charge, *jah*? If things were left up to us, why, nothing might happen."

Miriam was right. Was it worse to feel in charge but have one's life so well organized that nothing unexpected ever happened . . . or to actually be open to new things, both good and bad?

"I think I need to pray some more."

Miriam smiled. "I hope the Lord gives you some guidance . . . or at least helps you feel strong enough to handle whatever He sends your way."

"Thank you. I hope so, too."

Miriam sighed. "I think I'd best be getting home now. Miles will arrive in two hours. Calvin's going to wonder what's keeping me if I don't return soon."

"Enjoy your first evening together, Miriam. And thanks for chatting with me. You helped me a lot."

"If I did, then I'm glad for it. Good day, Sarah Anne."

After Miriam turned away, Sarah Anne decided to head home, too. And then, because she was all alone, she started chatting with the Lord, asking Him to take on all her burdens.

And wouldn't you know it? By the time she walked in her front door, she felt much better about everything.

She also knew what she needed to do — call Pete and tell him she wanted to stop by his place. It was time to give him her heart, even if their future together was uncertain.

THIRTY-EIGHT

· **TIP #38** ·

When all else fails, buy a new outfit.

Calvin had been a nervous wreck all day. He didn't know how to be a father, and he certainly didn't know how to be a foster father to a boy who'd already suffered more hardships than he could imagine.

What in the world had he been thinking? He wasn't going to be any good for Miles! Even all the hours of prayer with the Lord hadn't helped. Only when Miriam returned home with the news that she'd spoken with Sarah Anne had he calmed down.

When Miriam had relayed that she'd shared Amanda's advice about expecting the unexpected, everything had finally clicked into place. Amanda had been right. After Miriam had shared her belief that placing her wishes and plans into the Lord's hands had helped, he decided to do the same. He felt fairly good about that decision, too.

That is, until Amanda knocked on the door. Then, all his doubts and worries came tumbling back and gathered weight, like a boulder rolling down a mossy glen. Insecurities gripped him hard.

"Oh, no you don't," Miriam said, practically pushing him toward the door. "That boy needs you, Calvin! Just as importantly, we need him. Stop worrying about what hasn't happened and let him in."

She was right. Calvin pushed aside his doubts, opened the door, and saw Miles holding a backpack and looking scared. Beside him, Amanda held an overnight case that was far too small to hold a ten-year-old's entire belongings.

At last, everything slid into place. "I thought one o'clock would never arrive," Calvin admitted.

Miles's eyes widened, then he visibly relaxed. "Me, too," he said.

"Me, three," Amanda added as she escorted the boy inside. "I picked up Miles at eleven and blocked off some time for us to have lunch together before I dropped him off here. I thought it would be just enough time."

"But we finished at a quarter to twelve,"

Miles said. "We didn't know what to do then.

Amanda looked down at him fondly. "We both thought it would be really rude to show up here early, so we've been driving around for the last hour."

"What? You should've just come right over," Miriam said.

"I've been doing this job awhile, Miriam. I know better than to show up an hour early. Anyway, it was just as well. We did find something fun to do after all."

"Oh?" Calvin asked.

Miles nodded. "We walked on a nature trail and then got sodas."

"So, it was a special time indeed." Miriam shuttled them in and shut the door. "Miles, you are going to have to help me figure out how to be a *mamm,* okay? I'm going to try my best, but I'm sure I'll make mistakes."

His eyes widened. Then Calvin saw the same thing that had happened to him when he first met Miriam happen to Miles. The boy gazed at his sweet wife with adoration in his eyes.

A second later, Miles stated the words that his wife had needed to hear. "I don't want a perfect *mamm.* Just a *mamm.*"

Miriam looked like she'd just won the lottery. After she gathered herself together, she cleared her throat. "Well. Now that we have that taken care of, let's go upstairs, and I'll give you some time to get settled." She took the suitcase from Amanda and led the way up the stairs, Miles following behind with Paddy by his side.

When they were out of sight, Amanda was looking at Calvin with tears in her eyes. "That's never happened, Calvin. It's always awkward, kids are running around, the parents are asking a dozen questions to both him and me."

"That sounds hard."

"It's not unusual, but it is hard for the foster kids, and especially for a sensitive boy like Miles. I've watched him cope by almost going on autopilot."

"Oh?"

"He would answer all the questions and nod in all the right places, but I knew he wasn't happy. Then, when the time came for me to tell him goodbye, Miles would look so resigned and stoic . . . It was painful to see." She shook her head. "Sometimes, it was all I could do to walk out the door."

"Hopefully we'll keep doing all the right things, then."

"Miles's words were spot on, Calvin. He doesn't need perfection. All he needs are two people who care. And, since you and

Miriam do, everything is going to be just fine."

"I hope so." He still had his doubts.

"Don't second-guess yourself. You're going to do fine, Calvin." She cleared her throat. "Now, let's get a couple of nuts and bolts out of the way so I can get out of your hair."

He sat down at the table with her, planned for her next visit, and signed two final papers.

When he was done, Amanda adjusted her glasses and put Miles's file folder back in her briefcase. "Now, one last thing before I go tell him goodbye." She sat up straight and suddenly looked about ten years older. "Calvin, if you and your wife change your minds about your desire to foster Miles, please call me immediately. I'll need time to place him in a suitable home."

"That won't happen."

"I know you are saying that now, and you might even believe it —"

"I do."

She continued, "However, the reality of taking care of a child is far different than the idea of doing such a thing. You might find it too difficult."

"We will not."

But it was as if she wasn't hearing him.

"He's a great boy, but he's not perfect. Sometimes he forgets to do his chores. He might talk back to you."

It was as if he'd needed to hear Amanda's skepticism to dispel every one of his doubts. "We want Miles, not a perfect child. Not only will we be fine, but he will be, too. I promise you that."

After meeting his gaze, Amanda adjusted her glasses and spent several minutes organizing her paperwork in her tote bag. "Well, um, now that that is settled, I better get on my way. With your permission, I'll go on up?"

"Of course."

Watching Amanda walk up the stairs, Calvin sat down and just gave thanks for the gift the Lord had brought them. They were a family now.

An hour later, after Amanda had left, they'd had some ice cream, and Miles had gone back upstairs to take a shower, Calvin found himself just sitting and listening to the new set of footsteps above his head.

Miriam, who'd been in the kitchen giving Paddy water, came out and looked at him curiously. "Calvin, what in the world are you doing, just sitting here in the dark?"

He looked up at her and smiled. "Giving

thanks."

Nothing else needed to be said.

THIRTY-NINE

· **TIP #39** ·
If you don't end up finding anyone who sparks your interest, don't despair.
There's nothing wrong with being on your own. It can certainly be less stressful!

One day, Miles thought, he might feel like he belonged with Calvin and Miriam. So far, though, it only felt like he was on a really good vacation.

Calvin and Miriam were really nice. Miriam had not only made him two new shirts already, but she'd also made him all kinds of special food — and there was so much of it! Never had he had so many serving bowls passed his way at a table or been told he could have as much as he wanted. Now, though, if he didn't take much, Miriam seemed to think he didn't like whatever she offered. He'd finally had to tell her that he wasn't used to eating so much.

Calvin was just as kind. Though he wasn't exactly plying Miles with food or clothing, he did spend a lot of time with him. He walked him out to view the corn and did chores with him, and at night after they ate supper and did the dishes, he encouraged Miles to get a book and read with him in the hearth room. That was Miles's favorite part of the day.

Miriam joined them, too, except she didn't usually read. Sometimes, she would just sit with Paddy on the couch and pet her, or she would sew or stitch or knit.

Just like she was doing at the moment.

"What are you working on tonight, Miriam?" he asked, watching her knitting needles fly.

"Baby booties." She smiled at him. "*Mei boppli* is going to have more yellow, green, and white little socks and booties than he or she will ever need."

Miles chuckled. "Do you want a boy or a girl more?" They'd never talked about which she was hoping the Lord would give her.

"I don't care. As long as he or she is healthy, I'll be pleased." Looking over at Calvin, she added, "What do you think, Calvin?"

"The same as you, Mimi."

Miles grinned at the dog, who was curled

up in a contented ball next to Miriam's hip. "Maybe the only one who won't be too happy about your baby is Paddy."

"I'm a little worried about that, too, but we'll take things one day at a time," Calvin said.

Miriam looked affronted. "I'm not worried. Not one bit. Paddy is going to be fine. She's a *gut* guard dog. And nice, too."

"I hope that will be the case."

"Just think how kind she was to Miles when he arrived," Miriam said. "Right, Miles?"

"*Jah.* She was real nice." It wasn't a lie, either.

Miriam gave her husband a know-it-all look. "See?"

"Oh, brother," Calvin said. "Miles, would you care to take this wonderful-*gut hund* out for a walk with me?"

"Sure." Grinning at the spoiled dog, he said, "Are you ready to go for a walk?"

Paddy jumped off the couch just as Miles was putting down his book on the table. They accidentally knocked into each other . . . and somehow their movements caused the kerosene lamp to rock.

Next thing Miles knew, the lamp crashed to the floor, leaking kerosene fluid all over the rag rug carpet . . . and igniting it.

It was just that quick. One second, everything was as calm as every night before. The next? The floor was on fire.

Calvin yelled for Miriam to get Paddy and move off to safety, then at Miles to do the same. He began stamping out the flames with Miriam's beautiful yellow and purple chain quilt.

"Come, Miles!" Miriam called out. "Now!"

But he froze. It was like his mind couldn't remember how to communicate with the rest of his body, certainly not his legs. He gaped at Miriam like a stuffed animal instead of moving to her side.

"Miles, please hurry!" she called again.

"But —" He drew in a breath, trying to convey that since the fire was his fault, he should stay and help Calvin. Shouldn't he?

"Boy, get out of here before my wife gets hurt!" Calvin yelled at the top of his lungs.

Calvin sounded furious. As the reality of what he had done — put Miriam in danger — hit him hard, Miles turned and ran toward her.

"Thank the good Lord," she cried as she reached for him.

Miles squeezed her hand back, then did what he should've done sixty seconds before. He helped her get Paddy, now whining

344

and petrified, outside. Then, he held Miriam's hand as they hurried to the edge of the cement slab patio outside. Miles took deep breaths of the cool night air and tried to figure out what he should do next. Was the barn in danger? Should he run out there to save the animals? Or would Calvin get mad because Miles hadn't stayed to protect Miriam?

As his mind ping-ponged from one duty to the next to, reminding him that the whole thing was his fault, Miriam patted his back.

"*Jah?*" he asked.

"It's okay, Miles," she said gently. "Everything is going to be just fine. Look. It's out."

He looked to where she pointed. And sure enough, the fire had become soggy-looking smoke. Instead of seeing flames, he only saw Calvin.

His new foster father was standing just a foot or so away from where the flames had been. He was looking at the ground intently. Then, as if he'd noticed Miles looking at him, his chin lifted, and their eyes met.

He looked absolutely nothing like the man Miles had come to know. Instead of a warm expression in his eyes, Calvin's brown eyes looked as cold as the bottom of the nearby lake.

Shame and panic coursed through him.

After all, why would Calvin have looked happy? Miles had almost burned his house down. This was one of the worst moments of his life.

"Miles?" Miriam asked. "Are you okay?"

"Nee," he muttered before he thought better of it.

"Nee?" She stepped forward and reached for him. "Are you hurt? Did the fire get you?" Her eyes widened. "The glass from the lamp!" She began running her hands down his arms and legs. "Are you bleeding? Did a glass shard nick you?"

He could hardly talk. He settled for jerking his head to the side, hoping it sufficed as a strong "no." She knelt so that they were eye to eye. "Then what is wrong? Did the fire scare ya?"

She was speaking to him like he was a baby, like a child who didn't know any better. But his transgressions lay heavy in his heart. He'd not only knocked the lamp over and caused the fire, but he had also put their house, Paddy, Calvin, Miriam, and their unborn baby in jeopardy! Everything they'd wanted so badly and loved so much had nearly been taken away because of him.

It was almost more than he could bear.

He had to get out of there, had to step away from Miriam's sweet, searching gaze.

346

From Calvin's thunderous expression.

From the smoke and the ashes and everything that he'd done.

If he was the type to run away, he would've done just that. But instead, he found his voice. "I'm gonna go check on the animals in the barn," he muttered. Then, without waiting a second, he took off and ran.

When he got to the barn, he pulled open the sliding door and slipped inside the almost pitch-dark space.

Windy spied him and whinnied a greeting. The hens in the coop clucked. Even the milk cow paused her chewing and looked his way.

"I know," he said, though he wasn't even entirely sure what he was going to say. But at least with the animals and the quiet, no words were expected.

So he finally did what he had wanted to do from the split second when he'd watched the kerosene lamp topple over. He sat down on the ground, pulled his knees up to his chest, wrapped his arms around them, and dropped his chin to his knees. Then he closed his eyes tightly and tried to pretend it hadn't happened.

It was what he'd done when he'd learned his grandparents were dead, when he realized that he didn't have a single person on

Earth who cared about what was going to happen to him.

Some habits were hard to break.

FORTY

No relationship, not even the best ones,
are all puppies and kittens. Have realistic
expectations.

He'd really messed up. Tripping and falling,
breaking the kerosene lamp, starting a fire.
It had been one of the worst moments in
his life, and he'd had quite a few of those.

But seeing the look of fear in Calvin's
eyes, followed by the way he'd glared at
Miles once the fire was out? Well, that had
been even worse.

About ten minutes after Miles had run to
the barn, Miriam had walked out to get
him. She'd said nothing other than that they
needed his help to clean up.

And so he helped.

To his surprise, there wasn't as much
damage as he'd thought. Miriam's rug was
ruined, and the couch and table looked a

little singed and sooty, but all in all, it was pretty evident that the whole house hadn't been about to burn down.

It could have been worse, though. He was absolutely aware of that. So, as he helped Calvin carry out the wet, ruined rug and sweep up the glass shards, he apologized about a dozen times. Calvin didn't seem to care about that, though. All he kept saying was that it had been an accident.

Later, when just he and Miriam were eating some chocolate ice cream, he'd apologized to her. But instead of looking pleased, she'd just shaken her head and said there was no need and that everything was fine.

But it wasn't.

He really knew it wasn't when he'd discovered that the reason Calvin hadn't been eating ice cream with them was because he'd gone down to the phone shanty to make a phone call.

Miles knew for sure that Calvin had called Amanda.

No doubt Miriam and Calvin were now just biding their time until his social worker could come and take him away to the group home. He deserved it, too.

But it was so hard.

That night, every time he thought about leaving his room — with the quilt Miriam had placed on the bed, and his desk, and the spot for his books — it made him want to cry. So did the thought of losing Paddy and having free rein over the house and not having to only eat at certain times of the day.

But most of all, he mourned the fact that he'd almost killed Miriam and her baby and had lost Calvin forever. He'd miss the only home he could ever remember being really happy in.

Miriam had walked him to his room about two hours ago and softly said that everything would be better in the morning. He'd nodded. But he didn't believe it, and he knew Miriam hadn't believed it, either. After all, Calvin had barely spoken to him much that evening.

Miles had tried to go to sleep, but it was hopeless. He had spent the last hour reading with his flashlight. He knew that was another thing he was going to have to give up when he left the Gingeriches, too. He was pretty sure no bookmobile visited the kids at the group home and even more sure that none of the kids there were going to be given flashlights so they could read or move around whenever they pleased.

But now, at almost midnight, Miles was thirsty and wide awake. He decided to go get a glass of water while he could.

After carefully lighting his way downstairs, he set the flashlight on the countertop and got himself his drink. Then, because he hadn't been taken away yet, he sat down at the table and looked out the window at the fields surrounding them.

The moon was out, illuminating the land. He could see the shadows of Calvin's corn softly swaying in the wind. He wasn't going to get to see him harvest it, and he sure wasn't going to get to help him.

Too late, he heard an upstairs door shut and two sets of footsteps walking down the stairs. Looking up, he saw Calvin, followed by Paddy.

Now he would likely be in even more trouble. He didn't know where to look or what to say, so he just hung his head and kept quiet.

"I thought I heard you down here," Calvin said. "You got thirsty, huh?"

He swallowed. *"Jah."*

"Have you been up for a while?"

There was no reason to lie. "I haven't been able to sleep."

"That makes two of us, then." Calvin walked to the cabinet and got himself a glass of water, too. "Are you still thinking about what happened this evening?"

"Jah." Suddenly an awful thought occurred to him. "Is Miriam okay?"

"Miriam?" Calvin smiled. "She's been sleeping like a log. This baby of hers makes her want to sleep all the time."

"So, she's not in trouble?"

"Trouble?" A line formed between his brows. "Oh, you mean about the baby?" When Miles nodded, Calvin shook his head. "*Nee,* Miles. She ain't in trouble at all."

"That's *gut.*"

"*Jah,* it is." Calvin leaned back in his chair and sipped from his glass.

The tension between them was new. It was like they both had a lot to say to each other, but neither of them knew how to start.

Unable to take it anymore, Miles decided to put it out in the open. At least then he'd know when to expect Amanda.

"Did you call Amanda earlier?"

Calvin sat up. He paused for a moment, then nodded slowly. "I did."

So he'd been right. The truth of it felt crushing, but he powered through. "Ah, when is she going to come get me? Did she say?" It was going to take a lot of prayer to be able to leave this house and go to the group home without crying like a baby at either place.

"She's going to — Hold on." Calvin set

his glass on the table. "What are you talking about?"

He thought it was pretty obvious. "I mean that I'm not sure when I should have my things ready for Amanda."

"You've lost me, Miles. What things do you need to have ready?"

"My clothes and my other stuff." Miles was getting kind of mad. Why was Calvin making him spell it out like this?

"Wait. Do you think you're going to have to move?"

"That's why you called my social worker, right? Don't you want me to leave?"

"Nee."

"No? Are you sure about that?"

Calvin stilled, then got to his feet. "Miles, come outside with me."

Miles followed him to the door, but he didn't know what to expect. Maybe Calvin didn't want Miriam to hear him yell? When they got outside, Calvin sat down on the worn edge of the wooden back porch.

"Come sit by me, Miles. I want you to see something."

Miles sat down next to him but didn't see anything beyond acres of farmland. "What?"

He chuckled. "It's pretty dark out, isn't it? But since we've got an almost full moon, the fields are visible."

"I know. I was looking at the corn earlier."

"If you were doing that, then you might have a pretty good idea of what I mean when I tell you that this field feels a little bit like our family right now."

Huh? "I don't understand."

"See, right now, it's me and Miriam and Paddy. We're in that line of light shining clear as day. But in the shadows of that ray is you . . . and Miriam's babe."

"I don't understand."

"You're as much a part of our future as that baby is, Miles. We're planning on you living with us forever." Calvin paused then added, "Or at least until you're ready to live on your own."

"You mean that?"

"I do. I called Amanda because I knew you might need her, because you've known her a lot longer than us and might feel better talking to her. But I also called her because I asked her to see if she can put a rush on the adoption papers."

His heart just about fell out of his chest. "You talked to Amanda about adopting me?"

"I sure did. Miles, I don't want you to worry about your future anymore. I don't want you scared about an accident, or if Miriam or I get hurt, or if something else

355

unexpected comes along. I want you to feel secure."

"You really mean that?"

"Of course I do. And, just so we're clear, Miriam feels the same way."

"I didn't think that was going to happen," he murmured, half to himself. "I didn't think that at all." Taking a chance, Miles wrapped his arms around Calvin and hugged him close.

"I guess that's why the Lord made surprises, Miles. If we only got things we expected, the world would be a mighty boring place."

"Maybe a harder one, too."

Calvin nodded. "A much harder one. For sure and for certain."

FORTY-ONE

Dream about living your own happily
ever after!

From the moment the Schmidt triplets had
left the bookmobile, trailing behind Ruth
like a trio of ornery sheep, Pete Canon had
hardly stopped laughing.

If Sarah Anne hadn't been driving back to
the main library's parking lot, she might
have given in to temptation and slapped his
arm.

"Pete, they weren't that funny."

"Oh, yes they were."

She tried again. "I can't believe you were
so amused by those . . . those . . . tiny
children."

"I couldn't help it, Sarah Anne. They
really were as mischievous as you said." He
shifted, arranging his portable oxygen
device with him on the passenger seat.

357

After his diagnosis of COPD and their frank discussion, things had improved for Pete. Now that he was on better medicine — and had oxygen he was supposed to use several hours a day — his prognosis was better. Sarah Anne had gone to two doctors' appointments with him and heard the news herself. Though he did have a serious, chronic illness, it wasn't the terrible death sentence Pete had first feared.

However, the diagnosis was enough for him to retire. His children had encouraged it, for which Sarah Anne was thankful. Now Pete spent his days walking, seeing his children and friends . . . and spending as much time as possible with her.

Which was why he'd accompanied her today.

Returning to the conversation, Sarah Anne shook her head. "I'm sorry, but I don't think I ever referred to them as simply 'mischievous.' I believe I called them hellions, which wasn't very nice."

He chuckled again. "They don't even try to behave. I saw one of them simply gaze up at his mother while he dropped four books on the floor."

"That was Jonas," she said as she pulled into the parking lot at the back of the district library office.

"Well, Jonas and his siblings are going to be trouble when they're a little older." He smiled again. "It's hard to believe they haven't started robbing banks yet."

Still feeling guilty about how mean she'd sounded about such small children, Sarah Anne said, "They aren't all bad, of course. I shouldn't make them sound so awful. They're not."

Pete grinned. "You're right. They're only like, um . . . a set of feral cats on the loose."

"Maybe more like hamsters?" She laughed. "I'm sure each will grow up to be someone their parents will be proud of."

"One can hope and pray."

"Indeed."

"I do have to tell you that I get it now," Pete said as he unbuckled.

"Get what?"

"What your days are like. I'm a little ashamed to admit that I thought you might have been exaggerating a bit about how crazy your schedule is, but now I'm starting to think that you hadn't shared just how busy you are."

"I *am* busy."

"And those triplets aren't the only ones who give you a run for your money, either. Some of your other patrons seemed pretty snippy."

She waved that off. "Oh, everyone has their quirks — myself included! I truly love my job and the variety of people I see all day long. I wouldn't trade one of them . . . not even those triplets."

He leaned over and kissed her brow. "Thank you for letting me spend the day with you. I loved every minute of it."

She smiled up at him. "You were a lot of help. Plus, I enjoyed spending the day with you. I hope we can do this another time."

"Anytime you don't mind the company, I'm game." He winked. "I'm retired now, you know."

She was so happy he was retired . . . and very intent on making sure he concentrated on his health and happiness, not her work. "Maybe we can work something out. Perhaps you can come with me once a month."

"That's it?" When she shrugged, he reached for her hand. "Maybe one day I'll be able to persuade you to lighten your workload, too."

She wasn't ready to step back yet, but there were days when Sarah Anne could admit she'd rather be going out to lunch or tending her garden. Or, simply reading a book instead of shelving hundreds. "We'll see," she murmured. Realizing they were still sitting in the parked bookmobile, she said, "Well, I guess it's time to clean up."

"Sarah Anne, can you wait a sec?"

"Of course, but don't think I expect you to clean with me. You've done enough. We can get together later this evening."

"Actually, that's not what I wanted to speak with you about."

Pete looked so serious, she started worrying again. "Pete, what's going on? Has something happened with one of your tests?"

He hung his head. "I'm messing this up, aren't I?"

When she just stared at him, he said, "Sarah Anne, I actually went with you today for a reason, and it wasn't to meet your patrons." He took a deep breath. "It's because I wanted to ask you something here, where we met."

She still wasn't following him. "We didn't meet in this parking lot, Pete." Then, she realized he was talking about the bookmobile. Of course he was talking about that! "Ask me what?"

His warm brown eyes filled with amusement again. "Do you really have no idea?" He reached for her hand. "Sarah Anne, I know we've got a lot on our plate . . . but I think we need to make ourselves official."

She gulped. " 'Official'?"

"One day, I want to marry you."

"You want to get married?" And yes, she sounded like Minnie Mouse.

"I do . . . one day. But for now . . . How about we go steady?"

She giggled. "Pete Canon, are you asking me to be your girl?"

"I think you know I am, unless I'm really doing it wrong. So, what do you say?"

"I say yes." Beaming at him, she reached for his other hand. Pete had practically read her mind. She knew she loved him, and she knew she wanted to be by his side for as long as that was possible. But she wasn't quite ready to get married.

Not yet, anyway.

Pete grinned. "That's it? Really?"

"Really. I don't want to play games. The fact of the matter is that I would have never met you at Scarpetti's if I hadn't thought something great could happen between us. I would have never had pizza with you in my living room if I knew things weren't serious. I would've never gone on so many dates or spoken to you on so many nights . . . or introduced you to my patrons if I hadn't known you were special to me." Looking at their hands linked together, she added, "And that's what you are, Pete."

"I fell in love with you when I saw you sitting outside this big old bus, looking as happy as most people look on their first day of vacation."

"I fell in love with you when I realized you'd gotten to Scarpetti's early because you were nervous."

"I guess we were meant to be, then."

She nodded, just before he pulled her close and kissed her. She wrapped her arms around his neck and kissed him back. Right there in the parked bookmobile.

It felt sizzling and new and perfect and surprising. But then again, that was perfectly normal. After all, they were going steady now.

FORTY-TWO

· TIP #42 ·

Don't be offended if people don't want to
follow your advice. Sometimes all you can
do is simply sit back, hold on tight . . .
and watch what happens.

Two Months Later

Miriam had planned a special surprise for
Calvin and Miles. She could hardly stand
it, she was so excited. Her surprise had
taken a bit of time and quite a bit of
underhandedness, too! Thank goodness
she'd been able to enlist her whole family
to help. Once she'd told them about her
idea, all of them had gotten just as excited
as she was for the big event.

After lots of conversations on the sly, they
had a plan. In order to get Calvin and Miles
out of the house, Miriam's father and
brother-in-law had invited them to go to a
festival in Charm.

Though Calvin hadn't seemed too thrilled about the idea, he'd been game, especially since Miles had been really excited. The two of them had walked over to her parents' house at eight that morning. Two hours later, Eli, Bethy, Lavinia, and her mother had arrived at Miriam's house. So had the driver from Zeiset's Furniture Store.

The driver and some men from the store, along with Eli, had unloaded the most perfect picnic table and chairs right onto her front lawn. The workers had seemed confused about where they were supposed to put it, and one of them had even tried to tell Miriam that the set would look far better on the patio around the back of the house. But Miriam had held firm. She wanted the table directly in front of her kitchen window so she could stand at her sink like she always dreamed she would. She wanted to be able to look out there and see Miles . . . and one day their other children as well.

After the table delivery, Bethy's brother Abel stopped by. Together Abel and Eli had worked more wonders. They dug a bed, planted some boxwoods, and then carefully arranged the paver stones they'd hidden behind the house two days before. It was hard work, but it had achieved amazing results.

Two hours later, Miriam had a true seating area complete with greenery and a darling walkway leading from the table to the house. She thought it looked even better than she had dreamed it could.

While the men were outside laboring, Bethy, Lavinia, and her mother helped her with the picnic preparations — and with the quilt she and her sister had been stitching in their spare moments.

Then, at three o'clock, everyone had left. She'd hugged them all and promised to give them a report on how Calvin and Miles reacted.

With butterflies in her stomach, Miriam pulled out a book and a glass of lemonade and sat outside on the front porch to wait for her men.

She didn't have to wait long. Right at four o'clock, just over the crest of the hill, Miles and Calvin appeared. They were walking side by side, smiles on their faces. Miles was holding a stuffed animal like those they offered as prizes at some of the games of chance at the fair.

When they got even closer, she hurried out to meet them, Paddy on her heels. "You're back!" she called out.

Calvin's face broke into a huge grin when he got to her side. "I haven't seen you hurry out to meet me in years! Miriam, you must have missed us."

"I did." She kissed him on the cheek. Smiling at them both, she added, "I missed both of you."

"You should have come with us, Miriam," Miles said. "We had a great time. It was *wunderbaar!*"

"I'm so glad you had fun." Impulsively, she leaned down and lightly kissed Miles's cheek as well.

He groaned, but his smile told another story. "Another kiss?"

That was their game now. He pretended he was too old and grown up to receive kisses from his adopted mother, and she pretended her gestures of affection bothered him. With a sigh, she attempted to frown. "I'm sorry, Miles. I guess I forgot you don't like your mother's hugs and kisses."

He looked just about to say something when his eyes got big and he stopped. "What's that?"

Trying her best to hide her grin — she was truly a terrible actress — she said, "What's what?"

Miles rolled his eyes. "You know what I'm talking about, Miriam." His voice rose.

"Calvin, did you look? Do you see that?"

"I do, but I can hardly believe my eyes." To her delight, Calvin really did look just as shocked as their son. "Miriam, what have you been up to today?"

"A whole lot. I planned a surprise for you two."

The three of them were still standing in place, Paddy staring up at each of them in confusion. "But there's furniture in the middle of our front yard," Calvin said.

"I know. Zeiset's delivered it a couple of hours ago."

Miles started running ahead. "And chairs! There are chairs, too!"

Miriam laughed. "I figured a table was no good without chairs to go around it."

"And bushes! And flowerpots! And a walkway!" Miles called out.

"It does look nice, doesn't it?" Miriam smiled at her husband.

"It looks very nice indeed. Amazing, really." Reaching for her hand, Calvin continued to gape at their brand-new front yard oasis. "Miriam, how in the world did you manage this?"

"I asked my family for help. Every one of them wanted to be a part of the surprise."

"They must have been here all day."

"Oh, they were. They arrived soon after

you and Miles left. Even Bethy's brother came over."

They were at the table now. The furniture was made of a special material that could withstand rain, snow, and just about anything Ohio weather could send their way. Miriam had ordered the table in blue and the four chairs surrounding it in different colors. The whole set looked bright and cheery and welcoming.

"Can we sit down?" Miles asked.

"Of course, silly. Pick a chair," Miriam said.

When all three of them were sitting, Miriam held out her hands, one for Miles and one for Calvin. "I wanted to have a special place for our family to sit. Miles, I want you to be able to bring your friends over and sit out here, and one day you and our babe can sit here whenever you felt like it." Smiling, she added, "I wanted a place for our family. For our new, improved family."

"I like it," Miles said.

"Me, too," Calvin said.

"If you like it now, just wait until you see what else I have planned."

Miles's eyes widened. "There's more?"

Feeling a bit like Santa Claus, Miriam nodded. "There is. My *mamm* and Bethy and my sister helped me make a big picnic that we can eat out here. And I even have a pretty quilt to put on the table for now . . . and we can wrap the babe in it when he or she comes."

"I *canna* wait to see it," Calvin said.

Miles jumped to his feet. "Can we eat soon? I'm starving."

"As soon as you clean up, you two can help me carry all the food and plates out. I'm starving, too."

As Miles ran with Paddy toward the door, Calvin helped Miriam to her feet, then wrapped an arm around her shoulders as they walked on the new stepping-stones leading to the front door. "This was a terrific surprise, Miriam. You never cease to amaze me."

"I feel the same way about you, Calvin. Because of you, so many of my dreams have come true."

He stopped just outside the front door and gave her a kiss. When he pulled away, he ushered her inside. "Well, I best go hurry and wash up. I've heard you're practically starving."

"I am eating for two, you know," Miriam teased.

The laughter that rang through the house filled every room. And her heart.

EPILOGUE

· TIP #43 ·

Don't forget to be happy.
There's always, always something to be
thankful for.

Nine Months Later

God was so good. Sarah Anne reckoned He truly enjoyed placing surprises in people's lives, just to see how they would handle them.

And handle them they did. In one way or another, every man, woman, and child dealt with whatever the Lord gave them. Sometimes it was to His glory. Other times, all a person did was simply survive.

But today, watching Miles Gingerich approach the bookmobile, Sarah Anne knew this was one of the Lord's triumphs. When the boy was close enough to hear her, she called out to him and waved a hand for good measure.

"Good afternoon, Miles!"

He grinned and tipped his hat. "Hiya, Sarah Anne. You got here early."

"Traffic was light. Plus, I was anxious to see you," she added as Miles allowed her to give him a quick hug.

"Because?" he asked as soon as she dropped her hands.

"Because . . . I brought you something."

His eyes widened. "What is it?"

"I'm going to make you wait a bit. Why, chances are good that if I show it to you now, you'll likely leave to go show all your friends."

He grinned. "It must be mighty special indeed, though I *canna* think of what I've done to deserve such a thing."

"Two words for you." She lowered her voice. "Schmidt. Triplets."

He laughed. "What have they done now?"

"There's no telling, but Ruth did tell me she was coming to story time today. She's excited to hear you read to all the *kinner.* She said she wouldn't miss it for the world."

Miles blushed a bit. "It will be *gut* to see them."

He followed her inside, and seeing the way he now filled the small bus, Sarah Anne's heart filled with joy.

Miles had surely come a long way from

the first time she'd seen him trailing behind the rest of Ruth's brood. Gone was the shy, rather scrawny boy who didn't want to be noticed. In its place was a young man who had easily grown four inches, put on twenty pounds, and now carried himself like he was worthy of love.

"So, how are things at home? How are Andrew and Pearl?"

He smiled. "They're *gut*. They're six months now."

"Are you getting any sleep?"

"Me? Oh, for sure. Calvin and me built me a new room off the kitchen. I'm far away from the *bopplis*." He took a breath. "But I don't mind the babies none. They're cute and they make Miriam happy."

"I heard you make her happy, too."

To her amusement, he blushed. She knew he loved having a "real" mother who cared about him.

"Well, I reckon Ruth is going to be here soon, so I better give you your gift before we lose our chance." She opened her tote bag, which was next to the driver's seat, and pulled out a box she had wrapped last night. "Here you go, Miles."

He held the box carefully. "I don't understand why you got me anything at all."

"Sometimes I see something that suits a

certain friend of mine to a T. That was the case with this. Well, I thought so, anyway." She waved a hand. "Now, open it before I open it for you."

Carefully, he pulled off the paper, looked at the box curiously, then opened it up. He pulled out a package of labels that she'd had made up.

Each one was about two inches square, blue and gold, and had the words "Property of Miles Gingerich" emblazoned in the middle. Below his name, "Gardner Way," the name of Miles's street, was neatly printed.

His brow wrinkled. "What are these?"

She pulled out his second gift, a new book about the states and the National and State Park in each. "Open up the front cover."

He lifted the cover and saw she'd placed the first sticker inside of it. "I . . . I still don't understand."

"I ordered you a set of bookplates, Miles. It tells a person who borrows the book who it belongs to, and, in your case, it lists your street so they can find you."

"Oh."

She thought he didn't like them at all, until she saw him stare hard at his name and street.

"This is me now, isn't it?" he asked, his

374

voice filled with wonder.

She knew how he felt. She felt that way about her life as well. Sometimes she found it hard to believe she'd found love again — just when she'd least expected it. And that just last week she and Pete had gotten officially engaged.

Examining the bookplates again, Sarah Anne said softly, "That sure is you now. And I have to tell you that the Miles I've come to know is pretty spectacular." Smiling, she handed him the book. "I hope you'll enjoy the book as well."

"Danke." He smiled up at her. "One day I aim to go to every state in the country."

"If that's what you want to do, then I'm sure you will. I have a feeling, Miles Gingerich, that you're destined for lots of good things."

Hearing the telltale clatter outside the bus, she added, "And speaking of good things, Mrs. Schmidt is here!"

One of the triplets clambered in, spied Miles, and ran to him. "Miles!"

"Hiya, Jonas."

And so it continued. One by one, Miles hugged Jonas, Mary, and Ian and said hello to Ruth's babe before giving Ruth a hug.

"Are you going to read to us today?" Mary

375

asked, just as two more Amish families came in.

"*Jah.* Everyone gather around, and I'll get started."

Sarah Anne winked at the mothers who'd just arrived as Ruth sat down in a chair with the baby in her lap.

Satisfied that everything was as it should be, Sarah Anne brought over the chair by the small desk and sat down.

She smiled at Miles and listened. When he was on the sixth page, she at last pulled out her phone. She'd heard it *ding,* signaling an incoming text, while she and Miles had been talking.

After checking once again that no one needed her, she read the text.

As she had guessed, it was from her fiancé, Pete.

So, did he love it?

Beaming, she texted him right back.

He did. At least I think so.

What time should I pick you up for dinner at Scarpetti's?

Six o'clock. This is my last stop

376

for the day.

Can't wait. See you soon, gorgeous.

As she slipped her phone back in her pocket, Sarah Anne knew if she'd been alone, she would have giggled. She wasn't gorgeous. She never had been. But with Pete, she felt gorgeous and special.

Smiling at Miles, at the boy who had lost so much . . . then gained more than he'd ever imagined was possible, Sarah Anne realized that that was what love did. Love simply made everything better.

Which might have been the biggest surprise of all.

ACKNOWLEDGMENTS

This year, with the pandemic going on, I've been even more grateful for the great lengths to which everyone at Gallery Books has gone to ensure the publication of this novel. First and foremost, I'm so grateful to my editor, Sara Quaranta. Sara has become a wonderful sounding board for new ideas, a skillful editor of my sometimes clunky writing, and a caring advocate for my novels. Even in the midst of living in multiple places in a pandemic, she always answered my emails. Thank you, Sara, for everything you do.

Big thanks also go out to Christine Masters, who shepherds the manuscript through all stages of production, and to the whole marketing and publicity team, especially Sydney Morris, who really is amazing — and amazingly nice.

No acknowledgment letter would be complete without thanking my wonderful agent,

Nicole Resciniti; Lynne, my first reader, who always makes books better; my street team; the Buggy Bunch; and the many readers who've continued to read my books and even take the time to tell me what they thought of them.

Finally, I'm so thankful for my husband, Tom, for more reasons than I could ever name.

READER QUESTIONS

1. Do you enjoy surprises? What is something unexpected that happened lately that took you by surprise?

2. There were three story lines in this novel: Miriam and Calvin's marriage, Miles's hope for a better life, and Sarah Anne's romance with Pete. Which one did you enjoy the most?

3. So many people had to step out of their comfort zone in the novel. When was the last time you did that? Are you happy you did?

4. The following verse from Psalms guided the writing of this novel: "Open my eyes to see the wonderful truths in your instructions" (Psalm 119:24). When has the Lord opened your eyes to see His wonderful truths?

5. The Amish proverb I found for this novel made me smile. What does this saying bring to mind for you? "One of the most complicated tasks modern man faces is trying to figure out how to lead a simple life."

6. One of the reasons I've enjoyed writing this series is that I've always loved visiting libraries and discovering new books there. Do you have a favorite library? If so, what has made it your favorite?

ABOUT THE AUTHOR

A practising Lutheran, **Shelley Shepard Gray** is the *New York Times* and *USA TODAY* bestselling author of more than one hundred novels, translated into multiple languages. In her years of researching the Amish community, she depends on her Amish friends for gossip, advice, and cinnamon rolls. She lives in Colorado with her family and writes full time.

The employees of Thorndike Press hope you have enjoyed this Large Print book. All our Thorndike, Wheeler, and Kennebec Large Print titles are designed for easy reading, and all our books are made to last. Other Thorndike Press Large Print books are available at your library, through selected bookstores, or directly from us.

For information about titles, please call:
(800) 223-1244

or visit our website at:
gale.com/thorndike.

To share your comments, please write:

Publisher
Thorndike Press
10 Water St., Suite 310
Waterville, ME 04901